BODY AND SOUL

Frevisse overtook Dame Claire at the cloister gate. They came out into the courtyard together and crossed the yard. In the guest hall most of Lady Ermentrude's people had sat down to supper at the trestle tables. Heads turned as Frevisse and Dame Claire passed through. Frevisse glimpsed Sir John rising from beside his wife at the head of one table as she and Dame Claire reached the door.

Dame Claire's sharp stop in the doorway forced Frevisse to sidestep to avoid her. Then she stopped as sharply, too.

Father Henry was rising from his knees beside the bed, shaking his curly head with dazed disbelief. The patient lay propped up on her pillows, head rolled to one side, her hands still holding the crucifix, her mouth open, her harsh breathing filling the room. On the floor between her and Father Henry sprawled another woman, her legs straddled wide, her mouth agape and clogged with foam, her hands looking like claws in the rush matting, her eyes bulging, blood-suffused, in the strangled, dead purple of her face.

THE NOVICE'S TALE

MARGARET FRAZER

BERKLEY PRIME CRIME, NEW YORK

THE NOVICE'S TALE

A Berkley Prime Crime Book / published by arrangement with the author

PRINTING HISTORY
Jove edition / August 1992
Berkley Prime Crime edition / September 1993

For information address: The Berkley Publishing Group, a member of Penguin Putnam Inc.,
375 Hudson Street, New York, New York 10014.

The Penguin Putnam Inc. World Wide Web site address is
http://www.penguinputnam.com

ISBN: 0-425-14321-X

Berkley Prime Crime Books are published by
The Berkley Publishing Group, a member of Penguin Putnam Inc.,
375 Hudson Street, New York, New York 10014.

PRINTED IN THE UNITED STATES OF AMERICA

10 9 8 7 6 5

Help us, Seinte Frideswyde!
A man woot litel what him shal bityde.

Geoffrey Chaucer

THE
NOVICE'S TALE

Chapter 1

Mid-September in the year of Our Lord's grace 1431 had perfect weather, warm and dry. There was a drowse of autumn to the air, and in the fields beyond St. Frideswide's priory walls the harvest went its steady pace under the clear sky. There had been rain enough and sun enough since mid-July to bring the grain full ripeness. Now most of it lay in golden swaths behind the reapers or was already gathered into shocks to dry.

All month long the days had become familiar with the calling of the men and women back and forth at their work, the cries of children scouting birds away, and the creak of carts along the tracks to bring the harvest home.

Inside St. Frideswide's walls there was awareness of the harvest but none of its haste or noise; only, as nearly always, a settled quiet. A sway of skirts along stone floors, the muted scuff of soft leather soles on the stair; rarely a voice and then only briefly and in whispers since the rule of silence held here, except for the hour of recreation and the proper, bell-regulated hours of prayer sung and chanted in the church.

A Benedictine peace ruled there, Thomasine thought as she paused to gaze out the narrow window on the stairs to the prioress's parlor, a plate of honey cakes in her hands, still warm from the oven. She had been told to hurry with the cakes, that they were meant for an important guest, but she could not bear to pass this view over the nunnery's cream-pale stone walls. Framed in the narrow window was a scene of stubbled fields scattered with shocks of grain and small-with-distance figures bent to their work. Beyond them was the green edge of the forest, and over all the Virgin-blue of sky, all of it as finely detailed and remote as a miniature painted for a lady's prayer book, precise and wonderful to look at.

And soon to be far beyond her reach.

Slender with youth and the haste of growing up, narrow-boned from many childhood illnesses, and desperately pious, Thomasine meant to be a nun before autumn was done. In two weeks and a little more, on St. Michael's day, she would finally kneel before the altar to take her final vows. She was seventeen and had been waiting almost nine years to be granted the precious black veil and to be safe behind priory walls for all her earthly days to come.

Through each day between herself and safety, Thomasine had been hugging that certainty ever closer to herself, and now with a deep breath of contentment, she leaned forward to look down at the little nunnery orchard just outside the cloister wall. Apple and cherry trees, unburdened of their fruit but dusty and weary with bearing, waited for autumn to further rob them of their leaves. Oh, bittersweet life, to be an apple tree! thought Thomasine. She could not have said for a thousand marks how an apple tree's life could be bittersweet, but it seemed a fine, even spiritual, notion. Soon she, like the apple tree, would be rooted in St. Frideswide's forever.

While the cakes cooled on their plate between her hands, remarked the more practical part of her mind.

A familiar pang of guilt shot through her; while she stood there gaping, she was failing the most basic of all the vows: obedience. With a penitent frown, she hurried up the last steps to Domina Edith's door.

There, not meaning to, she paused again. Her hand was raised to knock, but the sound of voices in the room beyond held her. Dame Frevisse's she knew—strong and very distinct from Domina Edith's age-dimmed, murmuring tones, which faintly followed it. Both of their voices were familiar, as everything in St. Frideswide's was blessedly familiar. It was the man's voice answering theirs, deep and amused, that froze her hand. In her year and barely more at St. Frideswide's, she had grown unused to men's voices; they had no place in a nunnery, where even the voices of women were supposed to sound only rarely, according to the Rule. She had been warned about their guest, but that had not been enough to ready her.

Her raised hand drew back from the door, going instead to make sure her hair was all pushed safely out of sight under her dingy white veil. Then she tugged at her faded gown, to be sure it hung loose enough around her and gave no hint of her shape under its shabbiness. Although she had come to St. Frideswide's well provisioned by her sister and brother-in-law, she had chosen to trade her goodly clothes for the most worn garments in the nunnery's chests. Intent on proving how worthy she was, and despite her sister's disappointment and a suspicion that the prioress did not completely approve, she had clung to the habit of poverty. Now she was truly uncomfortable wearing anything remotely fine.

Sure that nothing was amiss with her appearance, that she was sufficiently uncomely, she tapped with mouse quiet at the door.

Too quietly. Dame Frevisse continued speaking, her words unclear but her voice strong and certain, doing nothing to ease Thomasine's reluctance. Before she had come to St. Frideswide's, she had expected there would be no differences among the nuns, that vows and a life lived together would make them somehow all alike, and she had been unsettled to discover, despite being blended all together in a sea of black gowns and veils, their faces framed in white wimples, they were still individual. Especially Dame Frevisse.

From the very first she had caused Thomasine unease. The plainness of her habit made her age uncertain, but her face was too strongly shaped for mildness, her eyes too clever under their dark brows, seeing much and remarking on everything with subtle mockery. The only nun whose scrutiny Thomasine felt more sharply was the prioress herself, who, despite all her years and age-weakness, seemed to see more of Thomasine than Thomasine presently wanted seen.

The man's voice came again, answering Dame Frevisse's. Thomasine's hand trembled. But obedience was still pressing at her back and the plate of cakes still cooling in her hands. She tapped again, more definitely than before.

Domina Edith's faint blessing answered her. "Benedicte."

Holding the plate in front of her as shield, Thomasine opened the door and entered.

St. Frideswide's was not poor, but neither was it rich. The prioress's parlor was only by contrast not so stark a room as the rest of the nunnery. Among her duties were the receiving of important visitors and the conducting of such nunnery business as needed more privity than the general gathering at daily chapter, or required the regrettable presence of men within the cloister. For the dignity of St. Frideswide's, the parlor had the luxury of a fireplace, and actual glass in the three tall, narrow windows overlooking the inner yard. Bright embroidered cushions lay scattered along the bench below them, and a fringed carpet woven in a Spanish pattern covered a table set with a silver ewer and bowl. Because Domina Edith had been prioress for thirty-two years—coming to the office the same year that the Duke of Lancaster had seized the throne from Richard II and made himself King Henry IV—other matters more privately hers had crept in, too, including her own embroidery frame and the tiny, elegant, elderly greyhound curled in its basket by the hearth.

As the priory's only novice, Thomasine was often sent to fetch or carry this or that between places in the cloister; the prioress's parlor was too familiar to her to need her attention, and she paused correctly just inside the door, head bowed, waiting to be acknowledged. Yet she could not resist, now that she was there, the urge to peep sideways around the swung-forward edge of her veil, at the man seated not five paces from her on the window bench.

In men as men of course she took no interest, no heed if at all possible. But today an important man was visiting. Word had run along with the order for the honey cakes that it was Thomas Chaucer who was come to Frideswide's today, and even Thomasine in her determined unworldliness knew of Thomas Chaucer. Like the weather, he was a common topic of conversation in Oxfordshire, both because of who he was and how he had come to it. His father had been a poet and a customs officer, his mother the daughter of a very minor knight, but Thomas Chaucer, so the rumors insisted, was one of the richest and most powerful commoners in England. So powerful he could resign of his own will from the King's Council though he had been asked to stay; rich enough, it was said, that his purse-proud, wool-merchanting cousin, the Cardinal Beaufort, Bishop of Winchester, was pleased to ask his advice.

So it was vaguely unsettling to see him sitting at ease in Domina Edith's familiar parlor, looking hardly different from the way Thomasine remembered her father: a middle-aged gentleman with well-grayed hair and pleasant face, tanned with sun, moderately lined around the eyes and across the forehead; dressed in a green wool houpelande to his knees, split front and back for ease of riding, with lamb's wool budge at its cuffs and collar, his hood with its trailing liripipe laid to one side out of respect for Domina Edith and the warmth of the day. He wore a large ring on either hand but no gold chains or other jewels, and his high riding boots were only boots so far as Thomasine could tell, knowing nothing of cordovan leather or how much effort it might have taken to fit them so skillfully to the curve of his leg.

She looked and was, without admitting it to herself, disappointed; while he did not look at her at all but went on listening with concentrated politeness to Domina Edith insisting in her old and worried voice, "I've always been afraid they would want silk for him when he's still too young. Young bodies, even royal ones, need to be kept warm, you know. You're certain that he has good woolen undershirts?"

"I've seen the royal inventory and joined in the discussion of His Grace's clothing in Council myself," Chaucer said, reassuringly and with good humor. "He has goodly store of woolen shirts and wears them. And he's a strong young lad. At nine years old he can be taken for twelve easily. Nor has he ever sickened a single day I know of since he was a baby with colic."

Domina Edith nodded. "Just so he doesn't outgrow his strength, God save His Grace. That's always a peril in the young, outgrowing their strength."

She went on nodding as if agreeing with herself, but the focus of her eyes had begun to fade.

Thomasine with a flare of embarrassment realized that her prioress, here and now, in front of Master Thomas Chaucer, was falling asleep. Everyone in St. Frideswide's knew that in her seventy-ninth year, a fabulous age, Domina Edith came to sleep easily at almost any time.

"Always a peril," she murmured. "I remember my brother as a boy. . . ."

But age was stronger than memory. Her eyelids fluttered briefly and then drifted down with her voice. Her slow nodding subsided; her chin sank into the folds of the wimple below her throat, and silence filled the room, until after a few moments she drew a deep breath, far back in her throat and very nearly a snore.

Thomasine dared not move. She could only stand, embarrassed, her anguished gaze fixed on her prioress, until Master Chaucer leaned back where he sat, stretched his legs out comfortably, and said, his voice warm with amusement, "It's God's blessing to come to sleep so easily."

"She deserves God's blessing. She's a good, kind woman." Standing behind Domina Edith's chair, Dame Frevisse smiled at him, a smile so casual and familiar that Thomasine, shocked by it, let her dismay show on her face. Dame Frevisse, glancing her way, caught the look and said with a touch of asperity, "You may put the cakes on the table, Thomasine. And then surely you must stay, to keep matters proper between Master Chaucer and myself."

Thomasine, dropping her gaze back to the floor, obeyed, setting the plate on the Spanish cloth and stepping back with her eyes still down, to fold her hands out of sight, into her sleeves in front of her, mortified to hear Dame Frevisse explaining to Master Chaucer, "Thomasine is a trifle scrupulous, as befits a novice. She is nearly ready to take her final vows."

To Thomasine's dismay Master Chaucer's attention turned to her. In his steady, mild voice he asked, "Are you liking the life well, child?"

Thomasine was appalled to find her head lifting and her eyes coming around to meet his, drawn by his voice. Catching herself, she hastily returned her gaze to her toes and said, "Very well, if it please you, Master Chaucer."

"And when do you take your vows?"

"At Michaelmas, if it please you."

"If it pleases God," Chaucer corrected mildly.

Thomasine felt scarlet warmth flow over her cheeks and drew her head down, turtling back into her dress, not knowing how, or whether, to reply. He had to know that unnecessary conversation was forbidden to her. Or was it necessary now, to show him she knew perfectly well that everything was according to the will of God, that she had only been being polite? Or would that be a prideful display of knowledge? Tears of helpless confusion welled into her eyes, worsened by the fear he would speak to her again.

Casually rescuing her, Dame Frevisse said, "It should please God very well to take a bride like Thomasine. She's shown a true vocation for our life. Only she finds it somewhat difficult to talk to men. Which is as it should be."

Her tears stifled by surprise and gratitude, Thomasine looked up again, ready to face whatever came next. But their attention was gone away from her as simply as it had come, leaving her only an onlooker again.

"And you, Frevisse," Master Chaucer asked. "How goes it with you? You weren't hosteler when last I was here."

Thomasine wondered at the familiarity of his tone, but Dame Frevisse answered back as casually, "I came to it last quarter-day when we changed offices all around. It means less time in cloister, more time busy with outside matters, but I like it well enough for the while. Otherwise everything is as always, including the fact that I'm very glad to see you again. Are you missing yet your place on the King's Council?"

"Except that Matilda reminds me daily how much the decision lowers me in important men's esteem, I don't seem to find myself grieving for it."

"Poor Matilda."

Thomasine had been scandalized at the obvious ease between them, and her spine stiffened further at the note of laughter in Dame Frevisse's voice. Her eyes were still resolutely down and she did not think she had moved, but Dame Frevisse, with her discomfiting skill at knowing what someone else was thinking, said, still amused, "It's all right, Thomasine. Master Chaucer's lady wife is my aunt and I spent eight years of my growing up in her household. We're kin and have known each other for as long as you've been alive. Our laughter is simply because we both of us know that 'the esteem of noble men' ranks almost as high with poor Aunt Matilda as her hope of salvation."

"Poor Master Chaucer, rather," Master Chaucer said

dryly. "Your Aunt Matilda has a way of making an unhappy household when she's unhappy."

"But with Alice married now to Suffolk, she's surely a little more content?"

"With an earl for a son-in-law and the hope of lordlings for grandchildren, she's almost forgiven me my latest disappointing of her."

"You've not bought your way out of knighthood again?"

Chaucer gave a mock-sly wink. "Maybe out of something even higher."

Dame Frevisse shook her head. "Then even I must despair of you."

But she failed to sound despairing, and Chaucer chuckled.

"My place in the world would hardly change by my gaining a title. I'd simply add more duties to my life and my taxes would go up and that's an idiot's price to pay for fancying my name. Besides, it might mean my having to go back to watching Winchester and Gloucester make fools of themselves on the Council. I've had my share of that, thank you. And at any rod, with Winchester set in Normandy for this while, Gloucester has settled down to governing with some degree of sense."

"But not much?"

"He can't use what he does not have and 'sense' is high on his list of inadequacies."

Dame Frevisse stopped the soft beginning of a laugh with her hand and glanced toward the sleeping prioress before saying quietly, "It's good to talk with you again, even for this little while. Thank you for stopping."

"My pleasure more than my duty." Master Chaucer made a courtly inclination of his head, then twitched it sideways toward Thomasine, adding, "I hope we've not offended someone again."

Thomasine, drawn by their casual talk, found she had been listening avidly. Now, wincing at her conscience's sharp rebuke as much as at Chaucer's amusement, she jerked her gaze back down as Dame Frevisse said with some asperity, "I have Domina Edith's permission to talk with Master Chaucer. She knows how it is between us and finds no harm. Don't take it all so much to heart."

Thomasine swallowed hard past the tightness in her throat and whispered, "Yes, Dame."

With light amusement in his voice, Master Chaucer remarked, "Both heaven and earth rejoice when a saint escapes the earthly body: heaven because a soul has triumphed over the devil—and earth because a saint is a prickly person to live with."

Dame Frevisse looked over at Thomasine; her face echoed her voice's concern as she said nearly gently, "Sit, Thomasine."

Thomasine, who tired easily, sat gratefully on a stool beside the table, but her resentment lingered.

Dame Frevisse turned back to Master Chaucer. "We're all going to be very grateful for your gift. Blue silk was exactly our need for Father Henry's new chasuble."

"I'm told there'll be white of the same weight in a few months if you'd have a need for it."

"Far be it from me to say we've never a need for white silk!" Dame Frevisse said. "Dame Perpetua has a new pattern of grape vines that we could embroider. . . ." She paused, lifting her head to a bother of noise beginning to grow in the walled courtyard below the window. "Now what is that?"

The noise sharpened into a clatter of many hoofs on cobbles and rising voices. Thomasine jerked upright. One voice carried above the others and she was afraid she recognized it. Chaucer turned where he sat to look out, and Dame Frevisse crossed the room to join him. But Thomasine, sure now she knew who it was, huddled down onto her stool, as if hoping by some miracle a bush would grow out of the floor and hide her.

Dame Frevisse, peering out, said with a feeling plainly far from devout, "God have mercy on us."

Chapter 2

DOMINA EDITH, WAKING as easily as she had fallen asleep, lifted her head. "What is it?"

Dame Frevisse swung back in a gentle swirl of veil and curtsied, her face courteously bland. "Lady Ermentrude Fenner is just entering the yard."

"And seemingly she's bringing half of Oxfordshire with her," Master Chaucer added, not helpfully.

Thomasine, her heart dropping toward her sandals at this confirmation of the visitor's name, bit her lip against any sound. Domina Edith herself gave no sign beyond the merest fluttering of her eyelids before saying mildly, "I do not recall receiving any warning of our being honored with a visit from the lady."

Which was usual for Lady Ermentrude. She seemed to feel that the honor of her coming more than outweighed the burden of surprise. It may even have been that she enjoyed the frantic readying of rooms, the culinery desperation in the kitchen, and the general scurrying that followed her unannounced arrivals.

Domina Edith brushed at her faultless lap. "She'll wish, as always, to see me first. You must needs bring her, I suppose. But there's no need to hurry her, mind you. Take time about it if you wish."

If Lady Ermentrude so wished, was the more likely, thought Thomasine. But Dame Frevisse only said, "Yes, my lady," then hesitated in her curtsey and asked, "The guest hall kitchen . . . ?"

The guest hall was new and barely tried, so there should be no surprise that things were still settling over there. Still, it seemed cruel that something should shift in the kitchen chimney just before the arrival of an important lady who inevitably traveled with a large retinue. There would be no stonemason to repair it for at least a week, and in the meanwhile nothing could be roasted in the guest kitchen fireplace.

Domina Edith gestured with true regret. "We needs must use the priory kitchen. You should advise the cooks on your way to greet Lady Ermentrude."

Dame Frevisse nodded and went out. Thomasine, hoping to make Dame Frevisse's departure her own, rose to follow her, but Domina Edith said, surprised at her, "Stay, child. Matters must be kept decent between Master Chaucer and myself. And Lady Ermentrude will be asking to see you, as always."

Thomasine knew it. And dreaded it. Lady Ermentrude was her great-aunt only by marriage, but that was small comfort. Her first husband had been Thomasine's grandfather's brother. When he died young, she married back into her own Fenner family, but with the Fenners' inbred devotion to keeping tight hold on anything and anyone who might be of use or profit to them, she had not let loose her interest in her first husband's people. Thomasine's father had been raised in her household—something she had never let him forget—and for one miserable season Thomasine and her sister Isobel had been there in their turn, too, to learn highborn manners and a lady's duties. Properly, they both would have stayed until their marriages were made, but Thomasine's frail health had failed her and she had been sent home, leaving only Isobel to Lady Ermentrude's attentions. Now Isobel was six years a wife, and Thomasine nearly settled into nunhood, where she hoped to find herself beyond Lady Ermentrude's interference.

But St. Frideswide's was a particular charity of the Fenners and lately most particularly of Lady Ermentrude. Her gifts of food and money were always welcome, which gave her further excuse to drop in uninvited, and her visits always included a rude teasing of Thomasine, asking if she were ready yet to be taken away from this dull prison and given to a husband of good birth and manly vigor.

Now, Domina Edith said, "Go to the window, child, and tell me what's come with her this time." To Master Chaucer she added, "Pray excuse my unseemly curiosity, but Lady Ermentrude's visits . . ." She hesitated, seeking an explanation that would be both polite and accurate, and finally said, "Her visits sometimes put a strain upon us."

"She stayed a week with my lady wife and I one Christmastide," Master Chaucer answered, his tone making very clear he understood all she had not said.

Thomasine, having gone carefully to the window farthest from where he sat, reported dutifully, "My lady, there are at least ten men-at-arms come with her. And fourteen or fifteen outriders. I see five sumpter horses and two carriages of servants. Here are more sumpter horses coming."

"Is Lady Ermentrude on horseback or in a carriage?"

There was no difficulty finding Lady Ermentrude among the clutter of her baggage and people. "She's dismounting now, my lady. She was riding."

"Then she's feeling well." Domina Edith betrayed a faint regret at that. Lady Ermentrude enjoyed a touch of sickness as much as anyone could, keeping her servants and everyone else scurrying to fetch hot possets and cool drinks and an orange if they had to ride to Banbury for it, and cushions and blankets and her dogs to tumble and quarrel across her coverlet and someone to read her awake or sing her to sleep. But the only thing worse than Lady Ermentrude ill was Lady Ermentrude at her vigorous best, needing to be entertained late into the evening when all Christians should be in bed, and then betimes up and around, looking into every nook and cranny of nunnery affairs as if the bishop had sent her on a visitation in his place.

"And baggage wagons besides the sumpter horses?" Domina Edith asked. The length of a visit could sometimes be guessed by the number of the lady's chests and boxes.

"Yes, my lady. They're still coming through the gateway, but there are three so far." Domina Edith could not hold back a faint sigh. "And two men with her dogs," added Thomasine. "Hounds and lapdogs both."

Domina Edith sighed again. The hunting hounds would go into the kennels, but the lapdogs were tiny terrors that followed their mistress nearly everywhere, even into the church for Mass. "And the parrot?" Domina Edith asked. "Did she bring the parrot as well?"

Thomasine looked among the women climbing down from the first carriage. "I don't see . . . ," she began but saw something worse, paused to be sure of it, and then said rather hopelessly, "There's a monkey."

From other times, St. Frideswide's knew that Lady Ermentrude's occasional monkeys were the most thieving, noisy, dirty, troublesome creatures ever to come inside the nunnery's walls. Every one of them had been wicked, nasty servants of the devil whose single grace seemed to be that they rarely lived long.

"A monkey," Domina Edith repeated, sounding as if she had been given a second hundred years in Purgatory.

Master Chaucer's shoulders twitched, and he found it necessary to extract a handkerchief from his undersleeve and blow his nose.

"That's very well for you, Master Chaucer," Domina Edith said sternly, "since you're meaning to ride on this afternoon." Then to Thomasine, "Is Dame Frevisse to the courtyard yet?"

Among the bright milling and shifting of people, wagons, and horses and the scurry of priory servants come to sort the rout into guest halls and stable, Thomasine was easily able to recognize Dame Frevisse, tall and black-gowned among the brown and cream livery of Lady Ermentrude's servants and the brighter colors of her ladies. As Thomasine watched, she moved with direct purpose through their chaos to reach Lady Ermentrude, also easily seen in her trailing gown of sheeny apricot-and-blue silk, arrayed with great hanging sleeves and a fashionable padded headdress airy with yards of floating veil.

How did she keep from frightening the horses? Thomasine wondered uncharitably. Dame Frevisse, having reached her, bowed a graceful greeting and began with only a word or two to draw her back from her busy shouting and gesturing at everyone in the yard.

"She's speaking with Lady Ermentrude just now," Thomasine dutifully reported.

"As you can tell by the sudden ceasing of the lady's voice," Master Chaucer added.

"But are they coming this way yet?" Domina Edith asked.

"Now they are."

"The monkey, is it coming with her?"

Thomasine hesitated. Close behind Lady Ermentrude were two women, one keeping well away from the other, who carried the long-tailed brown monkey perched on her shoulder. It had pulled her hat sideways and was shrieking in what seemed to Thomasine close imitation of its mistress. Both women moved as if to follow Lady Ermentrude, but Dame Frevisse lifted her arm in a polite but definite gesture. Thomasine could not hear what she said, but the women nodded and turned away to follow the flow of furnishings and people toward the guest hall.

Master Chaucer, who had risen to his feet to watch along with Thomasine, said admiringly, "Frevisse could command armies. A pity she's a woman."

Thomasine frowned at him, and beyond him caught an expression flitting across Domina Edith's face that showed how little she thought of that remark also. But before his quick glance could see her disapproval, Thomasine smoothed it away and said, "The monkey is not coming, Domina. Nor any of the dogs."

Domina Edith gave a relieved sigh. "I should have made her hosteler long ago." Master Chaucer looked pleased at this compliment of his niece, and she elaborated, "Lady Ermentrude had our last hosteler in near hysterics within a half day of her coming. And that time she had for once sent word ahead that she was coming." She shook her head regretfully at the memory. "Sister Fiacre is much more content now as sacrist. Neither the altar linens nor vestments nor candles nor lamps shout at her, no matter what she does or doesn't do. Shouting hurts Sister Fiacre's feelings." Domina Edith gazed off thoughtfully at nothing in particular. Thomasine hoped she was not going to sleep again. "But the monkey is not going into the new hall, is it?"

St. Frideswide's had two guest halls now, both within the priory's inner wall. Travelers and visitors could stay the night or longer in them, enjoying the priory's Rule-directed charity but leaving the nuns in peace inside their cloister. Only Dame Frevisse as hosteler needed to deal daily with them. Lesser sorts of travelers and superfluities of servants stayed in the old guest hall to the north side of the inner gateway, with its large single room for everyone to sleep in. The new hall to the gateway's south was of stone and better built, with separate chambers off its central hall for noble guests and their near attendants. It meant that St. Frideswide's charity was less evenhanded than it had been, but it still never failed, still always offered a roof to every head and food for every belly, charging only what the visitor cared to pay, even if it were nothing.

But just now anyone who chanced to come would have scant comfort; Lady Ermentrude and her traveling household were rapidly filling up both guest halls at once.

"The monkey and lapdogs are all going into the new hall," Chaucer said.

Domina Edith murmured, "God help our clean new floors."

Lady Ermentrude was out of sight now. Thomasine drew back from the window and said hesitantly, "Lady Ermentrude will be here on the moment. Should I go to the kitchen?"

She was assigned to help in the kitchen today, and surely she would be more needed than ever now, with all the guests come and the guest-hall kitchen useless.

But Domina Edith merely said in her faded voice, "Be sure the basin's water is clean and the towel folded best side up."

So Thomasine took up the towel Dame Frevisse must have brought for Master Chaucer. Refolded and laid over her arm, it showed no use. And the water in the silver pitcher was still mildly warm as she poured it into the silver basin on the table. Burying a craven urge to flee, she took the basin and went to stand by the thick wooden door, bracing herself.

Lady Ermentrude's shrill voice was already rising from the stairs, complaining of the ineptitude of servants, the dusty roads, the complications of travel in hot weather. As always, the sound of her made Thomasine's stomach knot; with an effort she kept her face under control as the door opened and Lady Ermentrude swept into the room in an excess of skirts and veiling and voice. Paying no heed to Thomasine, she paused to thrust her hands into and out of the basin, shook them briskly to make the droplets fly, and dried her fingers with little dabs at the towel while gazing around the room.

There might have been a time when her features could have been called beautiful. There were fine bones under the aging skin and traces of rich natural coloring. But years of self-indulgence, most particularly in her famed ill temper, had creased lines more deeply down her face than need have been there, drawn out and narrowed her mouth, given her eyes a beady eagerness to peer and judge. She was still, as she had always been, elegant in bearing and dress; however, greed and selfishness had made a thin, brittle veneer of her good manners. And now she said, still eyeing the room, "Nothing changed. Even the dog in its basket the same. You are like God's Holy Church, everlastingly unchanged!"

She made it sound a doubtful virtue for anyone to have and certainly not one for which she personally had much use. Before Domina Edith could respond, Lady Ermentrude recognized Master Chaucer standing at the window and, tossing the towel at Thomasine's face, advanced on him, her voice brightening. "Master Chaucer! What good chance to meet you here! We can have a fine exchange of news from Court and Queen."

With what looked to Thomasine like something less than pleasure, Master Chaucer took the plump hand held out insistently under his nose and kissed it before replying in cool tones, "I've long since left my service at the court and any word I've had of Her Grace Queen Catherine is third hand at best."

Thomasine had the small, sharp, sinful satisfaction of seeing her great-aunt very slightly disconcerted. Whatever Master Chaucer's connections, he was nonetheless of common birth and should be more flattered by her attentions than he was showing. But he was too unexpected a windfall in the predictability of the nunnery—and too rich and too close to nobility far higher than her own—for Lady Ermentrude to take offense. Instead, with a condescending familiarity meant to make up for his own lack of enthusiasm, she exclaimed, "Dear man! You know full well I've been these past few years with Her Grace as one of her ladies-in-waiting." To Domina Edith she added, as if she had not mentioned it on every possible occasion whenever she had been at St. Frideswide's, "I've been with Her Grace now and again ever since she left the court to live retired."

She settled into the room's second-best chair—Domina Edith had made no move to rise from the best—and turned her attention back to Master Chaucer. "I was with Her

Grace not above a week ago. But I've left her service for good. Did you know that—and why?'' She leaned toward him, a glitter of gossip in her eyes. ''I told her my age was wearing on me and she gave permission for me to leave.'' A beringed hand smacked a silken thigh. ''Ha! I'm as young as ever I was. No, there's going to be a scandal in that household. And the wise know better than to be near the mighty when there's a fall from grace.'' Lady Ermentrude's head cocked sideways like a clever crow's. ''What rumors have you heard, Master Chaucer? About one thing or another?''

''I've heard no rumors nor talk of scandal. And since you're surely to be counted among the wise, you know the unwisdom of retelling any such to me or anyone, even our good Domina Edith, soul of discretion though she is.''

His voice was mild, but Thomasine thought there was warning in his eyes. Lady Ermentrude paused before drawing a deep breath, her mouth opening to reply. Before she could, Domina Edith, apparently unaware of anything at all beyond the casual conversation, said, ''My lady, I think you've failed to recognize your niece.''

She gestured to Thomasine, and Lady Ermentrude turned to stare at her as if demanding how she had dared to go unnoticed. Thomasine, to cover the sick tightening of her stomach, stepped forward and set the bowl and towel on the table, her head bent to avoid her great-aunt's gaze.

But there was no avoiding her shrill summons. ''Thomasine! Come here, child! Let me see you better!''

Thomasine came as she was bidden and curtseyed, all outward politeness, but her hands were clenched up either sleeve, her eyes held carefully down to keep them from betraying her feelings.

Lady Ermentrude took hold of her chin and twitched her face up and from side to side, eyeing her with the same scrutiny she gave a horse she was thinking to buy. ''Indeed no, I hardly know you even when I look at you. You've sunk so far into nunhood you're becoming quite a little worm."

She released Thomasine's chin. Thomasine stepped out of reach and dropped her gaze back to her feet. "Yes, Aunt," she whispered.

"Pah!" Lady Ermentrude's disgust was plain. "You become any meeker you'll cease to breathe!" There was a familiar smirk to her voice as she added, "But you're a novice yet and it's not too late. There's many a fine and lusty young man to be had. Half a dozen I know who'd have you at my word. And some two or three not so young but rich enough you'd find the marriage honey-sweet one way or other. Whatever way, I could have you married before Christmas if I set to. Master Chaucer and I, we made a goodly marriage between your sister and Sir John. She'd not be a knight's wife now if it weren't for us, and we can do as much for you, I warrant. Eh, Master Chaucer?"

Young Sir John Wykeham had been Master Chaucer's ward when Lady Ermentrude's attention lighted on him. With no marriageable daughters or nearer nieces of her own to hand just then, she had decided Isobel would serve to bring him into Fenner circles, and since the marriage was in the young John's interest, too, she and Master Chaucer had brought it about. The title of Lord D'Evers had died with Isobel and Thomasine's father since there were no sons of the blood to carry it on, but the remaining inheritance was considerable, and with Thomasine purposed even then to be a nun, it would not be divided, only a smaller sum set aside to dower her into the nunnery. In every practical way, the marriage had been an excellent alliance. That Isobel and Sir John had fallen in love with one another between their first meeting and their marriage had been of no consequence one way or the other, merely a comfortable chance. More important was the fact that they had so far managed to have two sons and a daughter to secure the inheritance.

But the success of it all had given Lady Ermentrude ambitions to do it again. Now she prodded Thomasine.

"Here, girl! Come to your senses! There's no need to leave all that property to your sister and her get by losing yourself behind these sad walls! Come out and have your share of it and the world, too!"

Thomasine, knowing too well that there was no defense against her great-aunt in this mood and that she would only stop when she was sated with the game, bent her neck and said with forced mildness, "I thank you for your kindness, Aunt, but am content here where I am."

"Nonsense—" Lady Ermentrude began.

But Domina Edith, in her soft, aged voice, cut across her strident tones as if unaware of them. "Thomasine, tell her why you are content."

Thomasine, disconcerted, looked up into her prioress's gaze. Age had faded Domina Edith's eyes to paleness, and her much-wrinkled face seemed to take its shape more from the confining wimple than any strength left in her flesh, but her look held Thomasine's, steadying her out of her angry helplessness. "Tell her," Domina Edith said again, and Thomasine, goaded into nervous daring, looked from her to Lady Ermentrude.

Her great-aunt looked back, thin eyebrows raised as if she were unsure what was to happen. Thomasine, her voice trembling a little but sure of the words, said, "I've chosen my bridegroom, Great-aunt, and there's none more fit than Him. I've wanted to be Christ's bride since I was eight years old. I'm taking my last vows in less than two weeks time, at Michaelmas, God granting it, and then I'll be beyond any marrying with mortal man, thank God!" Finishing on a strong note, Thomasine felt her head lift, and she dared to look her aunt in the face.

Lady Ermentrude drew herself up with a sharp hiss of disapproval, but before she had regrouped herself to make reply, Domina Edith, apparently oblivious to any possibility of offense, said, "Thank you, Thomasine. You still have duties in the kitchen, do you not? You'd best be back to them, I think. Dame Frevisse, pray serve the cakes to our guests.''

It was dismissal and diversion together, and Thomasine gladly used it, curtseying quickly before escaping out the door. Knowing too well her great-aunt's skill at anger, she had no wish to be there for it, and as she fled down the stairs, she wished she could flee as swiftly down the next two weeks to Michaelmas.

Behind her in the parlor Chaucer said musingly, ignoring Lady Ermentrude's ire, ''So earnest a lamb. Unfit, I'd judge, for the world beyond her cloister walls.''

''I've never seen a greater urge to give one's life to God,'' agreed Domina Edith. ''Never a more fervent vocation. Too intense sometimes, I think, but that's her youth. She'll surely be a blessing to our house.'' The prioress crossed herself.

Chaucer and Frevisse echoed her gesture. Lady Ermentrude followed them more slowly. There was a silence then, until Lady Ermentrude broke it with ''You're new as hosteler since I was last here, are you not, Dame Frevisse?''

Frevisse was reminded of a vicious dog who, balked in one attack, looks for another. But mild as milk, looking at the plate of cakes she now held, she said, ''Yes, my lady.''

''And you must serve as Domina Edith's body servant, too, it seems. I wonder how you manage your duties in the guest hall if you're so much busied here?''

''We all serve our lady prioress gladly,'' Frevisse said blandly, ''whenever the chance comes, and do all our duties as best we may. Will you have a honey cake?''

She held out the plate with proper meekness and downcast eyes. Lady Ermentrude gazed at her a moment longer than was necessary, then took one. Frevisse turned away to offer them to Chaucer, who took another, and while Lady Ermentrude examined hers on all its sides—looking for something to criticize, Frevisse thought uncharitably—

Chaucer took a swift bite of his and said, ''Delicious. You've a cook to be kept.''

Lady Ermentrude nibbled at an edge. ''Truly,'' she agreed. ''You do well for yourselves here.''

''God sends us generous friends.'' Domina Edith smiled as Frevisse held out the plate to her.

Frevisse added, with subtle malice, ''These cakes are a special matter. Master Chaucer sent word ahead of his coming, giving our kitchener time to ready them.''

''He is a thoughtful man,'' Domina Edith murmured. Her face and voice were a study in aged innocence. Frevisse smothered a smile, having long since learned that though Domina Edith's body was wearied with life's long journey, her mind was not. Chaucer, himself well aware of the strength of the prioress's mind, seemed to choke on a bite of cake and was forced to cough heartily behind his hand.

Lady Ermentrude sent sharp, darting glances at all their faces. Her mouth tightened. ''I shall be staying only a few days here,'' she declared. Their faces betrayed nothing but polite interest. ''I hope that will be convenient to you as hosteler, Dame Frevisse, and to St. Frideswide's, Domina Edith?''

''Truly,'' the prioress agreed. ''Dame Frevisse?''

''As convenient and pleasant as it always is to serve you, my lady,'' Frevisse answered.

Chaucer choked again, swallowed hastily as Lady Ermentrude's eyes began to narrow, and said, ''Regrettably I'll not be enjoying your courtesies as hosteler, Dame Frevisse. I must needs ride on this afternoon. There's a manor of mine I mean to reach this evening if I'm to see to all there is to do before I go to France.''

''France!'' Lady Ermentrude was diverted instantly. ''You'll be seeing the King then. So fine a young lad he is. You're meaning to go soon?''

''This month's end.''

''Pray, tell His Grace from me that his dear lady mother was happy and well when I left her.''

Chaucer inclined his head in acknowledgment. "Gladly. And is there aught else you might wish done over there?"

Lady Ermentrude smiled, pleased at being treated at last in the way she deserved. "Oh no, I think not. My matters are all well in hand. But thank you. And how regrettable you must go on, or we could chat the evening away."

"He comes to see Dame Frevisse, you know," Domina Edith said a little vaguely. "So very kind of him, I think, she being his niece and all."

"Yes." Lady Ermentrude's gaze flicked between Frevisse and Chaucer intently. "I think I knew you had a niece here but had forgotten her name, Master Chaucer. By marriage, I believe?"

"Yes, but nurtured in my own household from middle childhood, and in many ways a daughter to me." He smiled at Frevisse.

Frevisse smiled back, as perfectly aware as he of how unwelcome Lady Ermentrude would find this piece of knowledge. Anyone so close to Master Thomas Chaucer was an unsuitable victim for her torments.

"Ah," Lady Ermentrude said shortly. "I did not know that." Unexpectedly her face brightened. "I remember!" She turned to Frevisse. "Your mother made that unfortunate marriage to the younger son of someone or other. Most regrettable, it was thought at the time. And so you ended up in Master Chaucer's household when they could not keep you anymore!"

"My mother and father did not find their marriage regrettable," Frevisse said in a level voice. "And it was my father's death that brought me to Master Chaucer's and my aunt's household. Nothing else."

The crisp, steady words must have given Lady Ermentrude sufficient warning she should go no farther that way.

"How stand matters with your family?" Chaucer put in. "Did you visit at Fen Harcourt on your way from the Queen at Hertford?"

It was another well-chosen diversion. Lady Ermentrude

smiled with straight-lipped disapproval. "I paused there and meant to stay longer but I'm not so old I need to wait on their favors. They could not find it convenient to give me due respect and I've come away sooner than I planned. They'll not be happy when they find how much they've offended me."

"Harvest time can be a heavy matter," Chaucer remarked.

"So can my displeasure be." Lady Ermentrude eyed Frevisse as closely as she had eyed the cake. "My own house at Bancroft will be ready in two weeks so I'm thinking to spend a week here and then another week with Isobel. I'm minded to see the girl she had this summer. A girl child may be all right, and is no problem since they have two sons already and they're thriving, so I hear. Then I'll go on to my own manor, and my relations will see how welcome they are in their turn."

"Concerning sons," said Chaucer, "how do your own at present?"

"My Walter has been with Lord Fenner these two months past. Lord Fenner is dying now, it seems, and since the title comes by right of blood to Sir Walter, he's there to be sure not too much is lost when Lord Fenner makes his will, not all the property being entailed, you know. The title and its lands will be a great boon to our family, and it will be best if the wealth comes with them."

"And Herbrand?"

"In France, in my lord of Bedford's household still. He fights occasionally, I believe, and should have the captaining of one castle or another soon."

"Mayhap I'll see him while I'm there."

"Mayhap," Lady Ermentrude agreed with no particular interest. "If so, tell him I mean to see how his manors are doing come the spring. He's left them to others for too long, if you ask me, and I've no mind to let Fenner property go to the bad by his neglect."

"How fortunate that travel agrees with you," Domina Edith said.

"It would if it weren't for servants." Lady Ermentrude took up this theme as if on cue, as Frevisse suspected Domina Edith had meant her to, and set off on a long, well-practiced dissertation concerning the inadequacies of everyone so fortunate as to be allowed into her service. It went its appointed course while Domina Edith fumbled crumbs off the single cake her conscience would allow her and Frevisse poured wine for everyone. Chaucer was finishing his third cake when Lady Ermentrude ended with "But it's a common tale, and surely we've all suffered from such lowborn folk. Pray, what will you be doing for the King while you're in France?"

"Very little, likely. Mostly my own necessities draw me there, with some few other matters friends have asked of me."

"I suppose there'll be his French coronation soon so he'll be able to come back to England and be done with it? Is it the coronation you're going for?"

"There's no date set for it yet and a great deal of France still to recover. The Witch and her rebellion cost us men and money as well as territory, and even though she's burned, Bedford reports he can hardly be sure of passage to Paris yet, let alone to Rheims."

"A French coronation." Lady Ermentrude shook her head. "You'd think his English crown would be enough."

"Not for the French," Chaucer said dryly. "But among other things I'm bound for collecting Lord Moleyns's heiress. I've bought her wardship and marriage rights from the crown and her mother has asked I fetch her myself if possible."

Lady Ermentrude looked well impressed. "That's a wealthy wardship to lay hold of! You've a choice for her husband? I've possibilities if you'd be interested. How old is she now? She was born in France, I think?"

"Six years or nearly. Yes."

Frevisse turned to set the wine pitcher on the table and hide her face from Lady Ermentrude. It was not like her uncle to stay long after he had said he must be going. But now he settled back and went on easily. "And that reminds me that there's word, too, of someone you might remember. A youth named William Vaughan. He squired in your household, I think."

Lady Ermentrude frowned with thought before nodding. "I remember him, though his family was no one in particular. He went to France to make his fortune and died years back."

"Not so many years. Just two. At Orléans, during the siege."

Domina Edith made a sound of regret. The loss of Orléans to the witch-girl Joan of Arc and the English disasters in battles afterward had brought much tears and praying at St. Frideswide's. Chaucer turned to include her as he talked. "Lady Moleyns is very taken with his story. He was part of her husband's *meinie*, one of his household men, I gather. In the fighting at Orléans, when Moleyns went down wounded, young Vaughan fought his way to his side before any of his other men and stood above him fighting off the French like a champion from Froissart. He was on his knees and bloodied in a dozen places before help came."

"A blessing on his courage," Frevisse said admiringly.

Lady Ermentrude, apparently unmoved by a tale of courage without a Fenner name attached to it, picked a fragment off the edge of her cake.

Domina Edith murmured, "But he did not save his lord?"

"No, alas. It would be a better tale if he had, but they both died of their wounds. Lady Moleyns, as the only reward she could make to him, took Vaughan's son into her household and has been raising him."

"A blessing on his courage and her piety," Domina Edith said. "Vaughan married over there then? Surely not a French woman?"

Chaucer shrugged. "The boy bears his name. That's all I know. Nor has Lady Moleyns been able to find any English relatives of his father, but she remembers Vaughan talking of your household, Lady Ermentrude, and asked if I would make inquiries. Do you know if he has any family who might want the boy?"

Lady Ermentrude shrugged carelessly. She thought, then mused, "There was a sister, a nun at Godstow, but she died long ago." She frowned, running her large list of names and connections through her mind. "No, I'm sure there's no one to be telling he's dead." The cake continued to crumble between her fingers. "God give him good rest," she added perfunctorily. "At Orléans, you say." She dusted crumbs from her fingers and turned the talk to a subject more to her liking. "One of my sumpter horses has gone lame, Domina. I want your groom of the stable to look at him."

"As you wish." Domina Edith nodded.

Chaucer rose, gathering up his hood and beginning to fold it into a coxcomb hat, using the long liripipe to bind it in place. "Ah then, I suppose Lady Moleyns will have to go on keeping the boy."

"Hm?" said Lady Ermentrude. "Oh, yes, I suppose so."

"And I, to judge by the slant of sunlight through this window, had best take my leave. I've some few miles to go yet today." He turned to Domina Edith. "Thank you for your hospitality, as always good and gracious."

Domina Edith inclined her head to him and held out her hand for him to kiss. "You are always welcome, whenever you choose to come. Pray, make it often."

"As often as I may."

His kiss was warmer than the one he next dealt to Lady Ermentrude, though his leave-taking was as graceful. Her reply was formal but disinterested. Frevisse moved to the door to accompany him to the yard; at his gesture she preceded him down the stairs, until in the lower corridor they could walk side by side, not speaking, their silence companionable. In the eight years she had grown to womanhood in his household, they had become friends enough to simply enjoy each other's company without words; in the years since she had entered St. Frideswide's, their worlds had grown so far apart there was now little to be said between them, but the friendship held.

Not until they were nearly to the outer door into the yard, in hearing of Lady Ermentrude's people still unpacking, did Chaucer say, "My deepest sympathies on your current quest. Will you be able to survive her?"

Frevisse's smile was wry. "I think between you and Domina Edith, she's impressed enough to be a little cautious. Now that she's quite perfectly aware that I'm closely connected to your wealth and royal relations, she may even want to make a friend of me."

"My deeper sympathies for doing you such a disservice. You know she'd treat me badly if matters were only slightly different."

"If things were slightly different she'd never speak to you at all except to give you orders. Your father was a vintner's son who happened to write stories and your mother's sister had no more decency than to be a royal duke's mistress. I would despair of anyone ever making a respectable figure from that."

"The disgrace sits deep within my soul," Chaucer said cheerfully. "All those impressive half-royal relations of mine but not a single drop of noble blood to be found in my own veins. It's a shock to know that all this wealth and power I'm supposed to have comes from naught but my own wits and skill. Regrettable, I'm sure."

Frevisse tempered her urge to laugh into a wider smile. Chaucer smiled back at her and asked with quiet seriousness, "You're still contented here?"

"Most of the time. Would it be simplest to say that I'm content with being content?"

"If it's true, it's more than most people manage with their lives."

"It's true," said Frevisse simply.

They had reached the door. Chaucer took her hand in his. "We've come, one way and another, by the turning of Fortune's wheel and our own wills, to the places we want to be." He kissed her cheek. "God's blessing on you, my dear."

"And on you, too, Uncle. Keep safe and come again when you may."

"Be assured."

From the doorway Frevisse watched him cross the yard to where his own escort was waiting, collected neatly out of the disorder of Lady Ermentrude's people. Not until he had swung into his saddle and was riding out the gateway did she turn away, aware belatedly of someone bearing down on her from behind and surprised past words to find it was Lady Ermentrude, in full flow of veils and gown, striding toward her like a lord set on battle.

Frevisse had not anticipated facing the full rigors of her attention so soon. She sank quickly in a curtsey, bracing herself for whatever was coming. But Lady Ermentrude waved a dismissive hand at her and said briskly, "My plans have changed. I'm riding on to my great-niece Lady Isobel's today. It's hardly a three-hour ride. I'll be there before full dark if I leave now."

"But—" A variety of protests went through Frevisse's mind. She chose the simplest of them and said, "Your people are half unpacked by now and settling in. Surely—"

Lady Ermentrude was already going out the door, forcing Frevisse to follow her. "And they can go on unpacking. I want haste, not a clutter of idiots slowing me down. A few men-at-arms, two of my women, that will do. I expect to be back tomorrow. You there!" She beckoned demandingly at a groom nearby.

Frevisse, with the thought that Lady Ermentrude's going would leave her free to set straight certain matters concerning the guest halls and dogs and monkeys, contented herself with murmuring, "As you think best, my lady. We'll await your return."

"And have all in readiness, I'm sure," Lady Ermentrude agreed sharply. The groom was bowing in front of her now, and she told him peremptorily, "I want my horse saddled. Now. At once. Go on." Smothering a look of bewilderment, the man ran off. "Sheep-face," Lady Ermentrude snapped, and began shouting, "Maryon! Bess! Bertram!"

The courtyard shifted from disorder to chaos, but more quickly than Frevisse had thought possible, Lady Ermentrude was mounted and riding out the gateway with a small cluster of her people behind her.

In the intense gap of quiet left by her going, Frevisse drew a deep breath and turned away to the tasks next to hand.

Chapter 3

THE NEXT DAY was as fair as the days before had been, mild with September warmth and quiet in its familiar pattern of prayers at dawn, then breakfast and Mass, and afterward the varied, repetitious business that was the form and shelter of everyday security for Thomasine.

But she had stayed in the church after the long midnight prayers of Matins and Lauds, kneeling alone at St. Frideswide's altar in the small fall of lamplight, meaning only to give thanks for yesterday's gift of courage against Lady Ermentrude and then return to bed. Then she had lost herself in the pleasure of repetition, murmuring Aves and Paters and simple expressions of praise over and over until all knowledge of Self melted away, and suddenly there was the sharp ring of the bell, startling her, because it meant the whole night had fled. She went as quickly as stiff knees and sticky mind allowed to the church's cloister door, there to join the nuns in procession to their places in the choir to greet the sunrise with the prayers of Prime.

Now, as the warm day wore away, she was finding her temper uneven and her frequent yawns a distracting nuisance. There seemed to be constant errands to be run, few chances of just sitting at a table in the kitchen pretending to peel apples, and every time she went out into the cloister the sound of her great-aunt's people lofted over the wall. Heavy male laughter and the higher pitch of chattering women's voices had no place in St. Frideswide's cloister. They bruised the quiet and made Thomasine wish for a way to bundle them into silence.

As she hurried along the cloister walk to fetch ink for Dame Perpetua, the little bell by the door to the courtyard jangled at her, saying someone wanted in. Thomasine halted, exasperated, and looked around with impatient anger for a servant to signal to the door—then caught herself and offered a swift prayer of penitence. Anger was one of the seven Deadly Sins, and its appearance marked a severe departure from the holiness she was so desperate to attain.

The bell rang again, there was no servant in sight, and misery replaced her anger. Why were patience and courage always called for when there was the least supply of them available? She went to the door and opened the shutter that closed the small window at eye level. Peering through its bars, she saw no one, and the ends of her temper unraveled a little further. Then the curly top of a head bounced barely into view, and a child's voice cried, "Oh, please! Open, please open! I need help!"

The cry was piteous and Thomasine's annoyance dissolved into her quick sympathy. She unlatched and opened the door.

The little girl standing there wore a less-than-clean dress in Lady Ermentrude's livery of brown and cream. She was near to tears. "Please, m'lady, is Dame Claire within? I must s-speak to her!"

Dame Claire was the priory's infirmarian, tending not only to the nunnery's sick but anyone who came there asking help. Thomasine tilted her head inquiringly, asking to be told more without breaking the silence that properly held her.

"Please, it's little Jacques!" the child cried. Her tears had begun to spill now that there was someone to hear her. "He's s-sick like to die, and oh, m'lady, you don't know, it's my life if something happens to him! Dame Frevisse said to ask for Dame Claire."

Thomasine had had no idea there was a baby traveling with Lady Ermentrude. Or perhaps her great-aunt had acquired a dwarf since she was last here. Poor unhappy thing, to be sick in a strange place. Her sympathy for anyone hurting was as swift as her urge to pray for them, and she signed the child to follow her.

Dame Claire was, as nearly always, in her small workroom-storeroom off the infirmary, counting sheets this morning. She looked up as Thomasine tapped on the door frame, began to smile at seeing her, then saw the child's tearful face beside her and came quickly. Dame Claire was small and neatly made, precise in all her movements, with a quiet dignity that belied her scant inches, as deeply quiet in her ways as her voice was when she asked, bending down to the child, "What is it, lamb?"

"It's little Jacques," the girl sobbed. Met with such open kindness, she felt free to cry as fiercely as her fear demanded. "I fell asleep and he fooled his way into a box of my lady's sweetmeats and overate them and now he's sick and he's going to die and if he does, I will too, because my lady will kill me!"

"We have very good things for bellyaches," Dame Claire said soothingly. "I doubt he'll die. Come tell me about him."

She went to her worktable below the shelves of stored herbs and compounds and salves. The girl followed her, her sobs already fading as she looked around at the various bowls and pestles, the grinding slabs, baskets, and boxes that were outward signs of a high and esoteric knowledge that had always fascinated Thomasine, too, whenever she was permitted to help Dame Claire here.

Now she yearned to display some of her own little learning to the child, but instead remembered the rule about unnecessary conversation and held her peace.

"Tell me Jacques's size. How big is he? How old?"

The child, already calmer and beginning to hope, answered Dame Claire a little doubtfully. "A year?" She held up her hands perhaps a foot-and-a-half apart. "This big. I can carry him, he's not very heavy. But you have to be careful because he scratches. And bites. His tail is as long as he is."

Dame Claire's face froze in astonishment, but horrified realization broke on Thomasine. Before she could stop herself, she cried out, "It's Lady Ermentrude's monkey that's sick! Oh, I wouldn't have brought her if I'd known it was only that horrible monkey!"

Dame Claire swallowed her shock, then looked at Thomasine reprovingly. "Suffering is suffering and if I can ease it I will." Behind the reproof, amusement sparkled in her eyes, and Thomasine stifled further apologies. Claire turned back to the child and said gravely, "You've told me what I needed to know. Now here, you have this while I mix my powders and everything will be all right."

She gave the child a horehound drop to quiet her and turned to her shelves of herbs. "Angelica, perhaps," she murmured. "Or betony. Tansy surely." Then to the child, "Do you know when the monkey was born? It helps to make a cure if you know your patient's astrological sign at birth."

Eyes wide at such a notion, the child shook her head dumbly.

Dame Claire touched and crumbled into a bowl dried leaves from several hanging bunches, ground them to a mixed powder, and poured the mixture carefully into a little cloth bag. Tying it shut with a triple strand of tough grass, she said, "There now. That will be remedy for even a monkey's well-earned bellyache." She gave it to the girl. "It has to be mixed with wine. Does the monkey drink wine?"

"Oh, yes, my lady. Lady Ermentrude likes to make him drunk. He's very funny then."

"I daresay," Dame Claire said. "Then mix this powder

with half a small cup of wine and give it to him to drink.''

The girl reached to hand the bag back. ''Oh, no, m'lady, I daren't feed it! I was given strictest orders. All I must do is watch it. And this isn't even food but medicine! You must come and give it.'' Again she held out the bag.

But Dame Claire turned to Thomasine. ''I'm not yet finished with my morning duties and this is hardly something I can leave them for. You take the powder and see to its coming to Dame Frevisse with my instructions about the wine. Warn her it will make the monkey sleep, but this will secure the cure.''

Thomasine raised her own hands in protest. To reach the guest hall she would have to cross a yard full of noisy, horrid, common menfolk. Why, they might speak to her!

But Dame Claire took the bag from the child and handed it to Thomasine, and she, automatic in obedience, took it. Dame Claire, as if the task were already completed, returned to her sheets, leaving Thomasine facing the upturned, expectant face of the child and the plain fact that she had no choice but to go.

Necessity was a poor substitute for courage, but all her months at St. Frideswide's and her own will had been set to training herself to trust God and obey orders. Twisting her mind into a semblance of willing obedience, she went.

There were perhaps a dozen of Lady Ermentrude's men and a few of her women in the courtyard, most of them gathered at the well. With her head up, feigning the dignity Dame Perpetua insisted every nun should show to the world's eye, but her face already burning with shame, she took her first mincing steps across the cobbles toward the guest-hall stairs. The child trotted at her side, chattering happily, her tears forgotten now that it seemed the creature was going to be cured.

As they passed the well, one of the men there made a kissing sound and called, ''Hey, pretty one, stop and keep us company!''

Thomasine stiffened an already stiff spine and threw him

a frightened sideways glance before trying to shrink further into her gown. The child said blithely, "Oh, that's just Hob. He's lickerous as a rooster, Catherine says. I think he's a calf brain."

Thomasine walked faster, her eyes now so far down she was in danger of running into something. Someone sang a few lines about Alison who was a nun but not a very proper one, and another voice called, "Ask your sisters when they're coming out of their nest to us! If they're pretty as you, they'll be worth the waiting for."

A woman's voice said disgustedly, "Stop it, the lot of you!" but there was only laughter at her and more kissing sounds. Thomasine, caught between a swirl of anger and an urge to sob, endangered herself further by speeding up her walk. Cheeks flaming, she was nearly running, and only her youth's quick reflexes stopped her from tripping when the bottom guest-house step was suddenly within her gaze.

She heard the door at the top open and behind her an immediate deep silence fell.

Thomasine looked up to see Dame Frevisse standing tall and stern-eyed in the doorway, staring over her head toward the well. A quick glance backward showed everyone suddenly very busy and looking anywhere but at her.

The little girl announced happily, "She's brought the medicine for Jacques," and slipped past Dame Frevisse into the hall.

Resisting an urge to point but forgetting the rule of silence, Thomasine gasped accusingly, "Those men—"

Dame Frevisse held out an arm to bring her into the hall. "—are too bored and stupid to amuse themselves otherwise than by teasing you. They thought it funny to see how frightened they could make you. You responded splendidly."

"But what they said—"

"Can no more harm you than the monkey's jabbering does."

The warmth of Thomasine's cheeks deepened from embarrassment to dull-burning resentment. "I was frightened," she said sullenly.

"Of course you were. But they're only men, not lions. They know who you are and where they are. They won't touch you. They know the strength of this place."

"But what they were saying . . ." She hesitated, looking for words.

". . . was only words. Thomasine, you must stop seeing men as monsters or devils. A nun must learn to live aside from the world, not hide from it." Dame Frevisse clipped her words, very clearly in no mood for trifling. "Ignorance breeds fear. If you decide to be ignorant of men, you're going to be afraid of them, too. And so long as we must butcher, reap, sell our wool, pay our taxes, and repair our buildings, we must deal often with those fearsome creatures. Give me the medicine."

Thomasine closed her mouth over further protest. Her tiredness had betrayed her into the sin of anger again, and she would have to confess it along with other things in Chapter tomorrow. Now, ducking her head to hide her expression, she held out the little cloth bag and said with outward meekness enough, knowing the importance of a correct dose and correct instructions, "This in half a small cup of wine. Dame Claire said not to worry if the monkey sleeps. It's supposed to."

"There's a mercy. The idiot thing deserves every pain it has in its idiot belly but it's been repenting of its foolishness at the top of its lungs." The feeling in Dame Frevisse's voice offset her terseness of a moment before. "Thank you for bringing this and, pray, pardon my short temper. Between the monkey and expecting Lady Ermentrude's return, this isn't a pleasant morning."

Thomasine, daring to look up, began a hesitant smile, but Dame Frevisse was already not looking at her, saying past her in greeting, "Father Henry," to the priory priest just coming in the door.

He was a burly, deep-voiced young man, built more for

swinging a quarterstaff than a priestly censer. His black gown fit close to his muscled shoulders, and his golden hair curled up so vigorously around his tonsure it was nearly hid. He was not at all what Thomasine thought a nunnery's priest should be, and once she had dared to murmur to Dame Perpetua that he did not seem very learned. Dame Perpetua had replied that truly he was not among the scholarly but he did his duties well. "And there's no real harm in him. We're blessed to be in his keeping," she had finished, so firmly that Thomasine had never presumed to mention him again.

Now Dame Frevisse said, "Thomasine needs escort back across the yard to save her from rude attentions. Will you do it?"

Father Henry grinned, shifting his shoulders inside his Benedictine habit as if he would be pleased for an excuse to use his strength on someone. "Gladly, Dame."

Dame Frevisse, with a pleasant nod, went away, and he turned his companionable grin on Thomasine. "Now, then," he said and started down the steps.

Thomasine, with only a faint quiver of alarm, followed at his gown's hem, but no one seemed to see them at all as they crossed the courtyard back toward the cloister. Certainly no one said a single word at them. They were halfway to safety and she was beginning to feel its welcome reach when someone beyond the gatehouse to the outer yard yelled, "She's coming! She's riding in!"

There seemed no uncertainty about who "she" was. The quiet of the yard suddenly swarmed with men and women scattering to look busy or be out of sight. Thomasine hardly had time to grab Father Henry's sleeve before Lady Ermentrude's horse came at a staggering canter through the open gateway. Her two ladies, their veils and wimples disarrayed, and her escort of men-at-arms, sweat-stained through their gambesons, were behind her, all dust-marked with rough travel. Everyone's horse showed signs of a hard journey, and Lady Ermentrude's stumbled as she jerked it to a halt at the foot of the guest-hall steps. She was not wearing yesterday's finery but a more closely cut dress, her padded headroll tightly fastened by a veil whose dusty whiteness made sharp contrast to the red, clenched fury of her face.

She threw her reins at a man standing there, the lather from her horse's neck spattering his startled face with wet. Not waiting for any help, she flung herself from the saddle, swayed on her feet, clutched at a stirrup leather for support, and glared up the stairs as if seeking a foe to challenge. Finding none, she twisted away and lurched toward the cloister door across the yard.

She seemed not to see Father Henry until nearly to him. Finding his bulk in her way, she stopped, blinking, then put her hands on her hips and shouted into his face, "You! I mean to see your prioress! I want her on the instant and no feebleminded excuses! Tell her that! D'ye hear me! Go on!"

Father Henry fell back, not trying to hold his priestly dignity against her fury. "At once, my lady. Of course, my lady," he gasped, and made for the cloister door on the instant, leaving Thomasine with nothing to hide behind.

Lady Ermentrude blinked and grimaced at her—it might have been a smile but looked more a mix of pain and fury. Before Thomasine's sudden thought that she should also retreat had reached her legs, Lady Ermentrude caught hold of her arm. Thrusting her face at Thomasine, she exclaimed, "Out here alone, are you? By God's breath, that's a blessing and their mistake. Confident they are, with your time so near, but they're wrong. You'll be free of this place now. I'll see to that!"

The words and the strong stink of wine were spat into Thomasine's flinching face. Lady Ermentrude leaned closer, as if to share a secret, but her voice was loud enough to carry across the yard. "God alone knows what payments above the dowry they've offered to this sinkhole of corruption to have you here, but I've found their game! I'll have you out within the hour. You'll be safe. I'll see to it. You'd be better off with the Queen and her scandals than here, I promise you.''

Thomasine tried to pull free, but Lady Ermentrude's fingers dug more deeply into her arm. Thomasine looked around, seeking a friendly face. There was no one in the yard but Lady Ermentrude's people, and of them, the only one who seemed to be taking sharp interest in the struggle was the prettier of the two ladies in waiting who had ridden in with her, and she made no move to help. Thomasine gasped, ''My lady, you're hurting—''

''Oh yes, I'm hurting.'' Lady Ermentrude grimaced and nodded jerkily, her voice harsh. ''I've ridden too hard and I'll be sore for it tomorrow. I hurt.'' She sighed heavily. ''But it was for you, sweetling. You'll not be forced into those vows. Not now! Ha! I'll see to it. You'll be safe with me. You're free, or nearly.'' A lewd grimace, meant to be a wink. ''And I'll find you a lusty husband. You'll have a good one coming to you after this.'' She looked around. ''You, Wat! Bring my horse!'' she swung back to Thomasine. ''You get up behind, ride the crupper, and we'll be away before they know it.''

''Wait, no!'' Thomasine, in rising panic, tried harder to pull away. ''I can't go with you! I don't want to! Aunt, please, no!''

Lady Ermentrude's hold tightened, and she looked toward the sun as if to estimate the hour, but its brightness made her wince and shade her eyes with her free hand.

A low voice over Thomasine's shoulder said, ''It may be best if you just go with her.''

''There's sound advice,'' remarked Lady Ermentrude, gesturing at Wat to hurry with her horse.

Thomasine looked quickly backward to see who dared approach with advice. He was dressed in Lady Ermentrude's livery, a tall youth a little older than herself perhaps, brown-haired and quiet-eyed, so certain and unmocking in his tone and face that Thomasine forgot to be terrified of him.

"But she's taking me away! I don't want—"

"She's not well," he interrupted, but quietly. "A little in her cups, I would guess. She'll not be going away, with or without you. Help me with her into the guest hall while she's still on her feet."

"But her horse—"

But he stepped around her. "Here, this way, my lady," he said in a respectful tone, while waving Wat away. "You're tired. You should rest before riding on. And your horse could use a breath, as well. There's wine in the guest hall and a place to sit."

"What's that you say?" Lady Ermentrude muttered, fiercely at first, then peering at him. "What? Oh, yes, that would be good. To sit down. All's so bright out here. I need to sit, out of the sun."

The youth took hold of her elbow. "I'll help you, if it please you, my lady."

Lady Ermentrude, her eyes half shut against the sunlight, moved her head in long, slow sweeps from side to side. "Yes," she muttered. "Yes. But you—" Her grip on Thomasine's arm tightened remorselessly. "You come, too," Her voice swelled back into rage. "By God's breath, there'll be no sacrificing this pretty lamb! No vows this Michaelmas or ever!"

The youth looked at Thomasine and lifted his chin in a gesture of reassurance that she grasped onto with grateful eyes. She yielded as best she might to Lady Ermentrude's pressing fingers. Despite her heart's thudding with fear and revulsion, she even began to help guide Lady Ermentrude toward the guest hall. Lady Ermentrude's walk was increasingly near to a stagger the further they went. By the time they reached the steps, she was leaning on the youth hard enough that he had to brace himself with all his strength to keep her on her feet.

One of her ladies, her eyes frightened, hurried up the stairs to open the door. At the bottom Lady Ermentrude groped with her foot for the first step, missed it, tried again, and found it. The youth steadied her, murmuring encouragement. Muttering under her breath, Lady Ermentrude reeled up four stairs, swaying drunkenly on every one, first against the youth, then against Thomasine, but never loosening her hold.

Intent on her fear and disgust and Lady Ermentrude, Thomasine failed to hear the clatter of other horses coming into the courtyard until they were nearly to her and a familiar voice cried out, "Thomasine! What's amiss?"

With vast relief Thomasine recognized first her sister and then her brother-in-law as they reined in beside the stairs. Their matching chestnut horses were streaked and darkened with sweat, and Isobel rode astride as she only did when haste was more important than fashion. Behind them a clot of mounted men-at-arms and an ill-laden packhorse crowded the gateway.

"Isobel!" Thomasine called, holding out her free hand to them. Lady Ermentrude's head came up and swung loose-necked from one side to the other as she tried to focus on who had come. Then she thrust the boy aside and yelled, "Wicked! Wicked! You won't have her! You hear me? You won't have her!" Her voice dropped, and her eyes bulged like onions in her flushed face as she thrust her face close to Thomasine and hissed, "Stay close, you hear? Say nothing, nothing, nothing until we've reached the bishop. Then we'll see who's taking vows and who isn't, who goes into cloister and who doesn't!"

Wine fumes and fear made Thomasine back down a step, her stomach twisting. "Please, Aunt," she whimpered, hating the sound of her own helplessness. "Please, it's Isobel and Sir John."

"Wicked!" Lady Ermentrude shouted. "Keep back and out of this!"

"Aunt, listen to us," Sir John said calmly, strongly, but Lady Ermentrude's head came up as if at an insult.

"You listen!" she spat back, but then swayed, her eyes

unfocusing. Her mouth gaped and worked, then she swayed away without continuing.

Thomasine had never seen anyone so drunk this close before. It seemed a kind of madness that had her by the arm and would not let her go. Giving way to terror, she pried at Lady Ermentrude's clutching fingers with her own free hand, but to no use. Lady Ermentrude seemed not even to notice and reeled forward again, on up the stairs, dragging Thomasine with her. "Inside. I want in out of the sun."

The youth was back at her side, taking all her weight on himself but managing to say over his bent shoulder at Sir John and Isobel, "Stay back, pray you. Let me bring her in and settle her."

Thomasine, looking back, pleading for help with her eyes, saw Sir John place a restraining hand on his wife's arm, nodding his head. Then her aunt had her into the guest hall, out of the bright day into shadow. For a moment Thomasine was half blind. Lady Ermentrude herself came jerkily to a halt, leaning against the youth, pushing him into the stone-thick corner of the door frame. Her free hand to her eyes, she moaned softly, "Ahhhh. That's better. The sun was too strong. Ah, my head!"

"Come sit," the youth said quietly. "Rest."

"Rest," Lady Ermentrude agreed thickly. "Sit."

She let him help her, jerking Thomasine along, toward a chair set near the long trestle table in the room's center. She sank into its cushion with a groan, her eyes shut but her grip still strong on Thomasine as she growled, her voice distorted with anger, "They can't force you. Remember that."

"No one is forcing me to anything!" Thomasine cried. "Stop saying that!"

Lady Ermentrude, eyes tightly closed and breathing heavily, said only, "No ssssacrifice to wickednessss." With her chin drawn in toward her throat and her head moving restlessly from side to side, she drew the sibilants out like sizzling fat.

"Would you care to wash your hands, my lady?"

Dame Frevisse's voice was cool and smooth as silver, deep with respect. As Lady Ermentrude had sunk into the chair Dame Frevisse had come from among the gathered, staring servants and was standing now in front of her, a wide, shallow basin in her hands and a white linen towel over her arm. Lady Ermentrude lifted her head almost blindly, her eyelids half closed over her distended eyes as if the light were too strong for her even in the shadowed hall. There was an effort of comprehension behind her flushed face. Shaking her head, she let go of Thomasine's arm to feel with both hands at her throat with a bewildered and oddly feeble gesture. "Th-th-thirssss-tee."

Thomasine, freed, stayed where she was, held by a glance from Dame Frevisse and an uncertainty that her legs would hold her if she tried to move.

Dame Frevisse, speaking in her same careful voice, asked again, "Would you care to wash your hands, my lady?" and stepped forward to kneel before Lady Ermentrude, holding out the basin. Lady Ermentrude, answering familiar form with familiar gesture, let loose her throat to dip her fingers into the water. But the bewildered look stayed on her face, and her mouth, like a fish newly caught, opened and closed soundlessly.

"Thomasine," Dame Frevisse said softly, not taking her eyes from Lady Ermentrude's face, "would you fetch us a sop of warmed milk and honey to soothe my lady's throat?"

Thomasine dared back away a step, then another, and, safe out of Lady Ermentrude's reach, bobbed a quick curtsey before turning to flee from the hall.

In the enormity of her terror at Lady Ermentrude's drunken madness, she forgot to be afraid of the yard and everyone in it. A gabble of voices met her on the doorstep, but her only thought was of escape, however temporary, into the cloister kitchen, until her brother-in-law called out to her, "Thomasine! What's toward in there?"

He and Isobel were still mounted on their palfreys, their few followers clustered behind them. To Thomasine they were familiar and safe, and she went down the steps to them quickly, saying in hushed tones, "She's drunk. She rode in drunk and raving."

"About what?" Isobel asked with sharp concern.

"About my not becoming a nun. She keeps saying over and over again she means to stop it, that she won't let it happen. This is not like her usual teasing. It's worse. It's . . . different."

Isobel turned a worried look on her husband. His own face was as puzzled and concerned as hers, but it was Isobel who said, "She wasn't drunk when she came on us yesterday, but she was raving then. It must be madness."

Thomasine's eyes widened at this echo of her own thought. She whispered, "I thought that, too."

Sir John swung down from his horse. He was tall and tanned, with firmly drawn features, easily handsome. Six years of marriage and its comforts had begun to thicken his waist and soften the flesh along his jaw, but at nearly thirty he still had the clear, fair skin and easy eyes of youth, as if fatherhood and the responsibilities of lordship were not yet enough to settle him.

One of his men came forward to lead his horse away as he moved to his wife's side. She leaned forward into his hands, and he lifted her as lightly to the ground as if she were a child. She matched Thomasine with her fair hair and green-hazel eyes, but was five years her elder, had borne three children, and was more mature in face and body, a woman where Thomasine was still a girl. Her eyebrows were plucked into thin, fashionable arches, and her riding dress was in the latest style, wide-sleeved and belted high under her fashionably small breasts, the collar laid out neatly around her shoulders. She neither wore nor needed demeaning face paints; her complexion was nearly as fresh and clear as Thomasine's own. Now, with troubled expression, she turned from Sir John to Thomasine and asked, "But wherefore mad? She arrived yesterday without warning, already angry, and set to ranting before she'd dismounted. No matter what we said, she was cruel and harsh in her words all the evening and left in a fury this morning. Now she's come here, still angry, and would have nothing but you away from St. Frideswide's. That's all she's said? That she wants you out of St. Frideswide's?"

"She says it over and over," Thomasine said. "Her raging has her throat hurting and I'm to fetch milk sops and honey for it. I'll be back as soon as may be. Pray pardon me." Breathless with so much speaking, she curtseyed in haste and moved swiftly on across the yard.

Chapter 4

THE PLACE WITHIN the cloister where the world most boldly intruded was the kitchen. Not only in its shape: it was a squat, ugly room with two big roasting fireplaces and a bake oven in its farther wall, sturdy locked pantry cupboards against the other walls, and an array of heavy tables in its middle for the carving, mincing, kneading, mixing, setting out, and gathering in of whatever needed preparation for the meals of the day. No pious silence here: because there was such necessary work to be done—and mostly by lay servants not under vows—the rule of silence did not hold; instead of hand signals and nods, there was ordinary conversation broken by curt orders, the words mixed among a secular clatter of dishes, clang of heavy iron pots, ring of large stirring spoons tossed from pan to counter, slap of bread being kneaded, whisht of knives slicing at vegetables, and the occasional scraw of saws carving up some unfortunate pig or ox. And over all of that was almost always Dame Alys's big voice, stronger than the noise and kitchen odors.

Dame Alys was cellarer, second only to Domina Edith in the priory. She was in charge of overseeing labor, land, and buildings, and since St. Frideswide's was too small to have a kitchener under her orders, Dame Alys saw to that office, too—food and drink and firewood and so the kitchen itself.

Word of Lady Ermentrude's arrival had come this far already, and Dame Alys was in full cry. "So now we're bound to cater to her drunk as well as stupid, are we? Her and that mighty baggage of followers." Dame Alys slammed an iron stirring spoon down on a table to emphasize her wrath. Since she was a large-boned woman running to muscle rather than fat, the spoon bent visibly.

The three laywomen and the sturdy chief cook, a man, cast looks at one another and went on with their business. Dame Alys's rages were as immense and sincere as her penances, and she seldom actually injured anyone in them. But she was always more interested in venting spleen than in being soothed or hearing anyone's helpful replies, and no one bothered saying anything.

Now, straightening the spoon between her hands, she pointed it at Thomasine hesitating in the doorway and said, "You're come to tell me she's asking for her dinner already, aren't you? Well, you can tell her from me I need more warning than that to set a proper meal under her nose. Would to God it were in my power to serve her as she deserves. Spoiled fish and rotten apples, with ditch water for a drink, that's what she'd have. And I'd stand over her with a cleaver to make sure she ate and drank it all!"

She paused to draw breath. Into the momentary lull Martha Hayward said, without looking up from a mixing bowl and whatever she was beating in it, "That would be enough to start a real feud between the Godfreys and the Fenners."

"What say you?" Dame Alys said indignantly. "There's been no bloodshed as yet, but there's a feud all right. And the blood will come soon, too, if they don't stop pushing to take our property away from us!"

Martha, bold to grin at Dame Alys, said, "And meanwhile the lawyers' cost enough to break both families. Aye, lawyers love a good quarrel between great families."

"Never you mind lawyers! It's Lady Ermentrude who is the heart and soul of the Fenners' wanting to grab what isn't theirs. And may their souls be damned to hell for it and hers to the hottest part, amen. She's a Fenner who married a Fenner and bred Fenner brats and that makes her thrice as bad as any of them and now she wants her dinner, la-de-da. Ha!"

"She's no worse than many another great lady," Martha Hayward said stubbornly. She was shorter than Dame Alys but nearly as broad, bulked out in fat from taking a serving size instead of a taste of anything that she judged in need of sampling. Along with her kitchen duties, she had collected little responsibilities such as seeing to the prioress's greyhound, and so gave herself such airs that she felt secure enough to be rude to nearly everyone, save Domina Edith herself. Only three things kept her from being sent away: her light hand with pastry, her skill in drawing the maximum of flavor from a minimum of costly spices, and the fact that she was there at Lady Ermentrude's request, as she was always glad to mention, given the chance. "I was in her service most of my life and only left it because she lessened her household after her husband died, God rest him, and she was going to be a lady-in-waiting to the Queen. I'm here because she asked me to be, God bless her. So let me tell you if you don't know already . . ."

They did know already. Anyone who ever came within ear's reach of Martha Hayward for any time at all knew everything about her and all she knew of Lady Ermentrude and every great personage who had ever crossed her path.

Dame Alys slammed the spoon down again, this time onto a pot lid, which now would need a tinker to mend it, and said loudly over Martha's flux of words, straightening the spoon as she did, "So why are you standing there all baa-eyed, child? What's her ladyship wanting to eat this time? St. John's bread and fresh-whipped cream?"

"She's ill," Thomasine said hurriedly. "Dame Frevisse wants warm milk and sops with honey for her."

"Ill's a nice name for it," Dame Alys snorted. "The word that reached the kitchen was 'drunk.' So go on! You know how to do that much, don't you? No, not my new bread,'' she added as Thomasine moved toward the rows of cooling loaves that would go into the refectory for the nuns' dinner. ''Here, never mind, it will be quicker to do it myself.''

Talking half to herself, Dame Alys went to a shelf beside a cabinet and took down a half loaf of bread. ''Last week's will do more than well enough for someone too 'ill' to know the difference. It'll soften in the milk anyway. And where's that pitcher of milk— Ah.'' The small pitcher was on the hob, staying warm. Dame Alys took a clean pottery bowl from a shelf of them. She broke the bread into it and poured the warm milk over it. The honey was in another cupboard; she spooned a dollop into the mix and stirred it until the bread began to soften.

All the while, she and Martha Hayward traded comments about whether or not there was a feud and how seriously Lady Ermentrude had involved herself in it. Just as she picked up the bowl to hand it to Thomasine, they both stopped. ''Listen,'' Dame Alys said.

But they were already listening, heads turned and mouths open. Because somewhere someone was screaming. Thinned by distance and stone walls, a high and drawn out cry wavered, fell and rose again in agony.

''Stand where you are!'' Dame Alys slashed sideways with her spoon at the kitchen staff as they began a surge for the door. ''Whatever that racket is, it's no concern of yours, and they'll not be needing a gaggle of loons getting in their way! There's plenty of work to keep you all right here!''

The cooks and scullions halted—except for Martha Hayward. Already near the door, she kept going, with a speed and grace surprising for one of her bulk, not slowing even when Dame Alys shouted after her to return. Thomasine, the bowl with its warm milk, bread, and honey clutched in her hands, stood fast near a table, not daring to move—or wanting to, either. She had had enough of noise and madness this day.

But Dame Alys, glaring around, said to her, "Well, why do you stand there as if you've grown roots? Didn't they send you here to fetch that bowl of sops? Begone! If that unholy noise is from Lady Ermentrude, and likely it is from the ugliness of it, they'll be wanting something to stop her mouth."

She underlined her orders with a thrust of the spoon, sending Thomasine out of the room in haste. But out of Dame Alys's sight she immediately slowed. She could hear voices shouting in the courtyard beyond the cloister and slowed her pace more, but too soon she was at the door into the courtyard. It was wide open, with Martha Hayward standing just outside in happy admiration of the press of servants pushing among themselves toward the guest-hall steps, yelling their excitement or shouting an apt paternoster for salvation of the soul that was obviously being torn untimely from its mortal host. A half dozen of Lady Ermentrude's dozen small dogs, doubtless let go by someone's start of surprise, had tangled their leashes around legs in their flight and were now joyously fighting among themselves or yipping with pain at repeated kicks.

An angry groom was trying to bring Isobel's and Sir John's horses out of the sudden mob, and there would have been injuries if the frightened animals had not been too exhausted to do more than swerve and half-rear. Sir John and Isobel, whose presence might have brought order, were not in sight.

And over all the surge of noise and movement, from inside the guest hall scream after scream tore from a throat bursting with terror.

"Lord!" marveled Martha Hayward. "She's set them up right enough. Come, my lady, let's see what it's about this time."

Thomasine wanted to refuse, but had no excuse ready to hand. Besides, Dame Frevisse had told her to bring the milksops, and obedience was the one certain choice in this chaos. Clutching the bowl to her breast with both hands, she followed after Martha, a small boat in a barge's wake. Martha pushed her way easily through the tangled crowd of servants, who would have blocked the way of anyone smaller and less determined. Her heavy shoves broke open a clot that blocked the guest-hall steps, giving her and Thomasine clear passage up to where someone in Lady Ermentrude's livery was deliberately obstructing the doorway.

Around Martha's bulk, up the stairs, Thomasine recognized the youth who had helped her with Lady Ermentrude. Now he was refusing to let anyone in. Flushed with his efforts, his blue eyes bright with the challenge, he said, "Hold!" to Martha Hayward's wordless thrust. He looked determined to stand his ground, but Martha turned and took Thomasine by the shoulder, bringing her forward and saying, "No, see, I've brought Thomasine, your lady's favorite niece. Dame Frevisse bid her bring a milksop for Lady Ermentrude and here it is. Let us by."

The youth frowned, then nodded and stepped aside with a reluctant bow. Martha surged by with Thomasine in tow.

Around the hall were scattered some few of Lady Ermentrude's servants, frozen in listening positions. More were gathered gabbling at a far door leading to the hall's best chamber. The screaming came from there but was broken now, as if breath or strength was failing.

With no pretense of politeness, Martha bullied her way to the door and opened it. Thomasine tried to draw back then, not wanting to see whatever was beyond it, but Martha's arm was strong from her years of kitchen labor, and Thomasine a good deal lighter than a barrel of salt herring. She found herself dragged helplessly in to where she least wanted to be.

They must have brought Lady Ermentrude into the room with some thought of putting her to bed. Her shoes and stockings, hat and veil were off, her gown open at the throat. But they had gotten no further before the fit came on her. She was on the bed, her back against the high wooden headboard. Her face was purple with her mad effort and lack of breath as she flailed with arms and legs at anyone trying to come near her. And this close to her there were words caught in among the screaming, words pulled out of shape and torn to pieces, but it seemed she was ranting of fire and burning and her soul.

Dame Frevisse to one side of the bed and one of her ladies-in-waiting to the other were stretched forward in a desperate attempt to take and control her arms, but they had no chance against a strength gone past sanity. Their occasional graspings seemed only to send her into a worse frenzy. She wrenched a hand free of Frevisse's grasp to point wildly across the room at nothing.

"T'ave coooom! Ear's flaaaame!" she howled. Her eyes distended, her head thrown back to show the cords of her throat, she gagged for air, her wail raw with despair. She drew a fragment of breath and suddenly the words were clear: "God help! Save me!"

Frevisse, aware of someone coming into the room, looked up, and her eye was then caught by the large carved crucifix on the wall. She broke away from Lady Ermentrude to grab it down. The crucifix was painted in raw colors, heavy in her hands. She went back to the bed to thrust it before Lady Ermentrude's distended eyes. "My lady, look here!"

Lady Ermentrude, mouth gaping in a desperate attempt to both scream and draw breath for another scream, choked. Her unfocused eyes glimpsed the crucifix, recognized it, and her hands fumbled out for it, grasped it, and dragged it to herself. Awkwardly, desperately, she pressed it to her lips, kissing it. It slid sideways onto her cheek, but she went on clinging to it as air whistled through her nostrils in a long-delayed need to simply breathe.

In the trembling silence, with everyone around her frozen, waiting, Lady Ermentrude rolled her eyes sideways to Frevisse. Her jaw worked. In a barking whisper, she forced out, "Hell . . . fire . . . stop . . . it."

"It's stopped," Frevisse said. "We've stopped it." She kept her voice low, pitched for reassurance, but Lady Ermentrude's eyes remained frantic, demanding. Without changing tone, Frevisse said, "Someone tell Dame Claire to hurry. And find Father Henry."

Neither Lady Ermentrude's lady-in-waiting nor the maid, cringed back against the wall beside the bed, moved, probably in fear of setting off the screaming again. Frevisse understood the fear; she was standing quite still herself. But she risked looking away, toward Sir John and Lady Isobel. They had been trying to help bring Lady Ermentrude to bed when the frenzy started. Now they were standing against the far wall, Lady Isobel pressed close to her husband, held in the protective circle of his arms though his own face was strained with shock.

Beyond them, in the doorway, were Martha Hayward—of course, Frevisse thought—and Thomasine. Neither of them had had sense enough to close the door; staring faces crowded behind them, no one looking as if they had the wit to help.

"Martha," she said, still careful of her tone. "I need Dame Claire and Father Henry. Go *now*."

"Demons," Thomasine interrupted in a loud whisper. "She was seeing demons."

"She wasn't," Frevisse said firmly, her attention quickly back to Lady Ermentrude, who was still clinging to the crucifix, her eyes now tightly shut.

"Demons," Thomasine repeated and came nearer, still clutching the bowl, her pale face narrow and intent in the frame of her white veil. "She's evil and demons have come for her soul."

Lady Ermentrude began to whimper. All though the room and in the doorway hands moved, crossing themselves.

Frevisse said forcefully, "They have *not*."

Lady Ermentrude's maid gave a dry, terrified sob. "But she was seeing hellfire. She said so. And she couldn't stop screaming until you gave her the crucifix. We saw it!"

Lady Ermentrude began to wail softly, and Frevisse said, fiercely now, "If there were demons here the cross would keep them at bay! Martha, I told you, we need the priest and Dame Claire!"

Martha nodded wordlessly and backed out of the door. But they must have been already in the guest hall; she was hardly out of sight when Father Henry's voice was heard saying, "Yes, yes, Martha, you wait out here." And a moment later, spreading the crowding servants aside, he came in, tall and comforting, already wearing his priestly stole and carrying the small box that held all the articles needed for the Last Sacrament. Dame Claire, small behind him, carried her own box of medicines, and Frevisse could not have said which of them she was more pleased to see.

Father Henry closed the door on the avid faces, including Martha's. Lady Ermentrude's wail subsided into a faint moan, and Frevisse said slowly, smoothly and low-voiced, to Dame Claire, "She's drunk. She came riding in drunk a half hour or so ago and then fell into the screaming and raving."

"It's demons," Thomasine said.

"If you say that again, I'll see Domina Edith has you on bread and water from now to All Hallows," Frevisse said in the edged monotone she used when at the end of her patience.

Dame Claire, ignoring both of them, came to the bed, silently assessing Lady Ermentrude.

"She's m-mad," said Lady Isobel, the second word drawn out, thinned and broken. She hid her face against her husband's shoulder.

"Perhaps," Dame Claire answered in her deep voice. She reached out to feel Lady Ermentrude's face. "It is true that those who have drunk for years often come to be bothered with evil visions. She has a fever, too."

She touched the backs of her hands. Lady Ermentrude flinched, her knuckles whitening as her grip on the crucifix tightened.

"No, here, on her hands, she's clemmed with cold." Dame Claire looked at Frevisse. "Was she like this when you tried to undress her?"

Frevisse nodded. "Hot as new baked bread, cold as autumn earth."

Dame Claire looked to the lady-in-waiting beyond the bed, a handsome woman, probably, when not terrified. "Have you ever seen her this way before?"

The woman shook her head. "No, madam, but I've been with her this past week only." She was one of the women who had ridden in with Lady Ermentrude the half hour ago. Though plainly frightened, she was calming a little at the need to answer Dame Claire's questioning. Her wits come somewhat back to her, she continued, "She had a single bottle of wine with her on the road this morning. I don't know how much she'd drunk when she dropped it and broke it on a stone."

Martha, her head around the opened corner of the door, spoke up. "I was with her for seven years, and I can say she could drink several bottles at a sitting, but it was usually of an evening, at her own fireside. And she might grow boisterous at it, but I never saw her taken like this. When I heard that shrilling start and my heart went up into my mouth, I knew my lady was taken in pain like she's never been before." But she was staring at Lady Ermentrude with ghoulish satisfaction.

Frevisse caught her eye and frowned a hush at her. Martha frowned back, but retreated, pulling the door shut.

Dame Claire looked at Lady Isobel and Sir John. "She was with you last night? Was she drinking then? What did she eat? Was she drinking before she left you this morning?"

"She drank a cup of wine at supper, and she ate very little of what we all had," Sir John answered. "She was in a rage, too busy ranting at us to eat or drink much. She left without breaking her fast this morning, only took some wine and rode off."

"We were afraid for her," Lady Isobel said. She spoke rapidly, eyes shining with unshed tears. "She kept talking at us, not listening to our replies. She said wild, impossible things. Ugly things." Her head sank, and Sir John held her more closely, looking at the listeners as if his lady wife's trouble was their fault. Taking courage from his embrace, she lifted her chin and continued, "We tried to quiet her—the servants, you know; they will gossip, repeating all they overhear. But it was no use. She went at us until late in the night and again this morning. I doubt she slept much if at all, because she was in the same fury this morning. We tried to have her stay but she rode off still furious at us. We were afraid for her, John and I, riding off like that. Afraid she might be taken ill on the road . . ." Isobel gestured vaguely. "Her heart. Or a fall. She can be cruel to a horse when she's in a temper. She's not young, and not always careful of herself. We followed after her as soon as might be. And now Thomasine says she came here swearing she'd have her out of the nunnery. I saw a madman once. It was awful. It was like—" She looked toward Lady Ermentrude and fell eloquently silent.

"Whatever this is, she's very ill with it," Dame Claire said with flat calm. "And not in her mind only." She had gone on examining Lady Ermentrude as far as she properly could with men in the room. Now she gently urged her to straighten and lie flat, to be covered. "It's not her heart or she'd not be so violent. Or apoplexy because that leaves its victims helpless, and that she obviously is not. It may be a fever. But it's a strange fever that leaves the hands and feet cold." Dame Claire was clearly thinking aloud.

"Perhaps she is only drunk then," Sir John suggested hopefully.

"Drink can take people in different ways." Dame Claire nodded. "This could well be one of them. But whatever it is, she's quiet now and needs to be kept that way lest she make worse whatever is already wrong. Thomasine." She looked to where Thomasine still stood at the bed's foot.

Slowly Thomasine drew her eyes away from her great-aunt, to look at the infirmarian.

"Thomasine," Dame Claire repeated, "I want the box from the far shelf in the infirmary. The gray one with the borage flowers painted on its lid. You helped me make the compound, remember? Valerian for nerves and borage for melancholy. Bring it. And it needs to be given with wine. There's none left in the infirmary so you'll need all three keys to the wine chest. You'll have to ask Domina Edith for hers, and then Dame Alys, and Dame Perpetua."

Lady Isobel stirred in her husband's arms. "We have some malmsey with us. We brought it on the chance we could make peace with her. It's one of her favorites. I'll go for it."

But Sir John said with a gesture, "Wait. Malmsey may not be right for this."

"It should be fine, and save us time," Dame Claire said. "My thanks. Only the box then, Thomasine. What's that you're holding?"

"A milksop, my lady."

"Good. Leave it; we may want it. Now go. Be quick."

Frevisse reached out to take the bowl from Thomasine's stiff hands. Thomasine made the correct curtsey to Dame Claire, then backed away from the bed as if afraid to turn her back to Lady Ermentrude. Not until she bumped into the door frame did she turn to fumble the door open and leave so quickly she seemed as much in flight as in obedience.

Frevisse set the bowl carefully on the table along the wall. Father Henry, who had been standing to one side of everyone this while, praying under his breath, now lifted his head and asked, "Will she live?"

"I don't know. She's very ill," Dame Claire answered. "But blood and heart and breathing are all strong. And she's quiet now. That's to the good, if her mind stays unconfused."

Lady Ermentrude made a small moan and turned her head

toward the sound of Father Henry's voice, keeping her eyes closed. "Az devil 'mongst us," she croaked.

"Then you want our priest's prayers," said Frevisse sensibly.

Father Henry came to stand by the bed, fumbling his way into anxious Latin as he gestured a cross over it. *"In nomini Patris, et Filios, et Spiritu Sanctos, amen,"* he intoned.

Frevisse flinched at his inaccurate Latin, but Lady Ermentrude, with a deep, spasmed effort, broke one hand's grip from the crucifix and reached out to him, groping until she found his arm and dug her fingers into his sleeve. Her mouth worked, the cords of her neck stretching with tension, but all she managed was a gargling croak. Her eyes bulged with her effort and panic. The gargling changed to a hiss. Dame Claire moved as if to quiet her, but something in the sound made sense to Father Henry. Leaning toward Lady Ermentrude, he said, "Sin. It's sin that frightens you?"

Lady Ermentrude's head twitched in agreement. Her throat worked, straining.

"We all live in fear of that, my lady," Father Henry said. He patted her hand where it clung to him. "But I'm praying for you. Do you wish to make confession?"

"Sssinsss," Lady Ermentrude hissed. "Wwwwurrsss sssinns . . ." Anger darkened her face, and her gaze crawled around the the room. Her hand twitched away from Father Henry to claw at her throat. ". . . thannn miiine," she whined, high off the back of her mouth. "Wwwurrss thannn miiine."

There was fear mixed with the anger. It glistened in her eyes as she brought them back to the priest. She let him take her hand into his own as he said soothingly, "All sins come to God in time, and there are none that can't be forgiven, if we but ask. It's your own we need to care for now. Would you have me give you absolution?"

Unsteadily, Lady Ermentrude jerked a nod. Father Henry opened his wooden box and took out two small beeswax candles already in silver holders. He put them on the table, flanking the bowl of milksops, and Frevisse brought a scrap of kindling from the fireplace to light them while he took a small glass bottle of chrism, another of blessed water, and a fist-sized wad of fresh bread, his practiced movements somehow reassuring. In the few years Father Henry had been at St. Frideswide's, Frevisse had found that neither his mind nor faith went very far, but were strong so far as they went; and it was strength Lady Ermentrude needed just now.

Quietly Frevisse gestured to Lady Ermentrude's women, and Lady Isobel and Sir John, that they should go now. None of them seemed willing, until Dame Claire took Lady Isobel gently by the elbow and urged her toward the door. Sir John, his arm still tenderly around his wife, went with them, the maid close at their heels. Only the dark-haired lady-in-waiting continued to hesitate, until Frevisse made a sharper, demanding gesture at her. With a sidelong look at her mistress, she went. Frevisse followed to make sure no one lingered within eavesdropping distance.

The cluttering knot of servants outside the door drew back reluctantly, leaving them a little space. Dame Claire said to the lady-in-waiting and the maid, "She will not need you for a while. Go reassure the others that she's alive and quiet now, that she was in a nightmare, nothing else. We don't need foolish rumors running through all the priory."

The maid curtsied, but the lady-in-waiting said firmly, "I'm the lady of her chamber today. I'd best stay and go in again when we're able. You do as the lady bids," she added to the maid.

Clearly glad to obey, the maid walked away, immediately surrounded by the other servants. A little wave of low-voiced questioning followed after her, and Frevisse knew that despite Dame Claire's words, by dark word would have run all the way to the village that Lady Ermentrude had been surrounded by dancing demons and the flames of Hell and that Father Henry had driven them away with prayers and holy water.

Dames Claire and Frevisse started away from the door. Sir John stopped, putting his hand to his jaw and wincing. He asked, "She'll live?" in a voice stiff with pain.

Dame Claire thought before answering slowly, "There seems no reason why she shouldn't. Her heart and pulse are strong. It's her mind that seems gone most awry, and that will mend of itself if it's only drunkenness."

"Then she'll be all right?" Lady Isobel insisted.

"I think there's a goodly chance, though we may not know until morning. Or later. Thomasine, bless you for your speed." She held out her hand for the box Thomasine handed her, a little breathless with her haste. "There is this at least to bring on sleep, and that can be a better cure than most."

"The wine, I nearly forgot." Lady Isobel drew away from her husband. "I'll bring it."

"No, I will," he offered quickly, but winced again, and she placed a hand on his arm and smiled up at him.

"You don't want the outside air on that tooth. Besides, I know where in the saddlebags it is. You wait here, love."

Beyond the cloister walls the bell began to ring for late afternoon's Vespers. Dame Claire said, "You go, Dame Frevisse. Let Thomasine stay to help me. When Father Henry is through I want to give her the medicine and see if she will eat some of the milksop. We'll come when we can."

"I'll stay, too, by your leave," Martha Hayward put in, thrusting her way into the knot around Dame Claire. "I know her ways as well as any and can fetch things for her from the cloister better than her present people. That'll save Thomasine's feet a bit."

"And when I've brought the wine, I'll bide with her, too," Lady Isobel said. "Or we can be with her in turns. Whatever is the matter, she's my aunt and we owe her that much. If you think it all right?"

"Assuredly," Dame Claire said. "And good."

Frevisse, with the thought that they seemed to have the

matter well in hand without her, nodded her own agreement and left for the church.

Vespers was one of each day's longer Hours, with four psalms to be sung among its prayers. In her first months in the nunnery, as a novice with ideals but little knowledge, Frevisse had resented its intrusion into the routine of every afternoon. All the other offices had made sense and been a gladness to her, even Matins and Lauds, the twin service that dragged her from bed at midnight. Prayer then in the dark watches of the night, the church seeming full of otherworldly shadows, lurking around small hollows of gold candlelight beside the altar, and her mind withdrawn by sleep from everything but the need to chant the office and prayers, was a wondrous time, with God present all around them.

But Vespers came in busy late afternoon, with the nuns hurrying in to it from all parts of the priory and Frevisse almost always having to leave some task half-done behind her, and needing to go back to it, distracted, later. She had done silent penance for her resentment, but when that did not cure it, she had been finally forced to admit her feeling to Dame Perpetua, newly come then to being mistress of novices.

"It intrudes," she had complained. "It's in the way of whatever I'm about."

"But isn't prayer what we're supposed to be about?" Dame Perpetua had asked. She had an instinctive talent for knowing the best way to teach, based on a novice's needs and strengths. Some needed leading, others prodding. A very few could be challenged. "You have some business for being here other than serving God perhaps?"

Frevisse, goaded into looking at her mind and its habits, had come—less than graciously at first—to admit there were reasons for Vespers at the busy end of afternoons: a need to remember there were matters more important to the undying soul than the passing needs of everyday.

"A solis ortu usque ad occasum, laudabile noman

domini.'' From the dawn of the day until sunset, praised be the Name of the Lord.

They sang the words in Latin, but Frevisse turned them to English in her mind, partly from the little Latin that she knew but mostly from her much-treasured Bible, an object forbidden because it was a Wycliffe English translation. Still, she felt, understanding the glory of the words as she chanted them could not be sinful, no matter how she came by that understanding. She wove her voice with the other nuns into a curtain of praise, familiar and practiced, warm in the gray shadows of the afternoon church.

She knew when Dame Claire joined them, her surprisingly sweet, clear alto as precise on every note as she was precise with her medicines.

''Non nobis, Domine, non nobis: sed monini tuo da gloriamo.'' Not to us, Lord, not to us, but glory to your name, for your true love. Amen.

The last of the office sounded softly among the raftered roof and stone walls, then fell away to silence. Slowly, with the stiffness of age and sitting, Domina Edith rose, and they rose after her and in a hush of skirts and slippered feet made a procession out into the cloister. There would be supper soon, a familiar pittance of cheese and apples, with any bread saved from midday dinner, then a chance to rest or walk in the little garden or the orchard, to reflect on the day, and, by a relaxation of the Rule, to talk among themselves. Though today Frevisse would go back to the guest halls, seeing to what needed doing there. The day's last office, Compline, came after that, and then bed.

In the cloister walk they all knelt together for Domina Edith's blessing. She had raised her hand, had begun to speak, when the door to the courtyard slammed, startling them all in their places. Footsteps sharp with running came, and a woman in Lady Ermentrude's livery burst into the cloister walk's far end.

''She's choking!'' she cried. ''She's dying! The priest said come. Come quickly.''

Frevisse caught Domina Edith's raised eyebrows giving her leave to go. She left her place in line, but Dame Claire had not waited even for that and was already running down the cloister walk. The others started to rise, confused, but Domina Edith with a single gesture felled them and silenced them. Age had not lessened her authority.

Frevisse overtook Dame Claire at the cloister gate. They came out into the courtyard together, wasting no time on anyone as they crossed the yard. In the guest hall most of Lady Ermentrude's people had sat down to supper at the trestle tables. Heads turned as Frevisse and Dame Claire passed through, not running now but moving too fast to go unnoticed. Frevisse glimpsed Sir John rising from beside his wife at the head of the tables as she and Dame Claire reached Lady Ermentrude's door.

Dame Claire's sharp stop in the doorway forced Frevisse to sidestep to avoid her. Then she stopped as sharply, too.

Father Henry was rising from his knees beside the bed, shaking his curly head with dazed disbelief. Lady Ermentrude lay propped up on her pillows, head rolled to one side, her hands still holding the crucifix, her mouth open, her harsh breathing filling the room. On the floor between her and Father Henry sprawled Martha Hayward, her legs straddled wide, her mouth agape and clogged with foam, her hands looking like claws in the rush matting, her eyes bulging, blood-suffused, in the strangled, dead purple of her face.

Chapter 5

Frevisse stopped where she was, as much in disgust as horror, then crossed herself as much in penance for the disgust as for the repose of Martha's soul. Dame Claire, recovering from her own reaction, went to kneel where Father Henry had been.

Frevisse, almost as quickly, went to stand between sight of Martha's body and Thomasine, who was crouched too near it, whimpers crawling up from her throat and her face pressed against prayer-clasped hands. Carefully, not wanting to bring on hysterics, she took Thomasine by the shoulders and said as gently as she could, "Stand up out of Dame Claire's way."

The infirmarian was feeling for pulse and breath, looking for life where very surely there was none.

"Stand up," Frevisse repeated, wanting to get her away from the temptation to look again at Martha.

Thomasine responded, letting herself be helped to her feet. With an arm around her shoulders, Frevisse turned her away from both Martha and Lady Ermentrude.

"It was awful," Thomasine whispered, shaking in Frevisse's hold. "It was horrible. She had a . . . fit. She—"

Firmly across her rising voice Frevisse said, "It's over. She's not hurting anymore. It's finished."

Dame Claire sat back from her fruitless search for signs of life and looked up at Father Henry still standing above her. "What happened?" she demanded.

Dumb-faced and stunned, perspiring freely, he shook his head. "We were sitting here, the women and I. The others were gone to supper. Lady Ermentrude was dozing, all quiet. Martha was at her stories again, about Lady Ermentrude and what a willful woman she was. I was, God pardon me," he crossed himself fervently, "hard put not to be laughing at what she had to tell, until she grew too bold and Thomasine was beginning to be offended and went away to pray." He pointed to the prie-dieu in the far corner. "I asked Martha then to speak more seemly."

There was a growing murmur at the doorway, and they turned to see a clot of people come to gape. No more were they noticed than they were pushed aside as Sir John came through, with Lady Isobel behind him. "What is it?" he asked. "What's happened?"

Frevisse cut across his questions, pushing Thomasine toward Lady Isobel. "My lady, please, your sister has need of you."

"Why, what's happened?" Lady Isobel's question was sharper than her husband's. "Is my aunt all right?" She came to take Thomasine's arm as she spoke and over her sister's shoulder saw what lay on the floor. Her face went curd-pale. In a choked voice she said, "Martha Hayward."

"Help Thomasine," ordered Frevisse, shifting the girl into Lady Isobel's arms. "Take her away from here." Lady Isobel nodded distracted agreement, her sickened gaze still on Martha's body.

"She'd dead?" Sir John croaked the word disbelievingly, his gaze averted.

Frevisse thought dryly that he must not have received his knighthood for skill in battle if he were squeamish over so bloodless a death; she firmly pushed both Thomasine and

Lady Isobel away to the side of the room, turning back as Dame Claire told Father Henry, "Go on."

The priest, uneasy at his growing audience and still shocked, obeyed. "She said she was thirsty, all dry from so much talking, and missing her supper in the bargain, and the sops were going to waste and," he gestured helplessly toward the empty bowl on the table, "she just ate them. She said she'd have a taste and then she ate them all."

"I dare say," Frevisse said with subdued irony.

Father Henry nodded vigorously. "She ate the sops, talking all the while, and then without my having any chance to stop her, she drank a great draught of the wine. I told her then it was meant for Lady Ermentrude and had medicine in it, so she made a face and stopped and went to talking again. In a while she said she was hot and opened the window, though I told her not to, and took to walking up and down the room. She was drunk then, I think, taking so much wine at once, for she wasn't making much sense. I tried to have her sit down lest she rouse Lady Ermentrude but—"

Father Henry stopped, embarrassment and uncertainty on his face.

"She pushed him," Thomasine said a little shrilly. "She laid hands on him and pushed him aside and kept on walking back and forth and Maryon said we'd best do something."

"Maryon?" Dame Claire asked.

The dark-haired lady-in-waiting stepped forward from beside the door. Frevisse realized she had been there all the while but so still she had gone unnoticed. "I'm Maryon," she said.

"And you were here the while?"

Maryon bent her head in acknowledgment. "I thought to be of service, if my lady should need me."

"What seemed the matter with Martha to you?"

"Too much drink," said Maryon succinctly. "I went to the door to send someone for some of my lady's men to have her out of here but while I was speaking to the woman, Martha behind me started making . . . sounds."

"Awful sounds!" Thomasine cried, and they turned to stare at her. "And, and clawing at herself." She made a feeble gesture at her chest and throat.

Her calm a decided contrast to Thomasine's edge of hysteria, Maryon said, "I told the woman to run find the infirmarian, that she would be in the church somewhere. When she was gone, Martha fell down and we couldn't help her."

"She was lying on the floor, kicking, thrashing . . ." Thomasine's eyes were full of desperate misery. "Father Henry went to help her, and I tried to pray, but it didn't help. It didn't help."

Father Henry said, "There was nothing I could do, but give her the Last Sacrament. There was time, barely. Just a general absolution and the anointing." He held out the small wad of bread that he had correctly used to wipe the last of the chrism from his fingers. His hand was trembling. He looked at it with surprise and then put it behind his back.

"But she just went on and on, kicking and choking!" Thomasine cried. "She couldn't stop. Until she—died."

"A fit," Lady Isobel said quickly, firmly, hugging Thomasine close. "A fit. Her heart, I would think. So fleshly a person easily might die like that. Here."

She moved Thomasine toward the table where a goblet sat beside the empty bowl of milksops. She pushed the goblet toward Thomasine's hands. "Drink this. It will steady you, child."

Thomasine's hands fluttered back, warding it off. "No. That's the wine with Great-aunt's medicine in it."

"Yes, but medicine for quieting nerves," said Frevisse, remembering. Which would do Thomasine no harm just now. "It's all right," she said reassuringly. "Dame Claire can mix more. Go on."

Obediently Thomasine reached to take the goblet from Lady Isobel. But her hands were shaking far worse than

Father Henry's; there was an instant's mistiming and the goblet fell, spattering the edge of Lady Isobel's gown and splashing the wine across the rush matting in a bright stain.

Isobel exclaimed in annoyance and backed away, shaking out her dress as Thomasine, wringing her hands, began a shaky litany. "I'm sorry, I didn't mean to, I'm sorry, I'm sorry—"

"Enough!" Frevisse said sternly. "The dress will wash and there was hardly any wine in the cup. Crying over spilled wine is as useless as crying over milk." She shifted her attention to Lady Isobel.

But she was already recovered, her dress forgotten as she came back to Thomasine's side. "It's all right. Come sit down. You're trembling so." She led her away to the bench at the window. Sir John followed them and put his arm around his wife's shoulders, holding her close while she held Thomasine. They were not moved so much by a servant's death, Frevisse thought, as by the bare fact of Death itself, and a dreadful one, unexpected, a hard thing to face so young as they were. Thomasine, apparently recovering a little, began to draw slightly away from her sister and averted her eyes. Frevisse, reassured by so typical a gesture and feeling the girl would do well enough for the time being, turned her attention back to Dame Claire, who had closed Martha's eyes and was straightening her limbs.

"It would seem it was her heart," Dame Claire pronounced, gazing on Martha's face. She crossed herself and rose to her feet.

"How does my lady aunt?" asked Lady Isobel.

Dame Claire turned and felt Lady Ermentrude's face and hands, and listened to her breathing before answering, "She seems to be doing well enough."

Coming near, Frevisse asked in a quiet voice, "Is it the medicine you gave her makes her sleep so deeply?" She was thinking that perhaps it was as well Thomasine had spilled it.

"She never had any of the medicine. I wanted the food in

her, to act against the drunkenness, and managed to make her eat a little, but by the time she'd finished being fed she was nearly stupored into sleep already and wouldn't drink. She just went to sleep without it.''

''What should we do?''

Dame Claire stood still, thinking; and after a moment gave a tiny nod of decision. ''Domina Edith must be told at once. Father Henry, will you do that? And Martha's body had best be taken into the cloister, away from here. Can you find men to do it?''

Frevisse turned to the door and pointed at four gawkers, who proved less willing to bear Martha's bulk than they had been to stare at it. But they were even less willing to cross Frevisse, and managed to take the body away with a semblance of respect.

With an audible sigh, Lady Isobel moved from her husband's arms, going to pick up the goblet from where it had fallen and partly rolled under the table. As she bent over and her fingers closed around it, she made a small sound of surprise and reached further under the table, then cried out sharply, ''It bit me!'' She jerked her hand back and clasped the fingers with her other hand. Blood welled and spilled over.

''What is it? What bit you?'' asked her husband, coming immediately to swing his foot under the table.

''That stupid monkey!'' she said, fierce with pain. ''That stupid monkey bit me!''

Sir John kicked again, hard enough to hurt, but the monkey, untouched, skittered out of hiding and scaled the bed curtains to sit on top, chittering in fright.

''I'll kill it!'' Sir John said. His gaze and hands moved, looking for a weapon, but Frevisse said firmly, ''We'll have it down later. You'll rouse Lady Ermentrude. Be quiet!''

He stopped, confused, as if uncertain whether to glare at her or at the monkey. The animal stared down at them silently, his tail wrapped up across his chest and around his shoulders in comfort.

"Please, John," Lady Isobel said softly, holding out her injured hand to him. His anger vanished like mist wiped off a mirror, and he went to her again.

"I'll take her to the infirmary," Dame Claire said. "To clean it and bandage it. Will you come, my lady?"

"Lady Ermentrude?" Lady Isobel asked. "Who will stay with her?"

"There's no worry about that," said the woman Maryon. "I'll remain with her."

"And so will I." Thomasine still stood beside the window, a slender child in her dark gown, solemn as if years of age were on her, her voice steady. "I need to make up for failing Martha."

"There was nothing you could have done, child," Dame Claire said. "Dame Frevisse, will you see to what needs doing? And Lady Isobel, if you'll come with me. When we have finished, doubtless Domina Edith will be wanting to hear from me about what's happened. By your leave."

Frevisse nodded her agreement. As Dame Claire left, taking Lady Isobel and Sir John with her, Maryon closed the chamber door against the remaining staring faces. Thomasine turned, her hands clasped imploringly, to Frevisse. "Please give me leave to stay. I've been angry at Lady Ermentrude. And at Martha. My staying will be penance for all of that."

"Otherwise you'll spend the night in church on your knees," Frevisse said dryly. Thomasine looked surprised, and a little abashed, at being so well understood, and nodded. "Then you might as well pray here as there, and be of some use in the bargain. My lady Maryon, can you find some of Lady Ermentrude's ladies to keep the watch in turns with you?"

"I can do it alone. I don't mean to sleep!" Thomasine cried out earnestly as Maryon nodded.

"I did not think you did. But I doubt Maryon or any other of your aunt's ladies will make the same sacrifice. They'll take their turns while you keep your watch. And your silence," she added as Thomasine opened her mouth to protest. "Go to your praying."

Frevisse ate her belated supper alone in the refectory. The lay workers' silence and long looks as they served her told they knew all there was to know about Martha's death and were feeling it, even if they knew better than to ask her questions.

When she had finished, Frevisse went to the church in search of Dame Claire. Martha's body, already washed, wrapped in its shroud, and placed in a plain coffin, was resting on a bier before the altar, candled at head and feet, with Father Henry too deep in prayer beside it to notice her. At Compline Domina Edith would divide the night into watches and set the nuns in turn in pairs to praying in the choir for the salvation of Martha's soul.

But Dame Claire was not there, and after a brief prayer for Martha's repose, Frevisse went out to the garden, where the nuns would be taking the last of their evening recreation before Compline and bed.

Dame Claire was not among them. Frevisse, pausing in the gateway to look for her, supposed she must be with Domina Edith and was thinking of going to join them when she noticed that the other nuns were not walking or sitting as usual but standing in little groups along the paths, their low talking—allowed during this one time of the day—underrun with excitement and pleasurable agitation. She knew Martha had never mattered enough to any of them for there to be much grieving for her loss. It was simply that so sudden a dying provided eager gossip for an evening, even better than Lady Ermentrude's regrettable behavior. Better that they gossip about someone beyond caring what they said, than about someone still able to be offended.

Then, before she could withdraw, Sister Amicia, among the nearest cluster of nuns, saw her and called out excitedly, "Dame Frevisse!"

Heads turned, and they all began to move toward her

eagerly, Sister Amicia first. With resignation, Frevisse waited where she was.

Sister Amicia, still the most eager, exclaimed, "Dame Frevisse, you were there! Nobody knows anything except she's dead. Tell us please, was it awful?"

With a quelling edge to her voice, Frevisse answered, "She was already dead when Dame Claire and I came in. Her struggle was over; she was only lying there. It was her heart, Dame Claire thinks. Have you seen her?"

"No, she hasn't been into the garden yet today."

The nuns crowding behind Sister Amicia nodded, making hypocritical murmurs of sympathy. Martha had been a fine cook, but fat, and not young, they agreed. A greedy stomach was bad for the heart.

But Sister Amicia, with widened eyes, leaned nearer to Frevisse and whispered in awed, carrying tones, the question they all wanted answered. "She saw demons, didn't she, come to torment Lady Ermentrude? Isn't that what stopped her heart, truly?"

Aware that everyone around them had heard that "whisper," Frevisse let her impatience show. "I doubt it," she said crisply. "There was distinctly no smell of brimstone in the room."

Irony was lost on Sister Amicia. She only blinked, a little disappointed. "But maybe there isn't always. Brimstone, I mean. Do you think?"

"Thomasine was there," Frevisse said shortly, "and said nothing about seeing demons."

"Oh, but she did," one of the other young nuns exclaimed gladly. "She said she saw them dancing all around Lady Ermentrude. She said that."

If talk of Lady Ermentrude's demons was already this far into the priory, there was no hope of stopping it, Frevisse thought angrily. Curbing the rumors was all that was left. "That was this afternoon when Lady Ermentrude first came," she said briskly. "Not when Martha was dying. And

Thomasine never said she saw demons, only that she thought Lady Ermentrude was seeing them."

"But that's nearly the same!" exclaimed Sister Amicia.

"Not remotely the same. My saying you've seen angels in the sky doesn't mean you've seen them, only that I think you have."

"But Lady Ermentrude was seeing something. She was terrified."

"She was seeing the effects of having too much wine in too short a time. Dame Claire will tell you that people who drink too often and too deeply think they see terrible things not really there."

Better Lady Ermentrude's weakness be known than to have the whole priory giddy with rumors of devils for a year to come, Frevisse thought. She was satisfied by the shocked intakes of breath at her bluntness. Before anyone, even Sister Amicia, could think of anything else to say, she added, "Here's Dame Claire come. I pray, excuse us."

She did not wait to be excused, simply took Dame Claire's arm—as the infirmarian, surprised at so many faces looking at her all at once, paused beside her—and walked her away from them. Frevisse could fairly guess what they would say behind her, but she had long since accepted that among the various things she needed to do penance for was a recurring great impatience with stupidity. And their childish desire for gossip was a trial she did not care to put Dame Claire through just at this moment.

She had glimpsed Dame Claire's face as she joined her, and seen that she was looking tired and inward-turned, as she always did when someone in her care had died. That was why Frevisse had gone looking for her, to see if there was aught she could do to ease her friend's heart.

Away from the others, Frevisse let go of her arm, tucked her own hands into her sleeves to match Dame Claire's quiet self-containment. "I know we always say this to you but it's true. There was nothing you could have done."

"I know. But it's wearisome, being able to do nothing.

And it was all so unlooked for. So sudden, with no time for being ready. I hate being able to do nothing.''

There was no answer to that except platitudes, which were pointless, and after a moment Frevisse said instead, ''Domina Edith has settled everything for the funeral tomorrow?''

''Not tomorrow.''

Frevisse looked at her, surprised. ''Her relatives in Banbury will be wanting to bury her?'' So far as she knew, Martha Hayward's distant cousins had never shown that much interest in her.

Dame Claire said, ''I doubt it. They might. But the crowner has to come.''

''Ah.'' Frevisse had forgotten that necessity. Martha Hayward had died suddenly, without being ill, and any unexplained death, whether by accident or illness or overt crime, meant the crowner was required. Though his proper duty was to determine if any fines or forfeits were due the king (with a portion going into his own purse), in order to do so, he had to ask questions, determine where any guilt lay. Or at last say there was no cause for any doubts, that the death was innocent, and give permission for the burial. Depending on where in Oxfordshire he was just now, and how long he took to arrive, the burial would hardly happen for two days at least, or even three. ''He's been sent for?''

''One of Lady Ermentrude's men has gone. And he's to tell Lady Ermentrude's son she's ill. So there'll be more trouble there, too.''

The message might bring every Fenner who possibly could make the journey to St. Frideswide's. Lord Walter would surely come, bringing Heaven only knew how many followers and friends. And the guest-hall chimney still needed repairing, and there was hardly room left for putting up a single poor traveler, much less another entourage.

But if nothing else, their coming might divert idle tongues from talk of demons and devils. There was some bit of comfort in that, Frevisse thought.

"And I should have told you already that Domina Edith wants to see you. Now, before Compline, if possible," Dame Claire said.

"Which gives me somewhere safe to go, and you had better find one, too, because Sister Amicia is strolling to intercept us."

"Oh merciful Heaven," Dame Claire said, and turned toward the church as Frevisse left her for Domina Edith's parlor.

The old greyhound had raised itself up from its basket and was standing beside the prioress's chair, accepting bits of biscuit when Frevisse entered. Domina Edith looked up and nodded, finished with the dog, patted its head, and told it to go lie down again, which it obediently did. "And you, Sister Lucy, may go walk in the garden with the others awhile," she said to her attendant. "Dame Frevisse will keep me company until Compline."

After Sister Lucy made her curtsey, Domina Edith gestured Frevisse to sit on the window seat across from her. Domina Edith sat as if sinking into sleep for a few moments before raising her head and saying, with no sign of sleepiness at all, "Martha ate and drank before she died. A milksop from our kitchen. Wine from Sir John. Herbs from our infirmary."

"Yes, my lady," Frevisse answered quickly. Then she made the mental leap to overtake the prioress's mind and said, startled, "Surely not!"

"Surely not," Domina Edith agreed firmly. "There was nothing wrong with any of it, but the crowner will be here, asking questions, and there will be talk. There is always talk when someone dies without obvious cause. I would like the answers known before the questions begin. Who made the milksop?"

"Thomasine was sent for it. I don't know if she or Dame Alys or one of the lay workers made it. It might have even been Martha herself."

''Do find out, please. And what particularly went into it. The wine she drank was Sir John's?''

''He brought it because it's Lady Ermentrude's favorite. It was to hand and easier to use than gathering the keys to the priory's supply just then.''

''Very reasonable and thoughtful. The herbs?''

''Dame Claire sent Thomasine for them. She was very specific which box she wanted, and was satisfied with what Thomasine brought.''

Domina Edith drew a deep sigh and let it out heavily. ''That all seems reasonable. It is only a pity that Dame Alys makes so great a matter of the quarrel between her family and the Fenners, and her wishing she could have a hand in it, since the food came from her kitchen.''

''True. But she may have had no hand in the milksop.''

''But Thomasine surely did. And with the medicine. She had both of them at one time or another, and everyone knows how plainly terrified her aunt had made her.

''Not terrified enough to kill,'' Frevisse protested.

''That is what must be made clear to Master Montfort when he comes. Thomasine is strung too high for her own health and an accusation of murder could destroy her.''

Frevisse, frowning, said, ''You don't think—''

''No. She has been here long enough for me to take her measure. She could not hide such a deed, if she had done it.''

''No,'' Frevisse agreed.

Domina Edith nodded her bobbing nod that sometimes led off into sleep, and her voice after a pause was dreamy. ''She has a holiness sometimes alarming to behold. Men have been killed in mishandling holy relics, you know.''

Frevisse hesitated, having lost the prioress's path of thought, wondering how far toward sleep she was. ''Yes?'' she said, prepared to slip away if there was no reply.

But Domina Edith looked up shrewdly from under her wrinkled eyelids, not sleepy at all. ''I would be more afraid than pleased to have a living saint on my hands. And if I'm afraid of so much holiness, how must she feel, finding God working within her? It's small wonder she looks half-sick with dread so much of the time. And now there's her talk of demons. What happens when Master Montfort begins questioning her?"

"I don't know, Domina."

"I want you with her as much as may be through these next few days. Where is she now?"

"With Lady Ermentrude. I gave her leave to stay. She wants to spend the night there, in penance for her anger at Lady Ermentrude and Martha."

Domina Edith smiled a small smile. "People who cause such anger so deliberately should be the ones to do the penance for it. Which I daresay Martha is doing now, wherever she is, may I be wrong." She crossed herself. "And Lady Ermentrude—but Dame Claire thinks she will live."

"It seems likely."

"And enjoy recovering her health among us, doubtless." Domina Edith quieted the grumble in her voice. "But may she live a good long while yet, she and her monkey and her parrot and her dogs, and visit us many more times after this, amen."

"Amen," Frevisse replied.

"You mean for Thomasine to keep watch all night?"

"Some of Lady Ermentrude's women will keep it in turns with her. Otherwise I think she'd spend the night on her knees in church and this seemed a better choice. By your leave."

"My leave is given. But bring her to Compline. And see that she eats. Holiness is no excuse for mortifying a body God has already seen fit to make so weak."

Lady Ermentrude still slept, to Thomasine's heartfelt relief. The crucifix lay on her pillow, ready to hand if needed; the goblet, with fresh wine and a new infusion of Dame Claire's quieting medicine, sat on the table along the wall. There was nothing she need do except pray. All the women had gone to the hall for supper and she was alone. The prie-dieu waited in its corner, but Thomasine stood at the foot of the bed, watching Lady Ermentrude's sleep and trying to form the words that, for once, disconcertingly, did not want to come. It was a relief rather than interruption when a small scratching at the door was followed by Isobel looking cautiously in and then entering, closing the door softly behind her. She came to stand by Thomasine and asked, "How does she?"

"Still sleeping. I think it's sleep. She breathes evenly and hardly stirs."

"What does your Dame Claire say?"

"That if she sleeps quietly the whole night, she will probably mend."

"You look as if you could sleep yourself. You've had a wearying day," Isobel said.

Thomasine shook her head. "I couldn't sleep. She needs my prayers. I need my prayers," she amended softly, then turned her wide eyes fully on her sister and said, "We all need everyone's prayers."

Taken aback, Isobel said, "What?"

Thomasine looked to Lady Ermentrude again. "Death struck at her, you know. Meant to take her but missed, and Martha was taken instead. Didn't you feel it?" She was very careful to keep her voice calm, but the calm was stretched taut over a hysteria she was unsure of holding. She looked again at her sister, who looked desperately anxious to understand. They had never been much together, never particularly close, but they were sisters and there ought to be a bond between them. "I keep watching her, wanting to see what it looks like to escape Death so narrowly."

"Thomasine!" Isobel breathed, with a kind of horror.

But Thomasine needed to say the words, was too wrought into her own feelings to stop, and continued despite Isobel's stare. "And I'm afraid Death will try again. I tried not to hate her but I did. I maybe still do, even after watching her suffer so horribly. It was ugly and awful, the way she suffered, but I had no pity at all for her. She'd been awful to me and I had no pity. I'm so wicked, there was no pity in me at all and I still don't think there is! Oh, Isobel, what am I going to do?''

Tears came then, with the last wailing question, and Isobel, who understood the tears if nothing else, put her arm around her shoulders and drew her backward to the bench under the window. ''Sit,'' she urged. ''Sit here with me.''

Willing to be told what to do, Thomasine obeyed. They sat down together, and letting go completely, Thomasine buried her face in her sister's lap and sobbed.

Isobel patted steadily at her shoulder until the tears eased and Thomasine made to sit up again. ''You'll need this,'' Isobel said, offering a handkerchief.

''I have my own,'' Thomasine sniffed, pulling a bit of cloth from her sleeve.

Isobel, noting it and the frayed edge of the sleeve, asked, ''Do you have to wear so poor a habit? We sent you good cloth; did they take it away from you?''

''No, of course not. But this suits me well enough. I gave my good handkerchiefs to Domina Edith. The ones we made before I came, remember? She said they were as fine as any she had seen.'' Sharing the memory strengthened the frail bond and steadied Thomasine. She had dried both nose and eyes when Isobel said, ''Did Lady Ermentrude truly say she meant to take you away from here?''

''Yes.''

''Did she say why, among all her other ravings?''

''No. She was too drunk, I believe, to think. She had the one idea and she kept saying it. But I've told her again and again that I want to be here.''

''Again and again? She's threatened this before?''

''Not truly threatened. She's only teased me, very meanly. But this time . . .'' Thomasine's eyes widened with memory. ''This time she truly seemed to mean it. And what if she still means it when she wakens? Oh, Isobel, I was so frightened!''

''There now,'' Isobel said firmly. ''You needn't be. She was just stupid with drink, and has no rights over you, whatever she means. She can't have you out of here if you mean to stay. Thomasine, do you mean to stay here?''

Thomasine firmed her mouth. ''You never have to ask that, Isobel. I want with all my heart to be here forever.''

''I trust you don't mean in this particular room,'' Dame Frevisse said from the doorway, ''because Domina Edith has sent me to bid you come to Compline now.''

Thomasine and Isobel startled at seeing her there, and the bell for the office began its sweet small chiming into the evening air. Thomasine convulsively gripped Isobel's hand, as if she would refuse to go, then let her loose, and, sighing, rose to her feet. Obedience came before inclination. With what might have been sympathy in someone else, Dame Frevisse said, ''You also have Domina Edith's permission to return here afterwards and stay the night, just as you wished.''

Supper in the guest hall was just ending, with only a few beginning to rise from their benches as Thomasine followed Frevisse out. Outside, at the head of the stairs, was the quiet-eyed youth who had helped Thomasine with Lady Ermentrude. He had not heard them coming, was standing with his face turned upward to the darkening sky, drawing a deep breath of the evening air, but was quickly aware of them and stepped aside from their way with a light bow.

Thomasine thought Dame Frevisse would have passed him with only an inclination of her head, but he asked in his warm and pleasant voice, ''How does Lady Ermentrude?''

Dame Frevisse stopped and said, ''Better, I think. She's sleeping deeply now and is likely to recover if all goes no worse.''

''God be thanked.'' His tone matched his words, pleasing Thomasine because, though she doubted anyone had any great affection for Lady Ermentrude, it was good he knew his duty. Then she saw his gaze had gone from Dame Frevisse to herself. She stiffened, but he said gently, so careful with respect she loosed a little of her wariness, "And I hope you're none the worse for the fright she gave you and for the other woman's dying, my lady?"

Her eyes wide on his face, Thomasine stared at him for a breathless moment, then looked hastily down at her hem and whispered, "Well enough, if it please God, thank you."

Before he could answer, if he meant to, Dame Frevisse said, "We do not have a name to thank you by," in an inquiring voice.

He bowed. "I'm Robert Fenner, if it please you, my lady."

"Thank you, Robert Fenner, for your quick help today. Now, by your leave." She went down the stairs, and Thomasine perforce followed her, stifling her urge to glance back to see if he stayed to watch them go.

Late twilight was deepening past blue to night as they crossed the courtyard to the cloister gate. Once inside, the rule of silence took hold and they could not speak aloud except to God. The nuns gathered in the common room for Compline instead of in the church. Frevisse, with too many other things to think on, including Robert Fenner's face when he had looked at Thomasine, was a little bewildered to find that the office's three psalms were finished and that she was singing with the others, "Before the last of light, we pray that in your mercy you will watch over us this night." Then they were through, and she gathered Thomasine up before she could be away to the guest hall and guided her firmly to the refectory.

Leaving her seated in the hall's echoing loneliness, Frevisse went on to the kitchen. The lay servants were still there, finishing the day's work and preparing for tomorrow's, still quieter than usual, visibly aware of the gap where Martha Hayward had been a few hours ago. They looked up a little warily when Frevisse entered, but she only nodded to them and went about her business. She returned to Thomasine with not only the pittance of cheese and apples that were properly supper, but warmed milk and a honeyed crust of bread. Thomasine began to gesture in protest, but Frevisse raised one hand in a silent asking for obedience. A stubbornness began to pout across Thomasine's face, but her young body's hunger won over her mind's demands, and with more haste than grace she took the food and ate. Having watched to be sure she finished, Frevisse gestured she would go to bed now, and that Thomasine was free to return to the guest house. Thomasine gestured that she had an errand to do first.

Perplexed, Frevisse raised an eyebrow.

Thomasine gestured a bowl in the air, stirred it, and made the sign for bread.

Another milksop, guessed Frevisse, and nodded permission. It was well thought of and would comfort Lady Ermentrude if she woke in the night.

Thomasine smiled her thanks, made a little bow, and went out.

Chapter 6

FREVISSE WAS AWAKE. Somewhere the last faint tendrils of a dream drifted and faded from a far corner of her mind, leaving no memory of what it had been. The hour was past Matins but still far from dawn, she thought. She raised her head a little, looking for the small window in the high pitch of the dormitory's gable end. By St. Benedict's Holy Rule all who lived in nunnery or monastery should sleep together in a single room, the dorter. But the Rule had slackened in the nine hundred years since St. Benedict had taken his hand from it. St. Frideswide's was not the only place where the prioress slept in a room of her own, and the dorter had been divided with board walls into small separate rooms that faced one another along the length of the dorter. Each cell belonged to one nun, and sometimes each had a door, or, as at St. Frideswide's, curtains at the open end.

There, in a privacy St. Benedict had never intended, each nun had her own bed, a chest for belongings, often even a carpet, and assuredly more small comforts than the Rule even at its laxest allowed. In Frevisse's, one wall was hung with a tapestry come from her grandmother's mother, its figures stiff, their clothing strange, but the colors rich and the picture a rose garden with the Lover seeking his Holy

Love. Across from it, beside her bed, there was a small but silver crucifix her father had brought from Rome.

It was all lost in near-darkness now. Through each night the only light for all the dorter was a single small-burning lamp at the head of the stairs down to the church, and sometimes moonlight slanting through the gable window.

As a novice, Frevisse had slept badly. She had been uncomfortable with the hard mattress and with sleeping in her underclothing as the Rule required, disturbed by the water gurgling through the necessarium at the dorter's other end, and at being roused at midnight to go to the church for Matins and Lauds.

Finally, over the years, she had learned to use her lying awake for prayer, or meditation, or remembering, or simply thinking. Now, waking in the night was no longer a burden but a gift for which she was often grateful.

Now with the last whisper of the dream drifted out of her mind, she lay looking at the high gable window, trying to judge the time, but there was no familiar star or any moonlight, only the rich darkness of sky, so different in its satin gleam from the dead black of the dorter's night. She pulled herself more closely into her blankets' warmth, settling into her mattress's familiar lumps. And found she could not settle. Whatever hour of the night it was, not only sleep but quietness had left her.

She stirred restlessly, realizing she was fully awake. Why? She roamed through her mind and found she was wanting—for no good reason—to go see how Lady Ermentrude was doing. And Thomasine.

Not Thomasine, her mind protested wearily.

Ever since the girl had come to St. Frideswide's, the talk had been of how near to sainthood she already seemed to be; even Domina Edith felt the child's holiness enough to be in awe of it. And surely it was a rare enough thing, especially in this less-than-holy time when women came all too often into the nunnery more because they were unfit for life outside it than because they longed for God's life within it.

For Thomasine, pretty and well-dowered, the nunnery was no necessity. She was here by her own plain choice, and there was no denying—no way to avoid seeing—how she flung herself at her devotions and duties with utter earnestness.

The fact that so much earnestness wore on Frevisse's nerves was her own failing, not Thomasine's. But that did not change the fact that she had avoided the girl as much as might be this past year. Now her conscience was telling her that she was awake and not likely to sleep again and so ought to go see how Lady Ermentrude and, yes, Thomasine were faring in these low-ebb hours before dawn.

Clinging to her bed's warmth a few moments more, Frevisse thought regretfully of how very rarely a sense of responsibility was convenient. Her own devotion to it came from her rarely convenient childhood. Carried along by her parents on their wanderings, she had learned responsibility as a kind of defense against their habitual lack of it, until now it had long since become a habit too strong to break. With a sigh for a virtue she often wished she did not have, she pushed her blankets away and rose into the darkness.

By touch she dressed herself: outer dress over the undergown she had worn to bed, feet into her damply cold shoes, set in their prescribed place beside the bed, wimple and veil managed without need of a mirror after doing them so often in the dark of winter mornings. Then, doubting she would be back before breakfast, she folded her blankets neatly down to the foot of her bed as the rules required.

The wooden curtain rings were nearly soundless as she left her cell. By the dormitory lamp and the one at the foot of the stairs she made her way into the cloister walk. There in the starlight, with no need for lamps, Frevisse paused, listening to the silence. The air was sweet with cold and the promise of a dawn not yet begun but near. The night seemed to breathe gently of its own where there was no harsher breeze to stir it. Around her the quiet stroked down the edge of nerves with which she had wakened. In her mind, to the silence, she breathed a prayer from one of the St. Gregorys. "Let me yield you today in its wholeness, no deed of darkness or shame to allow or to do, keeper of my own passions in service to you."

The guest hall was dark except for the low glow of coals on the hearth. By it Frevisse could make out a few sleeping forms humped on their pallets near what had been its warmth. Carefully she circled away from them, but someone raised his head to mumble at her questioningly.

"Only Dame Frevisse," she murmured back. "*Benedicite.*"

He mumbled again and subsided. Frevisse scratched at Lady Ermentrude's door and entered without waiting for an answer. Two lamps were burning there, one to either side of the bed, giving good light to watch the patient by while the partly drawn bed curtains kept it from her eyes. On a pallet beside the bed one of Lady Ermentrude's women lay sleeping, softly snoring.

Thomasine, at the prie-dieu in a corner, had turned as the door opened and was now rising from her knees. In the lamplight her young eyes were blurred with a need for sleep, but plainly she had been awake for a long while past. Frevisse noticed that she had not given herself even the comfort of a cushion under her knees and, with a small prayer for patience with her, went to the bedside.

Thomasine joined her beside the bed; together, in silence, they stood looking at Lady Ermentrude.

As nearly as Frevisse could judge in the lamplight and shadows, her color had faded to normal and her breathing was easy, as if she were merely sleeping instead of sunk in unconsciousness.

"How long has she been this way?"

"Since a little after Matins. She's never wakened but I've thought her sleep was less deep."

"Thanks be to God."

Thomasine crossed herself. "Maryon didn't think we needed to tell Dame Claire," she added doubtfully.

"No, I should think not, so long as her sleep is quiet and her breathing even."

Her assurance seemed to ease some worry in Thomasine. Frevisse moved away from the bed and Thomasine followed her. "Do you want to be here when she wakes or would you rather leave?" Frevisse asked softly. "Her mind may not be changed at all about taking you away. You can have a little sleep and I can watch until Dame Claire comes."

Thomasine shrank inside her habit. She whispered, "I want to be here when she wakens."

"I'll tell her you kept watch by her most of the night, if that's what you want her to know."

Thomasine shook her head. "I want to tell her I prayed for her life. Then surely she'll see my prayers are worth far more to her than my marrying would be."

Frevisse privately doubted that Lady Ermentrude believed God would presume to thwart her own notions, but only said, "She may. It's very possible." And added to herself that in any case Lady Ermentrude, waking sober and feeling the worse for it, was unlikely to want to argue over anything very soon.

"I'm going to pray some more," Thomasine said doubtfully, as if asking permission. Frevisse nodded, but before Thomasine could turn away, Lady Ermentrude made a sudden, spasmed movement, half rolling to her side. The crucifix, dislodged from her pillow, slid to the floor with a clatter that in the nighttime quiet might as well have been a cannonade. Frevisse started at the noise; Maryon sat up on her pallet exclaiming and crossing herself. Thomasine stooped to snatch the crucifix up from the floor and kiss it, and as she straightened, she came level with the pillows and Lady Ermentrude's protuberant eyes staring directly back into her own.

Thomasine's eyes widened with a kind of terror, and she jerked upright, crying, "Heaven bless me!"

"Not so long as you disobey your elders, girl," Lady Ermentrude croaked. But her gaze was uncertain, confused.

She lost focus on Thomasine, her head moving feebly on the pillow as if she were trying to decide where she was. Maryon had risen from the pallet now but, while showing no eagerness to come near her, kept a steady eye on the proceedings. Thomasine, rooted in speechlessness, simply stood holding the crucifix out to her aunt. It was Frevisse who leaned over the bed to say gently, trying to draw her attention, "It's all right, my lady. You've been ill but you're better now. You're safe in St. Frideswide's."

Lady Ermentrude drew further in from the vague edge of consciousness and focused on her, blinking heavily. "Why are you all red? Why's that thing all red?" She twitched one hand in feeble indication of the crucifix.

Thomasine turned it toward herself, staring at it, bewildered. Frevisse, glancing at it, saw only its wood and the painted figure on it. "You mean His wounds?" she guessed.

"No, I mean . . . I mean . . ." Lady Ermentrude licked dryly at her lips and lost the words.

Frevisse quickly took up the goblet waiting to hand on the table. Careful not to jar her, she lifted Lady Ermentrude's head slightly and held the cup to her lips. Lady Ermentrude drank, and when Frevisse had lowered her head to the pillow, her eyes went back to roaming the room. "It's the light," she croaked. "What are you burning in the lamp to make everything so red?"

"There's nothing wrong with the light. It must be your eyes. You've been ill and this must be some last effect. You'll be all right when you've slept again." Frevisse tried to make her guessing sound confident.

Lady Ermentrude let her eyes close. Her lips worked at words that did not come, and then she was still. Not sleeping yet, though. Her fingers pulled restlessly at the bedcover, and Frevisse had the impression that rather than sleep she was working to gather her strength and wits back to herself.

Carefully Frevisse looked at the waiting woman and whispered, "Please find someone to go for Dame Claire.

And tell Lady Isobel her aunt has awakened. She'll want to know."

Maryon nodded and left. Lady Ermentrude opened her eyes again and said faintly, "Where's Thomasine?"

"She's nearby," Frevisse said gently. "But never mind, you should try to rest."

"Rest." Lady Ermentrude's voice was a croaking whisper. "Where's Thomasine? All's lost in redness here. Whatever you burn in your lamps, you shouldn't. Where's Thomasine?"

Frevisse surrendered and gestured at the girl.

"Here, Aunt." Thomasine moved closer, to where Lady Ermentrude could see her. "I'm here and I've been praying for you to recover."

Lady Ermentrude focused on her, blinking owlishly as if her eyes were tender. "Praying. Yes, praying is good."

"Would you care for something to eat?" Thomasine took up a bowl from beside the bed. "I have milk and bread with honey for you. It will soothe your throat."

Lady Ermentrude appeared to wander through her mind in pursuit of the words before saying, "Milk and honey. Yes."

Frevisse helped lift her a little higher on her pillows, then left Thomasine the task of feeding small spoonfuls into her great-aunt's waiting mouth. For a few minutes there was only the sound of spoon on bowl, until Lady Ermentrude said, stronger, steadier, "Ah. That's better." She looked around herself as if seeing the room for the first time. "What is this place?"

"Our guest hall's best guest room," Frevisse said.

"St. Frideswide's guest hall?" Lady Ermentrude's voice scaled up with outraged disbelief. Her hand clawed down around Thomasine's nearest wrist, nearly upsetting the bowl. "Have they made you a nun yet?"

Thomasine's mouth opened, but no sound came. Frevisse, against the girl's panic, said soothingly, "There are days and days yet before Thomasine is to take her vows. You've time to rest, to sleep a little more."

"No, I will not sleep! I will not stay here! Neither of us will stay! I'll have us both away from here!" She moved as if to push herself up on her pillows, letting go of Thomasine to do it. Thomasine stood quickly up out of her way and Frevisse moved between them.

"You shouldn't try to rise yet. You should rest awhile, I think—"

"I want out of here! And I'm taking the girl with me, don't try to stop us! That bitch Isobel and her dog of a husband tried to make a fool of me. They're here, aren't they? Don't deny it, I saw them!"

Frevisse said lightly, wishing she understood what the matter was, "They came directly after you, afraid something might happen to you."

"Afraid? By God's great toe, I'll show them how to be afraid! Where's Thomasine gone now?"

"I'm here, Great-aunt." Thomasine, apparently recovering a little of her nerve, moved past Frevisse to where Lady Ermentrude could see her again.

Lady Ermentrude gestured for the goblet again, took it for herself from Frevisse, and this time drank without help. But her gaze remained on Thomasine, her eyes unblinking. "They shall not make a nun of you," she began. Then she frowned and seemed to lose the trail of her thinking. She sat peering into the depths of her goblet before pronouncing, "If this is supposed to be malmsey, the vintage is truly vile."

Frevisse said, "There's medicine in it, to ease you."

Lady Ermentrude cocked a wary and increasingly alert eye at her. "I've been sick."

Frevisse refrained from saying, "You've been drunk as your own monkey." She merely nodded.

"But I'm better now. It's Thomasine I must take care of. You're not keeping her, you know. I've told you that."

"I will pray for you, Great-aunt, if I stay," Thomasine offered.

Against the vastness of Lady Ermentrude's certainty and the wandering of her mind, it was a feeble attempt at argument, and Lady Ermentrude, even weak and lying back against her pillows, swept over it, saying, "We're past the time for praying. It's doing that's needed. A great deal of doing."

"But not just yet, Great-aunt, while you're still so ill." Lady Isobel stood in the doorway, dressed only in her loose and flowing bedgown. Her fair hair spreading over her shoulders made her look hardly older than Thomasine. Only a tired grayness around her eyes showed she too had had little sleep.

She spoke mildly, but Lady Ermentrude stiffened. She was one of the few people Frevisse had ever seen whose nostrils actually flared with anger; they flared now, and her breast heaved as she gathered force for her mounting anger. "I need no words from you, whore! Nor your presence. You lost your chance and it's Thomasine's now. When I have her out of here—"

But anger was no substitute for strength. In an effort to raise herself on her elbows, the better to rage at Lady Isobel, she lost breath to finish and fell back gasping, ashen, against her pillows. Frevisse moved quickly, rescuing the tilting goblet from her loosened fingers as Thomasine sank to her knees, crying prayers beside the bed. Lady Isobel started forward but Frevisse moved more quickly, intercepting her and turning her back through the doorway, out of her great-aunt's sight.

Thomasine suddenly found she was alone with the person she least wanted to face by herself. But she had seen enough to know that for now at least Lady Ermentrude could do nothing more than say words at her, and uncertainly she reached out with some idea of feeling for her pulse the way she had seen Dame Claire sometimes do with others. Lady

Ermentrude, drawing deep breaths and steadying a little, jerked her hand away and gestured in feeble demand at the goblet.

"Thirsty," she croaked.

Thomasine, in hope of the medicine sending her to sleep again, held the goblet to her lips. Lady Ermentrude gulped at it, seemed to revive a little, but did not try to rise again, only asked with a bitter edge of anger, "Your sister—where did she go?"

Thomasine said, "Dame Frevisse took her away."

"That's good. You stay away from her. She's vile. She wouldn't listen. You stay away from her." Lady Ermentrude kicked feebly at the sheet. "I want to go. Help me get up."

"No, Aunt, you're supposed to stay here!"

"God's eyes! Don't be telling me what I can do and not do! Help me up! Go fetch my women and tell them what I want. We'll be out of here by dawn and halfway to Lincoln and the bishop before sunset. Go fetch my women!"

Her hand had closed in a convulsive claw around Thomasine's wrist, dragging her close to drive the words and wine smell into her face, but with her last order she flung her loose. Thomasine backed quickly out of reach and scurried for the door.

But in the last instant she turned back to look and saw, to her horror, a small dark shapelessness flow from the shadows between the bed curtains and Lady Ermentrude's pillows. As she watched, a narrow black stick came out of it, and suddenly there was a small, almost-human hand at the end of it, stretching, reaching, for Lady Ermentrude's head. Thomasine gave a cry of terror and fled.

Frevisse patiently said again, to Sir John this time, come out in his bed robe to be sure all was well with his wife, "No, truly, she seems better. Muddled still, and weak, but very likely to live, I think. Unfortunately her temper is no better than it was."

"It is a shame, but very like her," Lady Isobel said sadly. She was leaning wearily against her husband's shoulder, his arm around her waist in support. "All this started before her drinking did yesterday. No, the day before yesterday now. But she drank all her medicine?"

"She drank much of it and should sleep. Now if you'll pardon me . . ."

She meant to return to Thomasine, but Thomasine was suddenly there, catching urgently hold of her arm. "I saw," the girl gasped. "I saw—" The word caught in her throat, then was cut off completely by a strangled, inarticulate cry from the room behind her, that scaled toward a wail and broke into a less-than-human caw of pain.

"Angels and ministers of faith, defend us," Sir John breathed.

Frevisse in her mind echoed him, riveted to her place by the same shock felt by them all. It was Dame Claire, coming unseen from the shadows of the hall, who moved past them toward the doorway, saying sharply, "She's in pain. Are you deaf?"

Behind her, forms stirred, jerked out of their sleep, and began to rise before they even knew why they were awake. Frevisse's own shock had been broken by Dame Claire. Quickly she followed her, saying over her shoulder to Sir John and Lady Isobel, "We'll see to this. Best you stay out of it. Thomasine—"

But Thomasine was already following Dame Claire. It was the woman Maryon at her elbow, and behind her Robert Fenner. The choking, stuttered cries from Lady Ermentrude broke and began again, and Frevisse whirled away into the room. Maryon followed, and Robert behind her slammed the door against anyone else who might come to gawk.

Lady Ermentrude was no longer lying feebly under her blankets but flinging from side to side on the bed, thrashing against her own strangled, croaking screams. Her body jerked in rhythm to them, and her bulging eyes stared frantically at nothing.

Dame Claire, with a tiny vial in one hand, cried out to anyone, "We have to hold her! I can't help her like this!"

Robert, already moving, crossed the room to fling himself over the bed, pinning Lady Ermentrude's legs flat beneath his body. She writhed, but he was too heavy for her to throw off. Frevisse managed to lay hold of her shoulders while Maryon grabbed at her arms. Between them they forced her down flat. She heaved under their hold, writhing and thrusting with strength she should not have had, still crying out. Her eyes were wild and unfocused with pain, and she was fighting not them but whatever pain was driving her as tears ran down her face, smearing into her tangled hair.

"Hold her!" Dame Claire pleaded, the vial still in her hand, held uselessly out of reach of Lady Ermentrude's flinging head. "If I can quiet her with this . . . !"

They held, but there was no holding her still, until quite abruptly she arched her body upward to what seemed a breaking point under the grip. She stretched out in a helpless spasm, her mouth open in a silent scream. Then she collapsed, rag-limp and gasping, staring upward at the ceiling, all the struggle gone out of her.

They waited. She did not move except for her breast's rapid rise and fall.

The vial now unneeded, Dame Claire said softly, "Let her go. Slowly. As careful as you may."

Carefully, poised to grab her again if need be, Frevisse and Maryon obeyed. Robert, as slowly and cautiously, rose, holding his breath until he was safely clear.

Across the room the door began to open. Dame Claire glanced at Frevisse and shook her head. With an agreeing nod, Frevisse backed hurriedly away and went to keep out whoever was meaning to come in.

"Not now," she whispered urgently, even before she saw it was Sir John.

His face all creased with anxiety, he tried to look past her into the room. "Is she . . ."

As he hesitated over a choice of words, Frevisse answered quickly, understanding. "She's alive. It was another fit came on her but she's quieted, sooner than before. She may be . . ."

"Dame Frevisse!" Dame Claire's voice was sharp with alarm and urgency, two things she rarely showed.

Forgetting Sir John, Frevisse rushed back to her.

"Her breathing is failing. And she's gone cold again. Feel her."

Frevisse felt Lady Ermentrude's face. It was still flushed with her panic but was cold as hung meat. Her breathing, which should have been steadying, was coming in small heaves, and her whole body moved as if to help her take each breath. At Frevisse's touch, her eyes swiveled toward her, pupils spread so wide the eyes seemed black with terror.

"Father Henry," Frevisse said. "We need Father Henry."

"I'm here," the priest said behind her, his box in his hands. Dame Claire surrendered her place to him, and by that single gesture Frevisse understood that there was no earthly thing left to do for Ermentrude. Whatever was happening was now God's business, with Father Henry as his intermediary.

Maryon, stricken and white with shock, had already withdrawn to the door. Sir John still stood there, with a crowd of faces behind him. Frevisse belatedly looked for Thomasine and saw her on her knees at the prie-dieu, her face pressed against her prayer-rigid hands, her lips moving silently. Robert Fenner moved as if to go toward her, but Frevisse's hand on his arm stopped him. Prayers were the most needed things now, certainly not his attention. He resisted, but at her subtle pull he retreated with her and Dame Claire to join the others at the door.

They waited, all of them and the crowding servants. For a mercy there was now no sign of Lady Isobel; Sir John, for the little that Frevisse was aware of him, seemed oddly incomplete without her. But her attention was drawn, as was everyone else's, to Father Henry. She heard his hurried words and the struggle of Lady Ermentrude's breathing. They were the only sounds in the room until Father Henry's words of Last Unction ran out, and then there was only Lady Ermentrude's breathing, until it caught and strangled to a stop. Her hands lifted, moved as if she meant to sign herself, or to seek for air no longer there, then were flung outward as her eyes rolled back and her body arched and stiffened one final time. Father Henry caught her hands and held them, but even as he did, all of her collapsed, her body falling loose and empty, her head rolling sideways, her hands no more than lifeless rags between his own.

In the utter stillness afterward, Frevisse knew that Thomasine had turned from the prie-dieu to stare as all the rest of them were staring. And it was Thomasine who whispered, even her softness loud in the stillness, "*In manus tuas, Domine, commendo spiritum eium.*"

Into your hands, O Lord, we commend her spirit.

And if ever a soul was dependent on God's mercy to enter Heaven, surely Lady Ermentrude's was, thought Frevisse.

Chapter 7

THERE WAS QUIET in the church now that the bell had ceased its tolling. The air still seemed to tremble slightly, remembering the fifty-seven slow strokes in memory of every year of Lady Ermentrude's life, but faintly and fading now. As memories of Lady Ermentrude would fade away in time, Thomasine thought, fade away and not matter anymore.

But they mattered now, lying sickly between her thoughts and her praying, even here in her best place, on the step below St. Frideswide's altar, where almost always she could lose herself in prayers and not think of the stone hurting her knees or the thinness of her hands clinging together or the two coffins waiting on their biers behind her.

She had helped wash and ready Lady Ermentrude's body for its shroud and coffin, had followed it across the yard and seen it set beside Martha Hayward's, and been given leave, after Prime, to remain in prayer for their souls. But the prayers she wanted seemed to be nowhere in her, only the thought of Lady Ermentrude's and Martha's bodies lying behind her, waiting for their people to come and take them to their final places. Lady Ermentrude would go to her own lordship's church and a grave beside the high altar, to rest there under a carved stone image of herself until Last Judgment Day. Martha Hayward would lie in Banbury churchyard, where she would molder into bones to be dug up and put with other moldered bones in a charnel house, to make way for someone else's burying.

They were both dead and in need of her prayers, and no prayers would come, only the thought of how suddenly dead they had been.

Their dying had had nothing easy in it; even completed death had failed to soften the engraved pain of Lady Ermentrude's harsh features before the shroud covered it. Surely a soul forced from its body by such an end desperately needed praying for, and Thomasine knew it. But the prayers would not come, not for her own sake or Lady Ermentrude's or Martha's. Only thoughts.

Of Lady Ermentrude's dying, of the small black creeping thing reaching out—from Hell?—toward her. . . .

A hand touched Thomasine's shoulder. With a gasping shriek, she lunged forward to scrape with both hands at the base of the altar, then jerked her head around to find Dame Frevisse standing over her, come quietly in soft-soled shoes.

Unseemly amusement twitched at the corners of Frevisse's mouth before she could control it. She knew Thomasine saw it but could say nothing to her, only gestured wordlessly for her to come. For a moment Thomasine seemed near to refusing, resentment and less readable things showing in her face. Then her expression blanked almost perfectly over whatever she was feeling, and she came away from the altar, following Frevisse across the church to the side door into the cloister.

Frevisse carefully kept from looking at her, wanting her to have time to recover the dignity she had lost in her panicked lunge. Frevisse remembered how painfully necessary and difficult dignity had been for herself when she was very young. That she had consciously ceased being very young years before she was Thomasine's age did not change Thomasine's need.

So because she was not looking at her, Frevisse was

unprepared for Thomasine's sudden, great sob as they stepped out into the cloister walk. It seemed to come from deep within the girl's breast, a burden too much to bear, crumpling her down onto the bench there, her face buried in her hands. Aware that sympathy might only make it worse, Frevisse said firmly, "What is it, child, grief for your aunt, or something that can be helped?"

Thomasine turned up a teary face and cried out, "Two small weeks! That's all there are until I'm safe. She can't touch me anymore!"

With more sleep or less fear behind her, she would never have said so much. And even so, the words were hardly anything at all, only more of Thomasine's tedious, too-passionate desiring to be a nun, and Frevisse would have let them pass except for the sudden, terrified widening of Thomasine's eyes as she realized what she had said.

Frevisse, with sudden suspicion, demanded, "Why are you so afraid of being taken away from here, Thomasine? Were you forced to come? Are you in danger if you leave? Is that it?"

Thomasine's face, usually smooth with youth and studied holiness, so bland she seemed to have hardly any expression at all unless she was nervous or exalted in prayer, changed swiftly to a desperate smiling that was all lies. "I'm not afraid." She shook her head vehemently. "No one forced me. Ever."

The cloister walk was not the place for talking. Taking the matter literally in hand, Frevisse grasped Thomasine's arm, pulled her to her feet, and took her along the cloister to the narrow passage between the church and the nuns' common room. Called the slipe, it led from the cloister to the cemetery, and brief, urgently needed conversations were allowed there. In it, still keeping hold of Thomasine's arm, Frevisse said, "Now, what exactly has you so frightened?"

Thomasine's gaze went everywhere except Frevisse's face, and she blurted out with a sharp confusion of fear and desperation, "I never said I was afraid. I never did!"

Frevisse shook her arm. "Are you here by fraud or force? By threats or trickery? What are you fearing?"

Thomasine clasped her hands prayerfully and cried, "None of that. I want to be here! I've wanted it all my life!"

"But there's a reason you could be forbidden your final vows and Lady Ermentrude knew it? If there is, you have to tell someone. Domina Edith or Father Henry or Dame Perpetua—"

"There isn't any! I swear it!"

Meaning to have the truth from her, Frevisse badgered relentlessly, "You know that taking your vows falsely is a sin as great as apostasy itself?"

Thomasine had never seemed to have any courage in her, had always seemed to be all nerves and prayers, but at that challenge she steadied as if struck. Straightening in Frevisse's hold, she said, her voice high and light with strain, "I know it. I'd never falsely swear to God."

"So there's no falseness in your being here?"

"None."

Not loosening her hold but more gently, Frevisse said, "But you're afraid."

Thomasine blinked on tears again, but fought them and said, "Yes. Will I be sent away for that?"

It was very clearly a question that had been hurting in her for a long, long while. Frevisse eased her hold and said carefully, "It depends on why you're afraid. Can you tell me?"

Thomasine drew a deep, unhappy breath. "If I'm not allowed to stay, I'll be married to someone and I can't marry."

"Because you secretly promised yourself to someone before you came here?" It was a stupid thing that girls sometimes did, plighting their troth secretly with someone unsuitable and then finding themselves bound for life no matter how they felt later. A promise of betrothal was, in the Church's law, as binding as a marriage vow and, like the marriage vow, could only be sundered by complicated legal means. If Thomasine had sworn such a thing, she had no right to be in St. Frideswide's.

But Thomasine, with shocked, wide eyes, vehemently shook her head. "Oh no, never anything like that! I would never, never, never promise myself to any man. I couldn't!"

"But why?" The vehemence was as confusing as the girl's fear.

Thomasine hung her head. "Babies." She mumbled the word. "I'm afraid of having them."

Nearly Frevisse laughed. And nearly said the obvious: that very many women were afraid of it. But for Thomasine it was clearly something beyond that reasonable fear. Frevisse held her amusement and waited. Thomasine touched a knuckle to one brimming eye and said tremulously, "I know how women die in childbirth. There was a servant at our manor. A big, strong woman, but she died when her baby was born. I heard her screaming. It was awful. And my sister. She's told me how she nearly dies each time she has a baby and she doesn't think she can have any more."

"Thomasine . . ."

"I know," Thomasine said quickly. "It's all in God's hands but—" She ducked her head and spoke to her toes, as if about a guilty secret. "With me it's something more. It's what the midwife said after my brother was born. I was there until they knew how hard it was going to be. Then they sent me out of the room, but I waited outside the door. They were all caring that it be a boy after only daughters, and it was a boy, and that was good. We didn't know he was going to die almost right away. And my mother was never well afterwards. She died before the year was out. But it's more than that." Thomasine said it hastily, cutting off Frevisse's half-formed reassurance. "It's what the midwife said when she was leaving my mother, when we still thought everything was all right. She was saying to someone that it was my mother's narrow hips that made it so killing-hard for her to give birth, and then she saw me standing there and said, 'There's another one will have it bad, and worse than her mother, belike, she's so narrow through all her bones and not like to outgrow it.' " Even after years Thomasine had the woman's words and their intonation. "And I never have," she finished miserably.

Frevisse, looking at her, understood what the midwife had meant. Under the several layers and deliberate shapelessness of her novice's gown, Thomasine was meager, thin all through herself and narrow in her hips. That was no sure sign childbearing would go ill with her; there was no sure way to tell with anyone until the moment came, but truly Thomasine believed it, had believed it for nearly half of her life.

Carefully, Frevisse said, "So you decided to become a nun and be safe."

"Oh no! I was already wanting to be a nun. I swear I was. I've wanted it ever since I was a very, very little girl. But it seemed—what she said—it seemed it was God's way of telling me that I was right. That I was meant to be a nun." Thomasine's earnestness faded to guilty sadness, and she whispered, "But I'm afraid of dying, too, the way my mother did, and in St. Frideswide's I'm safe from it. If I have to leave, they'll make me marry and he'll want children and I'll die. So I've tried so hard to be everything I had to be. But not just to keep from being put out!" She looked desperately at Frevisse. "I love God more than anything. I want to be here, truly I do. Only if Domina Edith or the others know I'm so afraid, they maybe won't believe me. And I want to stay, I don't want to have to leave. Do you have to tell them?"

Her tears were falling freely now. Gently, wondering how Thomasine had ever come to think that to be a nun she had to have no other feelings except love of God, Frevisse said, "Thomasine, isn't Dame Alys ranting in the kitchen a plain enough example of how far from holiness a nun can be and still belong here? No one is going to put you out because you're afraid. We're all of us here for more reasons than one, and for some of us the love of God is maybe the least of them. If only women who wanted nothing in life except to live in the cloister became nuns, there would be one small nunnery in all of England."

She was watching Thomasine's face and saw when she began to believe her.

Faintly, her eyes moist with tears, Thomasine asked, "Truly?"

"Truly. Why didn't you ask Dame Perpetua? She would have told you."

Thomasine looked down at her clasped hands. "Because you all think I'm so very good. I didn't want anyone to know I'm not."

So Thomasine knew what was said of her holiness. Dryly Frevisse said, "Goodness can be a very great burden, both to live with and to have."

"Will you tell them?"

"That you're not good?" She saw her intended humor miss Thomasine altogether and instead said quickly, "Thomasine, beyond all doubting you are meant to be a nun. No one is going to keep you from it, least of all any of us here. But you'll have to tell Domina Edith."

Thomasine's lips trembled. "Must I?"

"You must, to free your own mind if nothing else. I promise you, she'll not send you away. But you must tell her. If you don't, I'll have to, and that won't be so well."

Thomasine's hazel-green eyes, still swimming in tears, searched Frevisse's face as if for signs of trickery. Finding none, she whispered, "All right. I'll tell her."

"Good then. And now there's another matter to hand, the one that brought me for you. Master Montfort has come."

Thomasine looked at her questioningly.

"The crowner," Dame Frevisse said.

Thomasine remembered then. He had come to St. Frideswide's not long after she first entered, when a stockman had been found in a barn, dead, with a broken skull, and no one to swear how he had come by it. Master Morys Montfort had come then, it being his duty as crowner for northern Oxfordshire to view and report on any sudden deaths. So he had come and viewed and decided what everyone else was already certain of: that the stockman had last been seen somewhat drunk, was known to be more than a little careless at the best of times, and had gotten himself kicked in the head and half across the stable by a cow well known to be a kicker. Death by misadventure had been Master Montfort's decision, and the man had been buried, the cow as the instrument of his death duly slaughtered and its meat distributed to the poor. Since then there had been no need for Master Montfort at St. Frideswide's. Until now.

"He was sent for after Martha Hayward's death." For once Dame Frevisse's voice was bare of anything but the flat statement of facts. "Now he's come and must needs see to Lady Ermentrude's dying, too, and wants to talk to everyone who had attendance on her, you among them. He's in the guest hall."

They had begun walking as Dame Frevisse talked, Thomasine hurrying a little to match her long stride. Now she stopped short under the last arch of the cloister walk and asked quickly, "Do I have to see him? I can only tell him what everyone else will say about them both."

"You were the first to see your aunt when she returned here yesterday. And you were there at both their dyings, besides being with Lady Ermentrude all the night before her death. He wants to question you."

"Everyone knows what happened. Everyone saw the drink take her mind and then her body. There's nothing else to tell. And Martha's heart failed. Dame Claire will tell him that."

"Dame Claire says otherwise now."

"She does?"

"Yes."

Dame Frevisse's voice had a hard edge to it that said more than the word, but what the more might be Thomasine had no time to guess. Dame Frevisse went on, and she had to follow, thrusting her hands up either sleeve and tucking her head down resolutely low, not seeing anything except her feet as they left the cloister and crossed the courtyard to the guest house.

Its outer hall was crowded with people, mostly in Lady Ermentrude's livery. Their clacking chatter died away as Dame Frevisse entered. Thomasine's quick glancing to either side showed they were looking at her and Dame Frevisse, but Dame Frevisse passed among them with apparently complete disinterest.

At the threshold to the room that had been Lady Ermentrude's, Thomasine consciously braced herself for whatever might be there, but after all it was only a room, with the window shutters standing open to the warm day's sunlight, the bed freshly, neatly made—no sign at all that here had been two deaths so near together under God's heavy hand, and the bodies still lying within the nunnery walls, wherever their souls might be by now.

Thomasine's nervous glance around the room, from under the shelter of her lowered lids, showed her that Master Montfort wished to talk to what seemed a great many people besides herself. Dame Claire was there, and Father Henry, and Aunt Ermentrude's lady-in-waiting Maryon, who was studying Dame Claire like Dame Alys studied a butchered lamb before dividing it. Only the monkey was missing. Beyond them, seated on the bench under the window, with the sunlight aureoling his brown hair to auburn, was the youth called Robert Fenner. Thomasine had the impression that he was looking at her almost like Maryon was looking at Dame Claire, so she moved backward, putting Dame Frevisse between her and his gaze.

But there were not enough places to sit in the room, except for the bed, where no one seemed to want to sit, certainly not Thomasine. Father Henry was already standing. It was Robert Fenner who stood up quickly and said, "Here. Pray you, sit here, my lady."

He might have meant Dame Frevisse, but Dame Frevisse,

intent on going to Dame Claire across the room, said, "Yes, Thomasine, do you sit. We may be waiting for a while." She added to Dame Claire, "He's not finished yet with Sir John and Lady Isobel?"

"Not yet. The lady is still so shaken, he's talking with them in their room. But he can hardly be much longer." Dame Claire's tone, like her face, was rigid, withdrawn as if her thoughts were inwardly turning around something else.

Neither she nor Dame Frevisse were heeding Thomasine at all. With no choice, Thomasine went, eyes down, to take the place Robert Fenner had offered her.

Instead of moving away as she sat, he slid down on his heels beside her, his back against the wall. From there he could look up into her face whether she wanted him to or not. He smiled.

Thomasine deliberately shut her eyes, refusing to acknowledge that he was there, and began the Paternoster, the first prayer that came into her mind. Her lips moved on the "amen" though she did not mean them to, and he must have seen them because, before she could begin again, he said softly, "Dame Frevisse speaks to me."

Thomasine threw him an inadvertent glance, then shut her lips tightly over any words that might try to escape her.

"You heard her. She's fully a nun but she talks to me," Robert persisted.

"But I don't," Thomasine whispered back, refusing to look at him again. "Not to any man." The warmth left around her heart by Dame Frevisse's assurance that she was safe from being put out of St. Frideswide's made her less taut with nerves than she might have been, so she was able at least to tell him she did not want his attentions.

"My lady?" The quiet voice on her other side made Thomasine look up. The woman Maryon made a small curtsey with her head. "I hope you're well enough after all that's happened and last night?"

"Y-yes," Thomasine murmured. "Thank you. And you?"

"Well enough, I thank you." Maryon drew a deep sigh and smiled a little sadly at Robert, who had risen to his feet. "We are rather at loose ends for the time, my lord. What will you do now your lady is gone?"

Robert made a vague gesture. "There's no place for me at home. Mayhap Sir Walter will take me again into his household. I don't know."

"Nor I." She was a pretty woman, all softness and smooth skin, with dark hair and manners meant to please. She made Thomasine uncomfortable. "I left the Queen's service in hope of seeing something more than Hertford Castle, where she mostly wants to be, and now that hope has come to an end with Lady Ermentrude's dying. Though she wasn't an easy mistress, mind."

"No. She wasn't that," Robert agreed.

"I've wondered if it wasn't her wanting to leave the Queen, so much as the Queen asking her to go because of her tongue. Did you ever hear aught about that?" There was a curious cadence to her speech that made Thomasine wonder where she had been born.

"Never anything but what Lady Ermentrude said. That she was tired and wished to leave and Queen Katherine granted it."

"You never heard her speak ill of the Queen?"

"Never."

The conversation did not interest Robert. Maryon turned her attention back to Thomasine. "Or you either? Never any reason why she left the Queen except she was tired?"

Gossip of royalty was not common in St. Frideswide's. Thomasine remembered very well what Lady Ermentrude had said the afternoon she first arrived. "She said there was going to be scandal and she wanted to be away before it started."

Maryon's eyes, so gentle-humored and soft under their full lids until then, sharpened. "Did she say what sort?"

A little disconcerted, Thomasine said, "Oh no. She might have been going to but Master Chaucer said he'd heard nothing of any such thing and . . . ," Thomasine sought for exactly his reply, ". . . and that he was sure Lady Ermentrude knew better than to say anything about any such matter, to him or anyone."

Robert uttered a short sound of amusement. "How did she take that subtle hint?"

Thomasine looked at him, a little surprised. "How should she take it except agree?" She frowned, trying to remember. "Only I'm not sure she actually did. Domina Edith changed the subject right then, I think." She paused, thoughtfully—and remembered herself. With a blush and a sudden awareness of Robert's eyes on her, she ducked her head down again.

Maryon, not noticing and clearly in a mood for gossiping, said, "Well, it will probably be a relief for her sons, her being dead, after the shock is over."

That brought Thomasine's head up again. "What a dreadful thing to say!"

"Not really," Robert said lightly. "I was first in the household of Sir Walter, and many a time I heard Sir Walter complain that she was spending the family into poverty. 'Always the best,' he would shout, 'and never mind if she had to send to London, Bristol, or Calais for it.'"

Maryon's dimple appeared. "And I heard her complain that if her son had his way, they would live year round on bread and cheese."

"Her, perhaps," amended Robert. "Sir Walter believes a noble man's living should reflect his high station."

"Maybe he thinks those nearing life's end should begin casting off what they cannot take with them." Maryon's ironic tone scandalized Thomasine, who believed people shouldn't immerse themselves too deeply in life's pleasures to begin with, in fear of the deadly sin of sloth.

Robert, seeing Thomasine's expression, dropped out of

the wicked game at once. ''Even the greatest families have their troubles these days,'' he said.

''Indeed,'' said Maryon, unaware. ''Sir Walter has been sitting with such concern at Lord Fenner's bedside these two months past.'' She explained to Thomasine, ''They're cousins by Sir Walter's father—or, did you know that? Lady Ermentrude being your aunt, you probably did.''

''No,'' said Robert. ''Lady Thomasine takes very little notice of the matters of this world.''

''Of course, poor thing. Well, Lord Fenner has no sons and the title goes by the male line so Sir Walter will be Lord Fenner when the old man dies, which looks like it could happen any time. Property comes with the title, but Lord Fenner has other wealth, and Sir Walter wants to be sure it doesn't all get given away elsewhere. Interesting how he's been so concerned about that, and, now that his mother is dead, he comes by a fortune equally large. It appears Sir Walter will be doing very well for himself indeed.''

Maryon seemed to have acquired a wide knowledge of Fenner matters in the little while she had been in Lady Ermentrude's service. Thomasine felt some reproving remark was required, but before she could form one, Master Montfort appeared in the doorway.

He was a round, well-bellied man with small black eyes and fox-red hair unevenly thinning across the top. The long, pointed slope of his nose gave his face a sly, smiling shrewdness that Thomasine supposed was surely useful in ferreting out the facts behind unfortunate deaths.

Behind him a little dark shadow of a clerk, carrying pen and ink and parchment scraps, peered nearsightedly around the room for a place to put them. Master Montfort nodded him to the table by the bed and settled himself in the doorway, legs straddled as if to make sure they would all stay where he wanted them until he had finished his business.

In a full, self-assured voice, Master Montfort demanded, ''Which of you is the novice Thomasine?''

Thomasine was too surprised and nervous to move or answer, until Dame Frevisse said, "Thomasine," in a tone that brought her to her feet. Past hope of going unnoticed, she moved a little forward, made an uncertain bob of a curtsey, and whispered, "Sir."

"Look at me, child."

It was a straight demand, barely courteous. Drawing a deep breath, Thomasine looked at him.

"So," he said, as if that settled something. "You met Lady Ermentrude when she first arrived here yesterday. How did she seem to you? I want what you thought about it then, not what you think about it now. Well?"

Despite the clipped command in his voice, Thomasine waited, swallowing, making sure before she tried them that the words would come. "Excited," she managed at last. "Angry." And then because strict truthfulness was needed, she added, "I could smell wine on her breath. I think she was drunk." She glanced at the little clerk, who was busily writing her words on one of his scraps of parchment.

"She frightened you." Montfort reclaimed her attention.

Thomasine turned her surprise to him. How had he known that?

"I've already heard that from your sister." Master Montfort gave the information as if grudging it. "She says Lady Ermentrude appeared drunk. That she was dragging you by the arm. That you were frightened."

Reassured he was not reading her thoughts, Thomasine answered readily, "Yes, I was afraid. She said she was going to take me out of St. Frideswide's. She was holding onto me so tightly I couldn't break free. And she was talking so wildly. I think it was the drink in her making her talk so."

"Did you think so then?"

The question rapped at her as if she had said too much. Thomasine hesitated, her eyes darting from place to place around the floor as if the answer would be somewhere there.

"I was too afraid to think," she whispered at last. "I was too afraid."

"But you did not try to get away from her."

"She was hurting me. . . ."

Beside her Robert said, "I told her not to struggle."

Thomasine stared at him. She had not known he was standing so near to her, or that he would dare speak so strongly to Master Montfort.

"Who are you?" Master Montfort demanded.

"My name is Robert Fenner. I am in—was in—Lady Ermentrude's household."

"Fenner? Then you are related to her, as well."

"I am a great-nephew."

"You were in her service long?"

"Almost three years. I began in Sir Walter's household at age nine, but latterly his household became too large, and I was sent to Lady Ermentrude."

"There was no quarrel?"

"No."

"You got along well with Lady Ermentrude?"

"As well as any."

"You went with her when she rode to Sir John's manor?"

"No."

"But you were in the yard when she returned?"

"I heard Lady Ermentrude ride in. I was in the guest house and came out in time to see her send the priest away and take hold of Lady Thomasine."

His bright gaze moved to Thomasine, who instantly dropped her own. But there was no way to shut out his warm, steady voice.

"And how did she seem to you then?" Montfort demanded.

"Frightened. Very frightened. But she listened to me and helped me bring Lady Ermentrude into the hall."

"I meant, how was Lady Ermentrude?" Master Montfort said, his tone attempting to quell.

Not very quelled, Robert said, ''Drunk, I think. Smelling of wine, unsteady on her feet. Confused in her talking. But—''

''So she was drunk and feeling the effects of her hard riding that day and the day before,'' Master Montfort interrupted.

''She'd ridden that much and more on other occasions and not felt it. I don't know why she did that day.''

''But she did feel it, didn't she?''

''I don't think it was the riding.''

''The drinking then. She was not a young woman.'' He looked around the room and dared someone to gainsay him. No one did, and having asserted his authority, Master Montfort said, ''So it would seem safe to say it was her drinking and exhaustion that killed her, coming as they did after her raging of the day before. She was too old to indulge in all that temper and drinking. They made an end of her.''

Quite clearly he had the answer he was seeking. Now he would let them go, Thomasine thought, and gathered herself for the relief of dismissal.

''No,'' Dame Claire said in precise, deep tones, ''it was something else.''

Everyone's eyes went to her, but her own gaze was on the crowner, her face as set and certain as his own.

After a moment Montfort asked insolently, ''Something *else*, madam?''

Dame Claire said stiffly, ''She may have been drunk when she arrived here, but all her dying signs show something else. Her convulsions as she was dying. The manner of the pain and the way it took her. That was not her heart failing. I have had time since she died to look into my books. I've read—'' She drew a deep breath and forced herself to go on against Master Montfort's lowering look of displeasure. ''Lady Ermentrude was poisoned. That's why she died.''

Thomasine, caught in her own stillness, had not known how still everyone else had been through all of Dame

Claire's speaking. Not until now, when sharply there was movement and indrawn breaths, her own among them. Master Montfort's lower lip jigged up and down as if fighting with his mouth over whether he would speak or not. Finally he said tersely, "You think so?"

"I know so."

"And what makes you sure?"

"I would maybe not be sure—"

"Ah."

"But Martha Hayward's death was the same."

Before, there had been surprise in the movements around the room; that sharpened now into open consternation. Except from Dame Frevisse. Thomasine, despite her own alarm, was aware of the nun's stillness. Had Dame Frevisse known Dame Claire was going to say that?

Master Montfort had recovered himself.

"I've not turned to Martha Hayward's death," he said sternly. "So, you say it was suspicious, too?"

"Father Henry was there when she died," Dame Claire said. "And Thomasine. They can tell you the manner of her dying."

Master Montfort glared at the priest. "Well?"

Father Henry was clearly unhappy at being called on to confirm a dreadful truth. "We were watching by Lady Ermentrude. She was sleeping and Martha was talking. Martha's tongue went ever on wheels but this time she was gabbling, louder and louder, until I had to tell her to remember the sleeping woman. But she became excited, very lively. She would not sit still, walked around and around, still babbling, until the words began to catch in her throat and change to queer sounds. She grew flushed and she looked strange and then clawed at herself." Father Henry made vague gestures at his chest or throat. "She fell down kicking on the floor. Thrashing and choking until suddenly she wasn't . . . anymore. There was time for me to pray over her but only barely, and she died before help came."

There was perspiration on his forehead as he finished, his open face revealing his discomfort.

Thomasine was already braced as Master Montfort's displeased eye turned to her. "Well?" he demanded. "Was that the way of it?"

Feebly, biting her lip, she nodded. He glared at Dame Claire. "I was told it was heart failure. Can't that have been heart failure? The clutching at her chest?"

Before Dame Claire could speak, Dame Frevisse said in her light, clear, unemotional voice, "Father Henry, pardon me, but how exactly did Martha catch at herself? Can you show us exactly?"

The priest looked bewildered but complied, his big hands after a moment's hesitation going not to his chest but to his throat, and not clawing but grabbing and pulling as if trying to loosen something that could not be reached.

"Like that?" Dame Frevisse asked.

"Like that," Father Henry confirmed.

Thomasine nodded.

Dame Frevisse turned to Master Montfort. "So it was not her chest she grabbed for but her throat."

"And that proves?" he said shortly.

"The heart in final pain does not make someone catch at her throat," Dame Claire said.

"But this Martha woman died in minutes, by his account, and Lady Ermentrude was all night about it."

"Individuals have individual responses to poisons; what will kill one instantly may, in fact, only give another an hour's indigestion."

"Perhaps Martha Hayward took more of the poison more quickly than Lady Ermentrude did," Dame Frevisse put in.

"How's that?" Master Montfort snapped the words, upset that these women were defying him, and clearly more dissatisfied with them with every word they said.

Dame Frevisse seemed not to notice. "There was wine beside Lady Ermentrude's bed, with medicine to make her sleep, but she collapsed before having any of it." She looked at Father Henry again. "You said Martha helped herself to Lady Ermentrude's wine. She must have drank most of it. I remember there was very little left when it spilled."

Father Henry moved his feet nervously. "She ate the milksop and then drank deeply of the wine. I told her it had medicine in it and she stopped. I should have stopped her, but—"

But Martha Hayward had never been a woman easily stopped in her pleasures, said the look on everyone's face.

"She was always tasting or sipping at whatever came to hand," Thomasine offered softly.

Master Montfort's look suggested he did not want to hear about it. "So did anyone else drink any of this wine?" People began shaking their heads, but before anyone could answer, he rapped out, "You said it was spilled?" and looked at Dame Frevisse.

"In the trouble after Martha's dying it was spilled. So far as I know, no one else drank of it."

Master Montfort looked at everyone but received only shrugs or shaking of heads.

"So where did *Lady Ermentrude* have poison from, if poison it was?" he demanded.

Dame Claire answered that. "When she awakened in the night, not long before she died, she ate a little . . ."

"Of what?"

"Another milksop," Dame Frevisse said. "And drank a medicined wine Dame Claire had readied for her."

"What was in it?" Montfort glared at Dame Claire.

"Valerian, white clover, the usual herbs that give a soothing rest. Nothing that would do harm."

"And where's the goblet from that time? Did she drink it all?"

Dame Claire looked around as if thinking to see it somewhere in the room. "I didn't see it, after."

Dame Frevisse said, "Robert, who had the tidying here after Lady Ermentrude was carried out?"

"I did. I oversaw some of her women doing it. I don't remember the goblet. You helped in here, Maryon. Do you remember?"

Maryon raised her eyes from staring at the floor. "No. I don't. I emptied the bowl of sops down the garderobe."

"Where did the wine come from? Your stores?"

"It was a bottle of malmsey, supplied by Sir John and Lady Isobel." Dame Claire frowned. "I don't know where it went, either."

"But the goblet," Dame Frevisse insisted. "It was the goblet she drank from. Robert, Maryon, did either of you take it away?"

They both shook their heads. Dame Frevisse turned to Master Montfort. "Then we should look for it. And the bottle."

"Oh, by all means. We don't want to have theft on our hands, too, do we?" he said ironically.

But Robert was already moving to look behind a chair set crosswise to a corner, and Maryon behind a chest set against the wall. Master Montfort's face took on a dusky red hue, and Thomasine guessed that only his dignity kept him from tapping his foot with impatience while he looked for the right thing to say to stop what he saw as nonsense.

Before he found whatever words he wanted, Robert on his knees, groping under the edge of the bed, drew back his hand with a satisfied exclamation and held up the goblet.

Master Montfort was unimpressed. "So we don't have to take on theft, too. Simply carelessness." He nodded dismissively at Maryon. "See to having it cleaned and put safely away with her other goods, woman."

But Dame Frevisse intercepted Robert and took the goblet. She looked into it and turned it so Dame Claire could see to its bottom. The infirmarian shook her head. "There's nothing left to judge anything by," she said regretfully. "But it would be if we could find the bottle."

"Come now, woman." Master Montfort allowed his impatience to show around the edges of his vast dignity.

"We must stop talking nonsense before it makes unneeded trouble. The throes of apoplexy can look much like poison, and we have grounds for suspecting it was apoplexy and none at all for thinking it was poison."

Dame Claire drew herself up to the top of her diminutive height. "We have very excellent grounds for knowing it was poison. And assuredly it was never apoplexy. You'd have to find a quack doctor and pay him to say so if that's the testimony you want. Every symptom named for both the women cries poison, not heart failure."

Master Montfort glowered at her. "Poison is a cheap word. Can you be telling me what 'poison' it might have been?"

"Nightshade. I can show you the book and read you the words. They name the symptoms and they are very like what we saw."

"Very like—! You draw bold conclusions for a person of your sex and learning." He turned from her to address himself broadly to Father Henry, Robert, and his clerk. "It's a common problem with women kept with too little to do and too little to think about. They find excitement where they may."

Father Henry and Robert were too wary to make any answer to that. The clerk, whose pen had been scritching at parchment fragments all the while, did not write it down.

Master Montfort, noting he was being edited, strode across the room, snatched the parchment from the clerk's ink-stained fingers, glanced down at what he had last written, made a disgusted noise, and crumpled it. "No need to put her words down. Nightshade and nonsense. That's the kind of idle talk that blurs the straight facts of a case."

Dame Frevisse said quietly, "Neither her talk nor her facts are idle, and it would be ill-advised to ignore them." There was no hint of defiance or temper in her voice, but it held a confidence that with or without him, the inquiry would go on.

Master Montfort, puffed and red again, glared at her.

Dame Frevisse, unyielding, let him.

The unpleasant quiet held, the clerk's pen poised above another scrap, waiting for words. Then Master Montfort looked away, as if to check what his clerk was going to write, and said ungraciously, "I see I must prove you wrong. Very well, we'll have to begin my questioning again, it seems. Who was with her in the night. Who gave her food. Or could reach her goblet. And Sir Walter is coming," he added gloomily. "He's not going to like this. Not like it at all."

Chapter 8

When Master Montfort was through with them, there was need to tell Domina Edith what was happening, and what was likely to come of it. At Dame Claire's asking, Frevisse went with her, and afterward they stood together in the stillness of the parlor, waiting for Domina Edith to look up from her lap. The dog twitched in its sleep, a fly butted at a windowpane, and after a time Domina Edith raised her head.

"You have no doubt it was murder indeed?"

Frevisse inclined her head even more quickly than Dame Claire had. "Murder meant and planned and attempted twice, failing the first time, succeeding the second."

"So you think Martha's death was unintended?"

"I can see no reason for it being wanted."

"But you see a reason for Lady Ermentrude's?"

"Being Lady Ermentrude, there were probably any number of reasons and people wanting her death."

Two days ago Frevisse would have said it wryly, but there was no humor in it now. Someone had truly wanted Lady Ermentrude dead, wanted it badly enough that Martha's accidental dying had not stopped them, wanted it desperately enough they had tried again with barely a pause.

"What reason does Master Montfort see?"

''I think,'' Frevisse said carefully, ''that he is still wishing Dame Claire had kept her knowledge to herself.''

Domina Edith nodded gently. ''I knew his father as crowner before him. He was another who always wanted his problems kept as simple as might be. And would not hesitate to make them that way if he could.'' She shook her head slowly. ''People are often said to grow foolish with age, but it seems to me that many of us bring our foolishness with us out of our youth.'' She raised her gaze and there was nothing foolish in her own eyes. Her voice changed, becoming direct and firm. ''So since he cannot unsay Dame Claire's words, what is Morys Montfort to do?''

''He says he will set in again to prove us wrong. I am sure he wants to make an end to it, one way or another, before Sir Walter Fenner arrives.''

''Is it possible Sir Walter might hear the death of his mother was murder before he comes within our gates? How widely is it known already?''

Frevisse hesitated and glanced at Dame Claire, who answered, ''Once I was sure of it, I told Dame Frevisse. Until Master Montfort's inquest, only the two of us—and the poisoner''—Dame Claire was always precise—''knew of it.''

''Now everyone who was in the room knows,'' Frevisse said. ''Father Henry. Thomasine. Two of Lady Ermentrude's people. None of them are given to talk, I think.''

''But if Master Montfort has gone back to questioning people, as he said he would . . .'' Dame Claire said.

''Then it will shortly be known throughout the priory there was something wrong with the deaths.'' Domina Edith said it softly. ''And given the ways of servants and the nunnery, it will surely be but little time before word spreads to the village, and beyond. And as it spreads, the tale will grow.''

''I think Master Montfort means to keep it to himself until he has learned more,'' Dame Claire said. ''But with one thing and another—''

"And people's tongues," Domina Edith finished for her, "there is very little time before we and Master Montfort will be dealing with too much talk. And angry Fenners, for who knows which wild tongue will be the first to tell the tale to him?"

Frevisse opened her mouth, then shut it again.

"Say it, Dame Frevisse." Domina Edith's shrewd eyes were on her.

"Master Montfort—" She stopped again, uncertain whether or not to say it diplomatically.

Without emphasis or flinching, Domina Edith said, "—is a political creature who will discover that the sun rises in the north if he thinks it would please Sir Walter. You have already said he will look for the quickest answer. What will that be?"

Frevisse hesitated.

"Dame Frevisse," Domina Edith said, "you are an exemplary nun, but have come to it by the effort of your mind, not the simplicity of your spirit. And that may be just now for the best, since surely simplicity is not our need in this matter. What are you thinking?"

"That if I were Montfort, I would look first and hardest at Thomasine."

Dame Claire made a small, protesting exclamation.

But Domina Edith simply went on looking at Frevisse. Taking her silence for acceptance, Frevisse presumed to add, "So with your leave, I'll keep Thomasine with me as much as might be for these next few days."

"Oh surely there's no need," Dame Claire protested, understanding what she meant as readily as Domina Edith did. Then, less certainly, seeing their faces, she said, "Or if you think there is, then let her stay with me, out of sight in the infirmary. Or here with Domina Edith."

"That would but add to any suspicions Master Montfort may already have," Domina Edith said, before Frevisse could. "It will be better if she's ready to hand for any questions he may be wanting to ask, so long as you are with her to steady her in her answers, and meanwhile keep her safely from chance.'' She sat in silent thought a moment, then said, ''I think that with so many guests here and coming, Dame Frevisse, you are in need of help for these few days. Let it be Thomasine who goes about with you.''

She moved her hand in dismissal. They curtseyed, but Frevisse turned from following Dame Claire to ask, low-voiced, ''By your leave, Domina, may I ask questions as I go about my work? Rather than leave them all to Master Montfort?''

Domina Edith eyed her with quiet assessment, then inclined her head, giving permission without comment.

Frevisse found Thomasine halfheartedly at her lessons with Dame Perpetua.

''No, no, child, *pere* is father, not the fruit,'' sighed Dame Perpetua.

She was safe enough there for the while, decided Frevisse. She contented herself with beckoning Dame Perpetua out of the room and asking that she send Thomasine to her when the lesson was done. ''And if she is sent for to talk with Master Montfort, or anyone outside the cloister, have her come to me first so I may go with her.''

Dame Perpetua rarely looked beyond her books and prayers and pet sparrow, but her cleverness went deep, and she answered, as if understanding more than Frevisse had said, ''The child will go nowhere unless I'm with her, or I've brought her to you. Will that do well?''

''Very well. My thanks.''

Dame Perpetua nodded and went back to the thankless work of teaching French declensions, leaving Frevisse to face the guest halls and her duties.

In the while before Vespers, in between settling such matters as whose duty it was to see that the dogs were exercised outside the priory yard and where Master Montfort's men were to sleep, she began to gather the pieces.

Father Henry, when she happened to encounter him, was

the easiest. He was willing to talk about whatever she asked and apparently never wondered why she was asking.

"No, only Thomasine and Martha and I were in the room the while, after Dame Claire left to go to Vespers. Except the woman named Maryon. She was there at first, all about the room making sure everything would be well when her lady awoke. Then she went to supper. And Sir John and Lady Isobel, too. There seemed no need of them there while Lady Ermentrude was so deep asleep, you know." He seemed apologetic, as if perhaps he should have kept them there. Frevisse assured him it made sense for them to go. "And Lady Ermentrude never roused at all? Never drank or ate anything that was ready for her?"

"Never at all. She was as out of the world's troubles as if she were in her grave."

He heard what he was saying after it was out of his mouth and grew flustered, but Frevisse didn't have the time to listen to his apologies. She said briskly, "Neither you nor Thomasine had any of the sops or wine, only Martha?"

"Only Martha," he said, and went on to repeat what he had said before—that she had gobbled all the sops and drank he knew not how much of the wine, then grown loud and erratic and caught at herself and died. "Just as I told Master Montfort," he assured her.

"And as you must go on telling him that whenever he asks you," Frevisse said firmly. It would hardly do for Father Henry to begin trying to make something out of nothing.

Among Lady Ermentrude's and Master Montfort's and Sir John's people crowding the guest halls, she was unable to find Maryon. "Here just a minute or so ago," she was told so often that she began to think the woman was avoiding her. Time for finding her ran out when the bell rang for Vespers. On the way, she met Dame Claire by chance and asked if any of the herbs she had used in either of the sleeping potions could have caused death.

"Not even if you took them by the handful and ate them

down all at once. Except the poppy. Enough of that will cause a person to fall into a deep sleep, past all waking until the drug has run its course. And it is possible to take so much that sometimes the sleeper will die without waking. But Lady Ermentrude did not sleep her way to death."

After Vespers was supper, eaten in silence except for a nun reading the day's lesson aloud. The meal was finished, and they had cleared their places and were turning toward the garden for an hour's recreation, when a servant slipped quietly up to Domina Edith and whispered something to her. Everyone paused. The prioress nodded to whatever was being said, then pointed at Thomasine and at Frevisse, crooked her finger to tell them to come, and nodded for the rest to leave.

When they had come to her, she said, "Master Montfort has asked to see you, Thomasine." Thomasine dropped her eyes and made her turtling gesture. Without seeming to notice, Domina Edith went on, "Dame Frevisse and my blessing will go with you."

Thomasine's eyes reappeared to glance slantwise at Frevisse, then at Domina Edith. She appeared on the verge of pleading something, then thought better of it and only nodded. Frevisse controlled a surge of exasperation at so much shrinking humility, swallowed it, curtseyed to Domina Edith, and left, sensing Thomasine behind her like a lonesome shadow.

Montfort had taken Lady Ermentrude's former room for his own now. The table had been pulled out from the wall to be more convenient to the clerk, who was crouched there over his parchment when they entered. Poised, pen in hand and ink beside him, he did not bother with looking up when they entered, just went on waiting for whatever was going to be said.

Montfort, on the other hand, was looking for them, rolling forward and back on the balls of his feet, rubbing one hand around the other in anticipation. Frevisse's dislike of him had begun the first time she had ever met him and had not lessened with their distant acquaintance over the years. Now he looked at her with less than pleasure.

"I asked for the novice Thomasine. Is she coming?"

"She's here," Frevisse answered as shortly and stepped aside, revealing Thomasine.

"That's good then. There are things to be asked. And from you, too. Or perhaps you first. You were with Lady Ermentrude less and so there's less you know. You helped bring her to bed when she arrived . . . um . . . ill?"

"I met her in the hall. She was disoriented and in pain. Two of her women and I brought her in here, to be put to bed. We began to undress her, to make her more comfortable. She was calm at first, then became agitated, and at last flew into screaming and hysteria. Her words left her, and there was only noise—"

"Yes, yes. I don't need to hear every step of it. Keep it brief."

"Very well. She collapsed and I left Father Henry to take her confession and did not see her again until perhaps an hour later, when word was brought that someone was dying. We thought it was Lady Ermentrude, but it was Martha."

"And how was she then? Lady Ermentrude, I mean."

"Sleeping so deeply that Martha's dying had not roused her."

"When did you see her again?"

"Sometime before dawn. I awoke and came to see how she did."

"Was she still sleeping?"

"Yes. But she awoke a short while later."

"How was she then?"

"Quiet. A little confused but in her right wits and apparently recovering."

"But she did not recover, did she?"

Frevisse had the double urge to smack the self-pleased

condescension off his face and to verbally rip his illogic to shreds. She smothered the first desire but said astringently, not tempering her contempt, "She was better. Weak still, but coherent and recovering. I was several minutes out of the room, hearing nothing from her, before she began the screaming again with no warning at all. We found her thrashing and incoherent, in pain and struggling to breathe. It was poison, not her heart or temper that killed her and you will never bring Dame Claire or me to say otherwise."

Montfort's florid face turned more red as she talked, and darker red before she had finished. The suffusing color seemed to stop his words, even when she had sharply ended. The clerk's scratching pen trailed off to silence for lack of anything to write; then Montfort shifted his feet on the floor and said, but this time with almost no conviction, "You are not fit to judge."

"Perhaps not," she replied. "But you cannot make a lie of what I know to be true."

Montfort glared at her but said nothing. Unable to hold a stare without words to back it, he whirled toward his clerk. "From here on, be sure to take down everything these women say. They want the truth, they'll have it, and convict themselves with their own words."

He swung on Thomasine. "So what were you doing all night in your aunt's room? Just answer what I ask you. Don't go adding matters. What did you do?"

Thomasine did not lift her head. Toward the floor she said, "I prayed."

"That's all you did?"

"My lady aunt was sleeping. My great-aunt. By marriage. She was sleeping and so I prayed."

"And when she awoke?"

"I told her I had prayed for her." Thomasine looked up. On this at least she was confident. "I wanted her to know my prayers were worth more to her than any worldly marriage could be."

"And what did she say?"

Thomasine looked down again. Her voice was barely audible. "She insisted she would have me out of here."

"And you were angry with her. And afraid. Your sister said so."

"No. Not then. She couldn't take me anywhere, weak as she was. I didn't have to be afraid of her. I fed her and helped her drink her wine and hoped she would sleep again."

"But when Dame Frevisse left you alone with her, she worked herself into a temper nonetheless."

He said it with flat determination, meaning her to accept it.

Thomasine shook her head. "No. She was in no more temper than was usual to her. Not even really angry. Only determined she was going to leave. She sent me out to fetch her women."

"Out? You left her?"

"For only a moment. I looked back—"

"It doesn't matter for how long," he interrupted impatiently. "What you're saying is that when you left your aunt, she was in no fit."

Thomasine nodded her head wordlessly, her eyes fixed on his face.

"You're saying she was fine when you left the room. And that then, when you weren't there, she began the screaming and all the rest."

Thomasine nodded again.

Montfort stared at her discontentedly, then turned his attention to Frevisse. "Is that what you say, too?"

"I heard nothing from Lady Ermentrude after I left the room until Thomasine was standing beside me. She started to say something but Lady Ermentrude began to scream and we all went in to her."

"Who do you mean by 'all'? Be precise."

Frevisse answered levelly, "Dame Claire, Thomasine,

myself. One of Lady Ermentrude's women named Maryon. Have you spoken to her?"

"Of course I have. Go on. Anyone else?"

"Robert Fenner was with us. Father Henry came a few minutes later, in time to give her last rites."

"But Sir John and his lady were not there."

"I thought it better they not be, since seeing them had so angered her before."

"So you told them to stay out. You take a great deal on yourself, Dame."

"Yes," she said. "Perhaps I do."

She left it there for him to make of her reply what he would. But there came a hard rap on the door, and his attention immediately shifted.

"Come," he barked.

The lean man who entered was beyond doubting a Fenner, with Lady Ermentrude's height and arrogant nose. He was wide across the shoulders and his fair hair was cropped close. He was richly dressed in a buff linen houppelande, with a jeweled belt low on his hips. The garment's yard-wide sleeves were gathered at his wrists and slit from below the elbow nearly to the shoulder, to show the sky-bright cotehardie underneath. The cotehardie's blue matched his hose and shoes and the long liripipe of his hat. It was an easy guess, from his looks, his manner, and Montfort's sudden, deflated, respectful bow, that he was Sir Walter, Lady Ermentrude's older son.

Frevisse, sinking quickly in a deep curtsey, could not read in his face what he was actually feeling, even when she straightened to look fully at him. Not looking at them at all, he briskly acknowledged her curtsey, and Thomasine's, as well as the clerk's quick rising and bow at the table. His attention was all for Montfort, and he cut over the crowner's fumbled greeting with "We must needs talk. Are you nearly finished with these?"

"Quite finished, my lord. Done just as you were entering, Sir Walter." Montfort flicked his hand dismissively at

Frevisse and Thomasine. "You may go. You were satisfactory. You may go."

More than merely willing, Frevisse collected Thomasine by the arm and hasted her out of the room, leaving the door for someone else to close.

Chapter 9

OUTSIDE THE DOORWAY, they nearly collided with young Robert Fenner, who fell back, his eyes going to Thomasine. "I pray you pardon me, my ladies," he said.

Apparently Thomasine was no longer afraid of this particular male. She murmured it was no matter and shifted a little, as if she would continue going toward the outer door. But Frevisse held her where she was and said to Robert, "Do you know if word is out about Lady Ermentrude's death?"

"There's talk beginning. Montfort is known for quick decisions, but hasn't made one yet for this. People are starting to wonder, and once that starts it will spread like mold in damp bread." He nodded at the door behind her. "Sir Walter has only just come but he's even quicker to move than Montfort. If he believes the rumors about poison, he'll press Montfort into doing something as fast as may be. If Montfort resists, there will be as fine a display of temper as this place has ever seen. He has that other matter to hand, so he will be doubly anxious not to linger over this one."

"Other— You mean his uncle's dying? But surely . . ."

"A cousin. Lord Fenner. He's rich three times over, and Sir Walter is his heir. The title is Sir Walter's for certain but he wants to be sure there's no ill-written will sharing the wealth with others. He's been at Lord Fenner's sickbed this month past, and the talk has been that nothing short of Judgment Day could pull him away. But now his mother's dead of a sudden, so here he is. Not that Lord Fenner will be making any wills in his absence; he's taking his time about dying and won't make a will until the bishop himself has assured him there is absolutely no way he can carry any of it away with him beyond the grave. Still, Sir Walter will be eager to get back. He's a careful man and doesn't like leaving things to chance."

"Or being kept from what he wants."

"No. Best warn your prioress there is going to be hell to pay until his mother's death is settled." He looked at Thomasine and paused. This time Frevisse noted that Thomasine did not flinch from his look. More gently than he had been speaking to Frevisse, he said, "We are kin of sorts, my lady. Did you know that?"

"No," she said softly. Her gaze dropped, but then returned to his face. "How?"

"I'm one of Lady Ermentrude's rather too many great-nephews. So by marriage at least we're cousins."

Thomasine hesitated, then yielded to a worldly impulse and asked, "What will you do now that Lady Ermentrude is dead? Will you go into Sir Walter's household?"

Robert made a small shrug. "Most likely, since I have to go somewhere."

"And after all, it will be familiar," Frevisse said. "He's very like his mother, I suspect."

Robert's dryness matched her own. "You suspect rightly, my lady." He turned serious again. "I would suggest your lady abbess see to keeping everyone as close in as may be. The fewer people Sir Walter has to strike at when he knows the truth, the better. Pray pardon me, I have tasks to finish."

He moved away as Sir John and Lady Isobel approached. They seemed not to notice him at all as Lady Isobel closed on Thomasine and folded her in her arms, exclaiming, "Poor girl! How tired you look! All this has been too much for you. Haven't they left you alone today? That dreadful crowner, with his stupid questions, has he been frightening you? Can't they see how weary you are?''

Thomasine began removing herself gently from her sister's hold. "I'm well enough. It will pass," she murmured.

"You look none so well yourself, Sir John," Frevisse said. To her eye he looked gray and a little drawn.

"The toothache," he said. He nursed his jaw a little with one hand. "It comes and goes. That wretched mountebank said he had cured it, and he was gone with our good silver pence before we discovered he hadn't. All that smoke and seethe and froth, and now the pain's come back again." He glanced uneasily around to see that no one was near them, and said, low-voiced, "You know what's being said about her death?"

Frevisse indicated with a small movement of her head that she thought it best they move away from the door behind her. Its thickness was sufficient to mute but not muffle Sir Walter's voice.

Sir John flinched slightly, and moved away toward the hall's outer door, the other three following.

"Is it true, what's being said?" Lady Isobel asked. "That she was . . . was . . . poisoned?" Her cheeks' soft cream reddened at the word.

"Yes. Beyond all doubting," Frevisse said.

"But why? By whom?"

"That's what Master Montfort is trying to determine. Will determine very shortly, I trust."

"But how can he be so very certain it was . . . poison?"

"Because of all the signs of it on her. And because Martha Hayward died the same. There's no doubting there was something in her food or wine that killed her, and Martha, too."

"Not in the wine, surely," Lady Isobel protested. "We brought it. There was nothing wrong with it. We brought two bottles, and the twin of the one I gave to Dame Claire I poured out for John myself. And you drank it, didn't you, my heart, trying to ease your tooth?"

Sir John blinked, then said, "Yes, and there's naught wrong with me." But he looked alarmed and seemed to take a swift internal inventory. *Not yet* were the next words off his tongue, Frevisse thought, but he curbed them as Lady Isobel said, "So it must have been in her food. Who prepared it?"

"Thomasine," Frevisse said. "The poison may have been added to one or the other after both the wine and food were in her room."

They had reached the end of the hall now. For a moment there were no servants or anyone else near them and Frevisse asked, "How long were you with your aunt last night?"

"All the first watch," Lady Isobel answered readily. "Then one of her women came in, Maryon, I believe, and I went to bed. It had been a wearying day."

"Sir John, were you there at all, after Martha Hayward's death?"

"Only to ask if more wine was needed. Dame Claire said there was some left and it would do." His jaw was obviously aching and the words came stiffly.

"So the bottle was there then. Did you take it away, then or later?"

"No. But does it matter? Obviously it was emptied and taken away."

"I don't know what matters at present. But it is odd that it has disappeared and no one seems to know who took it or to where."

"I remember seeing it," Lady Isobel said. "It was there on the table, and I could see there was perhaps a third of the wine still left." She gave her husband a tender look. "I thought to take it for John. His tooth is like to trouble him after such a day as we had had and I thought he might need its comfort." Her hand reached sideways, feeling for his.

Their fingers intertwined affectionately. "But instead I opened the second bottle."

"And it worked. After Isobel came with it, I slept far better." He seemed to imply that it was as much her tender concern as the wine that helped.

Frevisse smiled despite herself. They looked hardly older than Thomasine, standing there hand in hand like young lovers instead of a long-married couple. The bell for Compline began to ring. "My thanks," Frevisse said. "I ask your pardon for troubling you. Now, pray, excuse us both. We're needed elsewhere, by your leave." At their mutual nods, she began to leave, drawing Thomasine with her, then on a thought turned back to say, "You should ask Dame Claire for something to ease your tooth. She surely has something better than your peddler's frothing potion."

And Lady Isobel replied, "That's a kindly given thought. I'll do so."

The next day was overcast at sunrise, still dry to please the harvesters but heavy with a warmth that promised to be rain later. Frevisse, moving among the necessities of nearly four score people, with their food and comfort and tempers all needing seeing to, and Thomasine silent behind her, felt a building tension as palpable as the day's heavy warmth. No open talk that the deaths had been murders had reached her yet, but an unease was there, and an awareness that Master Montfort was going on asking questions past when he should have stopped.

Near mid-morning she managed a quiet word with Robert, wondering how far rumor might have grown. He shook his head and said, "Sir Walter is in a temper. That bodes ill." His gaze, as usual, went past her to Thomasine. He seemed about to say something else, then thought better of it, bowed, and went about his business.

A little after that Frevisse overtook the woman Maryon. Seeing her go down the passage to the garderobe at the rear of the guest hall, she waited at its end, knowing there was no other way to leave. She was aware of Thomasine curious beside her but said nothing.

Maryon, returning, drew to a sharp stop as she saw Frevisse. Wariness froze her pretty face for an instant, before she smiled and came forward. "You startled me, standing there so still and waiting. You have need of me?"

"Only to ask you about Lady Ermentrude's last day and night."

Maryon made a graceful gesture. "As you wish." Her smooth, dark hair was swept neatly back from her high, white forehead. Her large gray eyes and small, red, shapely mouth were solemn but not taut with any grieving Frevisse could see.

"How long were you with her that night?"

"All the second watch. Lady Isobel was with her the first watch and Maudelyn with her after me. Lady Thomasine was with her all night, I think."

Thomasine nodded. Frevisse, already knowing that, paid no attention.

"Did you leave her at all? Or did anyone else come in?"

"No one came. That's the black depths of the night then. Everyone was decently sleeping, I think. And I never left the room. I slept awhile. Much of the while, most likely. But I would have roused if she had had need of me."

"But she didn't."

"She slept soundly, she did, poor lady."

Frevisse turned the possibilities around in her mind, forgetting she was staring at Thomasine until the girl shifted uneasily. More than once Thomasine had seemed so deep in prayer that she was unaware of anything around her. Frevisse faced Maryon again. "You've been helpful. Thank you."

Maryon nodded, began to leave, then paused. "You know Master Montfort is asking the same questions, my lady? He's asking everyone, to be sure who was there, and when."

"I know," said Frevisse. "And it might be well if he doesn't know that I'm doing it, too."

Maryon regarded her with bright, considering eyes. "Yes, my lady," she agreed.

Only as she started away did Frevisse think of something else. "What have you done with the monkey, Maryon? I don't know when I last saw it."

"It's been gone since Lady Ermentrude died. Or maybe before. So much was happening, I wasn't paying heed who had it instead of me."

"Is it capable of carrying off a bottle less than half full of wine?"

"Indeed. I was instructed to pay special mind to any open bottle of wine when the monkey was present, as it would surely try to steal it. It's a foul little beast. I'm hoping someone has taken their chance and wrung its nasty neck."

The only relief of the morning was that Sir Walter sent a man to Frevisse offering to send help as well as food to the priory kitchen because his coming had so overburdened St. Frideswide's. Frevisse gladly accepted on Dame Alys's behalf, and made bold to ask if there was anyone among Sir Walter's people who might be able to see to the guest-house chimney. The man said he thought there was, if it pleased her. Frevisse assured him it most certainly did. To have that chimney usable would ease at least some of the problems of the day.

By early afternoon the day's warmth had thickened to discomfort. The coffins would have to be sealed shortly, and Frevisse knew that beyond the priory walls the villeins would be driving themselves as hard as might be, to have as much of the harvest in as they could before the inevitable rain. But her own concerns were bounded by the over-crowded guests, and she was setting two of Sir Walter's men to the problem of the chimney when one of Master Montfort's servants came to say the crowner wished to talk to the novice Thomasine.

Caught up in the bother of her duties, Frevisse nearly said for her to go; she would come later. But as she turned to say it, she saw Thomasine's face, even more pale than usual, and thinner, tight around her bones, her eyes huge and dark. The girl had been no trouble to her all this while, following silently, doing whatever small things Frevisse asked of her, never asking why, suddenly, she was so needed. But clearly the tensions behind the day had reached her, and she was afraid beyond even her usual fears of going alone to Master Montfort's questioning.

Frevisse said briskly to the man she had been talking to, "See to it as best you may then. I'll be back shortly. Come, Thomasine."

Master Montfort had, of course, yielded the guest-hall's best chamber to Sir Walter. He and his clerk and their papers were now crowded into a smaller, darker chamber off a corner of the hall. It was private enough but not so suited to his own sense of dignity and worth, Frevisse suspected, and he was clearly beginning to use his temper to make up the deficiency. He glared at her as she entered.

"I only needed the girl, not you again."

"It is not suitable for Thomasine to be alone with men," Frevisse answered evenly.

"I'm hardly—" Master Montfort began. Then he thought better of it and said instead, "You can wait outside the door then."

"That would still leave Thomasine alone. I'll stay."

Her words were more blunt than she had meant them to be. Certainly they were not what Master Montfort wanted to hear. The blood began to build in his face, going from red to darker red as his temper swelled. Frevisse watched, interested, and said, just before he reached the point of words, "We can send to Domina Edith if you choose, and ask her word on it."

His face darkened further, but his lips closed down over what he had been going to say. He glared at her, his purpose diverted from Thomasine, and said sharply, "All right, but stand you in that corner out of our way and leave me to my work.''

Annoying him was not the wisest thing she could have done, Frevisse knew, but she did not suffer fools so calmly as a good Christian ought. A little regretful of that, she withdrew to the corner beside the clerk's table. Without looking up, he curled his arm around his present parchment scrap, to shield whatever he was going to write.

''Now, my Lady Thomasine,'' Master Montfort began sharply, ''I've talked to more than a few folk since last I saw you. I've learned things and heard things. So what's all this about demons at Lady Ermentrude's bed? You never said anything about demons before. Why not?''

Bright color appeared on Thomasine's cheeks, but she said steadily enough, ''You told me only to answer your questions. You never asked me about demons so I couldn't tell you.''

''I never asked—'' Master Montfort stopped, apparently unsure if he should be offended. Then he decided he was and barked, ''Well, I'm asking now. You say you saw demons. How many and what were they like?''

Thomasine's mouth opened and closed. She shook her head. ''I didn't—'' she began.

Master Montfort jumped at her words. ''So now you deny you saw them? But you said then, before witnesses, you were seeing them. Now you admit you were lying. Why?''

''What she said was that Lady Ermentrude was seeing demons. Not that she saw them herself,'' Frevisse said.

For a man with such an ample face, Master Montfort's black eyes were very small and hard. He narrowed them at Frevisse and demanded, ''There's a difference, Dame? And mind that you're here only so long as you keep out of my matters. You speak again and I'll have you out of here no matter how it displeases your prioress.'' He looked back at Thomasine with an avid gleam. ''So did you see demons or not? You said there were demons come to take Lady

Ermentrude for her wickedness and now you say there weren't. Which is the truth, and why are you lying?"

Tears welled and gleamed in Thomasine's eyes. She was trembling, but very firmly she said, "Lady Ermentrude was shrieking. She was pointing at something no one was seeing and she was afraid of it. I thought of demons and I said it."

"But you didn't see them? Tell me the truth this time, one way or the other, and be done with it!"

A tear slipped down her cheek. "I never said I saw any. Not that time. I didn't see any then. I only saw one and that was later. Not then."

They all stared at her, even the clerk raising his head stiffly from his parchment to gape.

"You saw a demon, Thomasine?" Frevisse asked. "When?"

Thomasine's lower lip trembled, but she said firmly, "When you left me with Lady Ermentrude, just before she died. She was rousing, wouldn't lie quiet. I was going to the door to find you, and looked back at her. And, there was a black . . . thing on her bed. Creeping up over the edge of her bed and reaching for her." Thomasine shivered uncontrollably the whole length of her body. "It was small and black and horrible, and reaching for her." The tears were gone. Only remembered horror was on her face as she said desperately to Master Montfort, "I didn't see them before. Not during the day. But I saw it then. I truly saw it! It was coming for her soul. I swear it!"

It was more than Master Montfort wanted to hear. He did not need the added problem of a demon in his investigation, but there was no apparent way out of it. His clerk was already recovered and scritch-scritching away at the parchment, putting down what Thomasine had said.

"So. So. You say you only saw one and not when there was anyone else around. Did you tell anyone you saw it? Did you say anything about it then, or save it up for now? To make me forget you'd lied before?"

Thomasine stared at him. Then her chin lifted. Her

trembling was gone. "I have not lied. Not before and not now. I did not see demons and never said I saw them, only that they must be there. Why else was Lady Ermentrude so terrified? But I saw this one. I'll say I saw this one, no matter what you say."

"But you never told anyone? All this while and you never told anyone?"

"I tried to tell Dame Frevisse then, but Lady Ermentrude began her screaming. There wasn't time afterwards. And then it didn't seem to matter. There were so many other things."

Master Montfort brooded at her, his little eyes half-hooded as he tried to turn this new thing to good account. But before he could, there was a rap at the door and a man, in Fenner livery with Sir Walter's badge on his shoulder, came in unbidden.

"Here's another body for you," he said and chuckled. He tossed a small, brown, furry bundle at Master Montfort.

The crowner threw up his hands, not wanting the thing. It struck his forearm, fell to the floor with a dull thump, and lay unmoving.

"It's dead," Master Montfort said distastefully.

"As old timber," agreed the man. "One of the men found it in the chimney they're supposed to be mending. On a ledge above the hearth. You know how they're made."

"I don't," said Master Montfort with asperity. "Nor do I want this thing. Take it away."

"Sir Walter thought since it was another body, you ought to have a look at it." The man was clearly amused.

The crowner was not. "Take it away and dump it on the midden. I don't deal with dead dogs."

"It's the monkey," Frevisse said.

Master Montfort glared at her. "A monkey? In your priory?"

"Lady Ermentrude brought one with her. It's been missing."

"And like the goblet, it's been found and no one's the worse for it."

"Except the monkey." Frevisse knelt down and prodded at it, then picked it up. It had been dead some while; it was cold and the death stiffness was gone out of it. "But its neck's not broken. And there are no wounds."

"Then it died of natural causes, the stupid thing, caught up in the chimney." Master Montfort gestured at the grinning man. "Take it out of here. I deal in human matters, not foul imitations like this."

The man picked it up by the long tail, dangling it head downward. Its thin arms fell loosely, limp and long, dragging on the floor. Thomasine drew in a startled breath.

"Close the door," Master Montfort ordered.

Frevisse obeyed.

"Now, Lady Thomasine. Back to the matter at hand."

But Thomasine turned her round eyes to him and said wonderingly, "That's what I saw on Lady Ermentrude's bed. It was the monkey, not a demon at all." She smiled with deep relief.

"How could you mistake a monkey for a demon?" Montfort rapped out.

"Because the monkey is brown, but what I saw seemed black. And when I saw it before it was all curled up on a servant's shoulder, and I didn't see how a monkey is all arms and legs. The arm coming out of the shadows was long, very long, and thin, and black. . . ." Thomasine's breath caught with remembered terror, then she blinked the memory away. "But it was just the monkey, looking black in the shadows. It was just the monkey, not a demon coming for her soul."

Master Montfort's frustration was written in large lines across his face. "So now you're saying you saw no demons at all? You're saying it was just a monkey coming for a visit?"

"It was the monkey coming for the wine," Frevisse said,

with sudden realization. "Thomasine, where was the wine when you left your aunt? Was she holding it?"

"I've told you you're not to—" Master Montfort began.

But Thomasine said, "Yes! She had been drinking it again after you left. She was holding the goblet. The monkey was after the wine!"

"And took it and drank it and left the goblet under the bed. And then it took the bottle, ran and hid while it drank it. And died of too much drink."

"Yes, very well, we're pleased to know that." Montfort smacked his fist on the table edge to have their attention. "But that's not the matter to hand here. You're saying there were no demons, correct?"

The bright relief went out of Thomasine. "There may have been. Lady Ermentrude was so frightened. She behaved so strangely when she first came."

"Ah yes." That pleased Master Montfort. "Lady Ermentrude's behavior. Her desire to take you out of the nunnery, back into the world. That frightened you, didn't it, child?"

Thomasine looked puzzled at his insistence. "I told you it did."

"Why?" he rapped.

"I want to be here."

"She promised you a husband, a fine marriage."

"I'm to be Christ's bride. I don't need a worldly marriage."

"She said she was going to take you away, whether you wanted it or not."

"She couldn't. She had no authority over me."

"She might have. She had powerful friends. You were afraid, your sister said you were afraid."

"Because my aunt was loud and hurting me."

"And so you hurt her back?"

Thomasine's face froze. Only after rigid seconds did she say, looking as if she wanted to faint, "No. I helped her come inside. I brought her warm milk and bread with honey.

I prayed for her. I watched by her bed. I would never have hurt her."

She knows, thought Frevisse. She knows what Master Montfort is saying, and is holding against it better than I thought she ever could.

But how long Thomasine's nerve would last was another matter, and Frevisse desperately wanted to have her away from him before the direct accusation came.

The unlatched door slammed suddenly open. Scarcely in time, Frevisse had her hand up to protect her face from it as Sir Walter strode forcefully into the room and without greeting, demanded, "Enough ring a ring a' rosy, Montfort! What's this tale I'm hearing run about my mother's death? You gave me a song yesterday about exhaustion and drink and temper that did for her, but poison is the word I'm hearing now."

Master Montfort had backed away quickly at Sir Walter's coming in. He was outranked and outtempered by Sir Walter and knew it. With hasty respect and a deep bow, he said, "My lord, we're about the matter now. If you would be so good." He gestured toward the room's other chair, which he had not offered to Thomasine or Frevisse.

"I don't need to sit. I need answers. My mother yielded to her temper all her life, drank more wine, and exhausted more horses than any man for years without tiring herself beyond what a day's rest would mend. Don't expect me to believe it was otherwise here. She came to take a novice out of this hole and now she's dead. There's fraud at the heart of it and you'd better have found out who's to gain from that fraud, because whoever killed my mother is going to hang!"

"My lord, the matter is well in hand. I was just questioning—" Master Montfort started to gesture toward Thomasine, who had shrunk back toward Frevisse.

Sir Walter cut across his words. "You've had a day of questioning. Where are your answers?"

"Not fully a day, my lord. . . ." Master Montfort tried again. He cast a desperate glance toward his clerk, who was racing his quill at full speed to keep up with their exchange. ''Stop that,'' he said a little shrilly. The clerk stopped, obedient but still hunched over his parchment, waiting for more. ''My lord, I've found out things but these matters take a certain time. I'm crowner here, responsible to his grace King Henry VI for justice to be done. I must have—''

''And I am Sir Walter Fenner, with two score men-at-arms camped in the field across the road. King Henry is nine years old and he and his government are in France and I am perfectly willing for another crowner to come and inquire about your broken neck if I don't have a poisoner in my hands before the day is out!''

Master Montfort was still stammering toward some sort of answer as Frevisse gathered Thomasine to her with a quick hand and pulled her backward out the door.

Thomasine went, thankful to be away. But brown-haired Robert with the quiet voice cut across their way to the outer door. Without the bother of greeting, he said to Dame Frevisse, ''Sir Walter knows.''

''We just heard.'' Dame Frevisse jerked her head toward the crowner's room and Sir Walter's rising voice.

''He's angry. And more angry for it not being Montfort who told him.'' Robert spoke at Dame Frevisse, but his gaze slipped to Thomasine. ''I'd not frighten you, my lady, but from what he said to me about it, he will revenge himself on someone. You'd best go into the cloister and stay there. I'll do what I may for you here.''

Thomasine wondered how Sir Walter came to think of her as possibly guilty of murder. Who had put that idea in his head? And what would he do about it? She met Robert's ardent gaze and said, ''Thank you for the warning, my lord. God grant us the courage to meet this challenge, I pray.''

She gave way then to Frevisse's pulling on her arm and went away from him.

The first rain was falling darkly on the cobbles as they hurriedly crossed the yard toward the cloister gate. Not until the gate was shut behind them did Dame Frevisse pause, draw a deep breath, and let loose of Thomasine's arm.

"Thomasine, you are not to go out of here again until this matter is settled. Do you understand? Not for any reason are you to leave."

Thomasine's fear was a swollen clot in her chest, making it hard to breathe or speak. So she only nodded to Dame Frevisse's order and, not knowing what else to do, followed her as she went on along the cloister walk.

They were nearly to the kitchen door, but came on Dame Claire before they reached it, tying a knot in the last towel to hang on the three hooks behind the stone lavatory outside the refectory. She glanced up at their coming. When Dame Frevisse made a small sign toward the narrow passage where they could talk, she nodded, finished her task, and came into the slipe.

The rain had thickened into a steady patter on the roof. Dame Claire glanced toward the sound and said, "That won't be good for the harvest."

"Most of it is in, I think," said Dame Frevisse. "And if this lasts only a little and the weather clears, the rest will dry. The monkey has been found."

Dame Claire followed the shift of topic poorly. "The monkey? Was it missing?"

"Since about the time Lady Ermentrude died. And now it's dead, too, and has been for quite a while. I think, from what Thomasine has told me, it drank the same wine as Lady Ermentrude did and died of it."

Dame Claire's reaction was complete stillness. She went on looking at Dame Frevisse, but her mind was clearly elsewhere. It was a thinking quiet that Thomasine had often admired.

"Then we can be sure it was the wine and not the sops," Dame Claire said finally.

"Nearly sure. From what I know of the little brute, it would not have bothered with anything so bland as milk and bread, but it surely would have taken to the wine."

"Does this change what you think about Martha's death?"

"No, I still think it was an accident. Like the monkey's. No, it was Lady Ermentrude who was meant to die."

"Has Master Montfort found the reason for it yet?"

"I think he thinks he has. And if he isn't certain sure, I'm afraid he's going to let Sir Walter tell him, and point out the murderer for him, too."

Thomasine did not flinch as they both looked at her then. But fear tightened her throat.

Very gently, Dame Claire said, "You're not the only one he can suspect, child. I mixed the medicine both times. And the wine was from Sir John and Lady Isobel. And there were others in the room who could have done it. You're not the only possibility."

But the unsaid words "Only the best one" were in Dame Frevisse's face, where Thomasine could read them as clearly as she had read them in Master Montfort's.

Chapter 10

THUNDER GRUMBLED. DAME Claire looked up as if it were reminding her of something. "I must go."

"One other thing," Frevisse said. "Sir John has the toothache. Have you anything to help it until he can find an honest surgeon to draw it?"

Dame Claire was always ready to talk of remedies; she brightened, thought for a moment, and said, "My oil of cloves is nearly gone but I'll have more from the Michaelmas fair. He's surely welcome to what I have left. Has he been troubled long?"

"Long enough that he bought a cure from a passing mountebank some time of late. He described it as all froth and little help."

Dame Claire made a ladylike snort of contempt. "I know of that false cure. All smoke and dwale and fancy words. Then they show you the gnawing worm they've driven from your tooth, but it's come out of their sleeve, not your mouth." Thunder muttered in the clouds. "If he's hurting, this weather will make it hurt the worse. Tell him to send to me for the oil of cloves when he wants it. Where are you bound for?"

"The kitchen, I'm afraid."

Dame Claire nodded her sympathy and went away.

Frevisse, drawn by duty and against her own inclination, went to see how matters were coming between Dame Alys and her unfortunate staff. Thomasine, as ordered, hung in her wake. There should have been no need of that within the cloister, but Frevisse felt uncomfortable unless she actually had the girl in sight.

The kitchen was crowded. Frevisse paused in the doorway, waiting to sort out what was happening, and saw that besides the priory's usual lay workers, there were three of St. Frideswide's nuns and a half dozen Fenner servants hurrying under Dame Alys's full-voiced orders.

The dame was presently declaring that the next hand besides her own that touched the pastry would be ground up and added to the meat for the pies, but her usual fury lacked full conviction.

"Here now, here now!" She poked one of the servants in the ribs with her bent spoon but scarcely hard enough to make the woman wince. "Do that chicken neck again! There's a fistful of meat on those bones! Pick it all off, pick it all! We've too many hungry mouths waiting to waste a morsel!"

She saw Frevisse, and turned on her, exclaiming, "So let's have a new chimney built if the other can't be repaired! It will take less time, I swear you. And now I'm feeding a troop of Fenners because one wasn't enough, and that one stupid enough to drink herself to death at our priory! Ah, I see you're bringing me Thomasine back, that's one good thing, because surely I've need of the girl. And you, too, if you've a while to spare."

Frevisse had spent her own apprenticeship in the kitchen and knew how much of that she could ignore. She said, "Thomasine is to be my help today. I've come to see how supper is going on. Will there be enough?"

"Enough. And maybe a little more." Dame Alys admitted it grudgingly. "Sir Walter didn't come empty-handed. He's given us a moldy cheese, one sack of flour, and a sick old ox." She jerked her spoon at the immense carcass turning on the great spit in the far fireplace. "I can make do."

The growth of mold on the cheese was smaller than the palm of a hand and the cheese itself was the size of a cartwheel. The spit in the fireplace was in danger of bending under the weight of the beef roasting on it. The single sack of flour was a very large one. It appeared from what Frevisse could see that there was more than sufficient food to satisfy all their enforced guests. And it would be delicious. Despite her tongue, Dame Alys would supervise the making of a meal for even an enemy to perfection. It would be as coals of fire on their heads for her to feed the Fenners well enough so they could have no complaints about St. Frideswide's hospitality.

But it must have been hard on her to be brought to this pass. Burdened with food enough and help enough and no more Lady Ermentrude to plague her, Dame Alys was woefully short of things to complain of.

"Have you people enough for serving the supper?" Frevisse asked.

"I'm having nothing to do with serving Fenners!" snapped Dame Alys. Then she conceded unwillingly, "Sir Walter has said that if we bring the food to the cloister gate, he will have people to take it to the guest halls, so that's settled. But there's more than enough to do, we'll be sore wearied doing our work in here. Sister Amicia, when I said I wanted those parsnips cut to finger size, I didn't mean a giant's fingers. Smaller, girl, or they won't cook till Hallowmas."

Because Frevisse was responsible for the feeding of the guests, she took a purely formal walk between the tables, looking at the cheese flans, meat pies, sauces, and other things prepared or in the making. There was a sweet, spicy odor of cakes baking. Dame Alys, carrying her warp-handled spoon like a baton of office, rumbled at her heels, pointing out that the Fenners' flour was over-ground to almost useless fineness and their beef hung too heavy on the spit, and the cheese they had brought was aged, which she declared made it evil to digest.

With Dame Alys distracted by Frevisse, the women set up small spates of talking among themselves, with one of the Fenner servants going so far as to giggle at something someone said. Dame Alys stopped her with a fuming look, but behind her back the murmured talk went on. Only Thomasine, standing at the edge of it all where Frevisse had left her, kept silent, her head down, hands folded into her sleeves.

Frevisse, under the burden of Dame Alys's complaints, forgot her. It was Sister Amicia who exclaimed in shrill tones easily heard across the kitchen, ''Well, crying all over the floor like a rag gone sopping. It's not like you cared for her, is it? Goodness!''

Frevisse's quick glance told her that Thomasine was indeed crying, shaking from shoulders to feet with her arms pulled tight against her to hold in the sobs. Not wanting her to lose the fight, Frevisse put down the spoonful of frumenty she had been about to taste, and swept between the tables to take Thomasine briskly by the arm and out of the kitchen before anyone could find anything else to say.

The slipe would be too chill after the kitchen's warmth; Frevisse took Thomasine around the cloister to the church, entering by the small side door the nuns used to come and go for their services. It let into the choir, an arrangement of stepped pews facing one another across the tiled floor. The altar of polished stone was to their right, raised on a dais three steps up from the floor, gleaming with white linen, gold, and brass. Frevisse firmly stopped Thomasine's instinctive turn toward it, led her instead through the choir, past the two nuns praying at the coffins, to the church's farther end, near the great western door that led into the courtyard and was rarely used except for processions on high feast days. There was a stone bench built from the wall on the great door's left side, on which the sick or weary guest could rest during services.

"Sit," ordered Frevisse.

Thomasine obeyed. Frevisse sat beside her.

"Now," Frevisse said, "if you need to cry, get on with it."

Thomasine did. She pressed her hands over her face and wept until the tears seeped between her fingers.

Frevisse waited patiently, until the sobs subsided to a few ragged hiccups and then silence. Thomasine's hands fell limply into her lap.

"I'm sorry," she whispered.

Frevisse waited, having no particular answer to that.

Thomasine hiccuped again on caught tears. Drawing a handkerchief from her sleeve, she wiped her face. "It was what Sister Amicia said," she whispered. "She was hoping their bodies would be taken away soon, so the harvest home feasting won't be spoiled by their being here. Lady Ermentrude's and Martha's." She nodded painfully toward the coffins, lidded now and nailed shut, then looked at Frevisse with huge, tear-swimming eyes. "Sister Amicia is wanting harvest home to be as ever it is, not thinking of them at all and that they're dead and won't see harvest anymore. It hurt so much so suddenly, thinking they'd never sit down with their friends anymore, I started to cry. They're dead and I'm crying when I should be praying."

Frevisse said, "No, you cried for good reason. Now you've finished and we've things to see to. Come wash your face so we can be on with them."

Thomasine raised her head. Her pale, thin face was mottled with the red of her crying, her eyes pained. "But I'm not supposed to feel these kinds of things! I'm not supposed to care about things like the body dying, or anything of world at all. I don't want to. I want to be away from it, not hurting for it. They've gone to God. I'm only supposed to pray for them, not cry."

Frevisse might have had compassion for the child if she had been asking for guidance, but her usual impatience at Thomasine's useless simplicity, and the pressure of too many things still needing to be done, made her ask sharply, "And what good do you think your prayers are going to be if you don't care about what you're praying for? We work and pray for more than just ourselves and well you'd know it if you'd paid any heed to anything at all besides yourself since you came here. What good do you think your prayers are going to be, if the only thing you care about is your own self? You cried because you were hurting for other people's hurt, and that's probably worth more than a hundred careful prayers with no feeling at all behind them. Now come. We've things to do."

Thomasine stayed where she was, staring with mouth slightly open, looking stupid. Or stunned. Then her mouth closed, and a slow flush of color crept up her face, covering the mottling of her crying. Her eyes lost the blur of tears and her mouth's soft line tightened, making her look more her age, a woman instead of a frail and cosseted little girl.

Frevisse half-expected some kind of answer from her, but after that first moment, Thomasine's gaze dropped and she rose to her feet, showing that she was ready to come, all outward meekness again. Only the stiffness of her shoulders and her rigid neck, the cringe gone out of it, showed that what Frevisse had said had struck deep enough to leave a mark. And something of the courage she had shown to the crowner had come back, too, because before Frevisse could turn away, she lifted her head and said quietly, "Master Montfort wants it to be me who killed them, doesn't he?"

There were ways around answering that directly, but meeting her gaze, Frevisse said levelly, "Yes. You're the simplest choice, and with Sir Walter snapping at him, Montfort is going to want the simplest choice."

Thomasine searched Frevisse's face, looking for hope. Frevisse did not give it. So far she had no idea who had given the poison, or why. Until she did, Thomasine was indeed the first, best choice. "Come now," she said. "All that may be done is being done. We must go tell Domina Edith how matters stand. She'll want to know."

The door to the prioress's parlor stood open, and from it Sir Walter's voice rumbled, raw with temper and bare of courtesy. "Hear me out! My mother is dead. By poison, Montfort says. Murdered. And from what I've heard, it was some one of you did it."

Frevisse flickered one hand in the sign for church, meaning Thomasine should go there and stay. Thomasine nodded and left without hesitation. When she was safely gone, Frevisse rapped at the door clearly enough to be heard over Sir Walter's continuing voice.

"*Benedicite,*" Domina Edith said. Her quiet voice carried with apparent ease over Sir Walter's, and Frevisse entered, head properly bowed but not so low she could not see all of the room from under her eyelids. Domina Edith was in her chair, drawn straightly up but facing Sir Walter with an expression that said he was far from overwhelming her with his noble temper. To her right stood Dame Claire, rigid with self-control; to her left was Father Henry, very pink with indignation, glaring at Sir Walter.

Beyond Sir Walter was Robert Fenner, standing statue-still, his face guarded. A freshly formed bruise showed dark along the side of his face. He glanced past Frevisse, looking for someone, and when he saw she was not there, set his eyes back to carefully not looking at anyone.

Sir Walter, with his mother's way of dominating a room, stood in the parlor's center, head up, hands on hips. He paid no heed to Frevisse but went on at Domina Edith, "My mother was never so drunk in her life she didn't know what she was doing, and there was naught wrong with her heart. It was poison, and someone here gave it, and the only one with reason enough to do it, Montfort says, is your novice Thomasine D'Evers. I want her to come away with me, now. Montfort says he's not done with his questions, but he's a fool and I am not. Are you going to give her over at my asking or do you want to make a quarrel of it?"

So it had gone that far already. Frevisse could not help making a tiny sound of disgust, and Sir Walter swung around to point at her fiercely, aware of her after all. "You! You're hosteler, right? My mother was in your keeping when someone killed her so you must share responsibility with that puling girl. I think you know more than you've told." He swung back to Domina Edith. "She's not a nun. You've no right to keep her. You can't protect her. I'll have her out of here if I have to take the place apart stone by stone!" His face was red, his light, protuberant eyes very like his mother's. "And if the King's man won't do justice, I'll have you all for sheltering her!"

Domina Edith raised her eyebrows very slightly. Father Henry, hands clenched into fists, stirred forward, but the prioress lifted a finger from the arm of her chair, stopping him. Very calmly she said to Sir Walter, "I am a professed nun, belonging to God. Not you nor Master Montfort nor the King himself, God keep him, can touch me. Or any of those in my charge."

Sir Walter's jaw worked, cutting off words not fit to say before he finally swung back at Frevisse and said sharply, "Produce the girl. For the sake of your soul and your prioress's peace. You know where she is. She's in your care—just as my mother was!"

"Your mother was also in mine," Dame Claire said firmly. He glared at her, but she went on, "We don't know who gave the poison to your lady mother. Or to Martha Hayward. We don't even know where the poison came from."

"You have poisons on your shelf, all 'pothecaries do. I dare you to deny it!"

"The poison that killed them was nightshade, and, yes, I have it with my medicines, for poultices and suchlike. But it also grows in any wood, for anyone to take if they trouble to look for it."

"And there's the matter of who could have given it, no matter where it came from." Domina Edith spoke in a cold, clipped, patience-coming-to-an-end tone. "I myself would think three times over before agreeing with Master Montfort on any conclusion, especially one so grave as this."

Sir Walter asked with his belligerence a little less certain, "You have some better ideas on the matter?"

"Dame Claire very sensibly points out that others besides Thomasine could have had nightshade. It might be someone among Lady Ermentrude's own people."

"So that's how you would have it!" Sir Walter sneered his scorn. "Blame it on a servant and not one of your own! Pah, a servant could have done it anywhere and more conveniently elsewhere than this. It wasn't one of her own people. It was someone here. Mayhap even one of you right in this room!"

He was stirring himself to fury again. Frevisse felt her own temper rising in answer to it, and saw that Father Henry was reddening, tensing to say something or, worse, do something. Quickly she said, "Then you'll have to tell us why one of us would do it, Sir Walter. Why would we want Lady Ermentrude dead when she's given so much to St. Frideswide's?"

Triumphantly Sir Walter sprang at the point. "Because she was meaning to take your novice out of here! She was going to take the girl away—and with her would go her dowry. Surely something you're not wanting to lose. A poor little place like this is always wanting money. You couldn't afford to lose the only dowry likely to come your way for a while, so my mother had to die. But you're going to lose more than the dowry now. There's not a Fenner will give a penny to this place when the truth's found out!"

Domina Edith flung up one hand to silence Dame Claire and Frevisse together. "Stay!" she snapped at Father Henry, already moving toward Sir Walter, his hands flexing at his sides. The priest stopped, but Frevisse heard his teeth grinding together. Domina Edith, her eyes fixed on Sir Walter with a chill and withering look, pressed her hands down on the arms of her chair and raised herself slowly, remorselessly, to her feet. She was not tall, but her force of will reached out and held them all until she had drawn herself up straight. In a tone to match her look, but not raising her voice, she said, ''If it were any business of yours to discover, you'd find St. Frideswide's has no need to go begging to anyone, or be bankrupt by a lost dowry. Our house may be small but we are not poor nor beholden to anyone, and you may take your Fenner pennies and your temper with them, for you'll not insult me and mine in my own nunnery. You are in sorrow and, by the Holy Rule, our guest for this time being, and will be treated so, no matter how we feel about it. But mind your tongue. Not even your mother in all her tempers ever presumed to speak to us as you have done. You have what answers we can give you here. Go back to the guest hall and leave us before even guest right and a knowledge of your grief aren't enough to make me stomach you. And don't come in my presence again unless you are on bended knee in sign of a contrite heart, asking my forgiveness. Go.''

Sir Walter drew himself up, breathing heavily through his nose, his mouth working around things he wanted to say while his mind visibly canceled them short of words. At the last it was probably the fact he had had to face his mother all his life that kept him silent against Domina Edith, and furious but unable to do else, he jerked his shoulders in a travesty of a bow and flung himself out of the door. Less headlong, Robert followed him, with a roll of his eyes and a raising of his eyebrows at Frevisse as he passed her. Frevisse looked at his bruised cheek and twitched her head at Sir Walter's back. Robert nodded, and was gone. She pushed the door shut after him and moved quickly to help Dame Claire ease Domina Edith back into her chair.

The prioress seemed none the worse for her effort, only a little breathless, and still annoyed. ''Worse manners than any Fenner, ever. And less sense. Half a mind would at least make up for lacking manners. A little.'' Her hand closed on Frevisse's wrist. ''There's going to be more trouble coming. We didn't satisfy him and he won't be stopped by what we've said. You're hosteler and must go out of the cloister yet again. Can you face him?"

"Yes, of course." She had spent all her childhood managing other people being difficult; she had small qualms about facing either Sir Walter or Master Montfort.

"That's good. That's very good. You can go then where you need to go, and ask what needs to be asked. Master Montfort will never find out everything, not now that Sir Walter has an answer that satisfies him. We can't depend on either of them for the answers."

"Yes, Domina."

"And Dame Claire," Domina Edith said.

"Whatever you need, Domina."

"Think harder on the poison and who could have given it. Was there a particular reason for it to be nightshade? Who, having chosen it, would have it to hand? Did they choose it suddenly because it was there? Or did they plan aforetimes to have it? Think of all of it, both of you. Father Henry."

The priest came eagerly to stand in front of her.

"Your prayers," she said. His face showed his disappointment at so inactive a task, but Domina Edith said firmly, "Your prayers. As many of them as you can manage, that we be allowed to find out whatever truth there is in this. Because," she added with a waspishness that must have been strong in her in her youth, however mellowed it had grown with age, "truth would have to stand up and bite Master Montfort before he'd recognize it. Go on now, all of you. I have a shameful need to sleep." Her attention sharpened again. "Where's Thomasine?"

"I sent her to the church when I realized Sir Walter was with you," Frevisse said.

Domina Edith nodded, satisfied. "Let her stay there. She'll do well not to be with you when you cross paths with Montfort or Sir Walter. Go on now."

They left her. At the foot of the stairs Father Henry went away toward the church, Dame Claire and Frevisse, of one accord, to the narrow slipe, where they could talk. But once there, they seemed out of things to say, and Frevisse wondered if the strain of the past two days showed as clearly on her as it did in the gray shadowing around Dame Claire's eyes.

Finally Dame Claire asked, "So what are we to do?"

At least to that Frevisse had an answer. "We do again what we've been doing, asking again where everyone was and what everyone did. And we seek to speak to those we've missed, to learn what they remember about everything that's happened. Someone had an urgent reason to have Lady Ermentrude dead, or they'd not have been so headlong about it, not after Martha's death. It would be among those who wanted her dead to begin with." Frevisse began to count off on her fingers. "Her son, Sir Walter, to inherit the money he feared she would spend before he got hold of it. Sir John and Isobel, with whom she rode off to quarrel and who came riding so fast after her when she left them. There's the servants she keeps close about her, Maudelyn and Maryon."

"Why them?" interrupted Dame Claire.

"I don't know. But every time something happens Maryon is there, peering and questioning. Except when I want to talk to her. Then she is not to be found." She switched hands to tap her other thumb. "Robert Fenner."

"That nice young man?"

"That nice young man began in Sir Walter's household, moved suddenly to Lady Ermentrude's, and now will go back. And it was after Sir Walter talked to him that Sir Walter began to suspect Thomasine."

"What about Thomasine?" Dame Claire's tone was reluctant, sober. "We even have to consider it might have been her, if only to prove it was not."

Frevisse nodded, but said, "She might kill in fear, or panic, and surely she felt both when Lady Ermentrude seemed grimly determined to take her away, but her conscience would drive her into agonies afterwards. She's the sort who does penance for spilling a bowl of soup."

Dame Claire smiled despite herself at the thought of Thomasine's excesses. Then she sobered. "There's Martha Hayward's death to be remembered, too."

Frevisse shook her head. "It was most likely not meant at all. If by some terrible mistake Thomasine killed Martha, then that death would have shocked her back to her senses. She'd never have tried again." She frowned. "Where did the poison come from? Is there any missing from your stock?"

"No. That is, I don't think so. I haven't used any nightshade in some while, so I am not sure whether my supply of it is a little diminished or not. The jar does not appear disturbed."

"Which it probably would if Thomasine, who would have been in a great hurry, rushed in to steal some of it. What about some other poison? Was there anything in the stomach-ache potion for the monkey that could have killed a person?"

"Nothing sufficient even to kill the monkey, let be a person. And nothing to bring on those agonies."

"So Lady Ermentrude came here drunk and we fed her milksops that Thomasine fetched from the kitchen." She tapped her right forefinger.

"Yes," nodded Dame Claire. "The feud between Dame Alys's family and the Fenners. She has often said she'd like to take a hand in that quarrel."

"But we're fairly certain it was the wine that had the poison, since the monkey is dead of it."

"Fairly certain, but not perfectly. Is it possible that the creature stopped to dip into the bowl of sops before rushing off with the bottle?"

"I suppose. We had best learn who could have handled the food at any time, as well as the wine. How long does nightshade take to kill?"

"Different times with different people and depending on how much and how fast they have it. Martha would have gulped most of the first goblet down at once, before Father Henry warned her it was medicine."

"And Lady Ermentrude only sipped at the other one again and again the morning that she died," said Frevisse, remembering. Her face stiffened with another thought. "The first one—the one that Martha drank from—Thomasine dropped it. Lady Isobel tried to give it to her but she dropped it. She is not usually so clumsy."

The two women regarded each other soberly.

"Presuming Lady Isobel would not deliberately try to poison her own sister . . . ," Frevisse said after a moment.

"Frevisse!" Dame Claire exclaimed. "That's not even to be thought on!"

"Everything has to be thought on. So let's suppose Lady Isobel did mean to poison Thomasine."

"That would mean she poisoned Lady Ermentrude too. And for what reason? Why would she want them both dead?"

"The wine was brought by her and her husband. And Lady Ermentrude was in a tearing rage at them, so bad they followed her here to try to settle it."

"They were worried she would come to harm on the road."

"I could be tempted to think they were more worried that she might say something about the quarrel," Frevisse said grimly. "We don't know why she was so angry. All they have said is that she wanted their marriage ended. I wonder why."

"They brought servants with them, and there were others with Lady Ermentrude. We'll ask them what they know and heard. But there were others in reach of the wine after it was set out."

Frevisse closed her eyes, trying to remember who had been in Lady Ermentrude's chamber anytime she knew of. "You and I were there. And Thomasine. And Father Henry."

"Now there's nonsense," Dame Claire protested. "He has no reason at all to want to kill anyone."

"We don't know why Lady Ermentrude was killed. Not knowing, we can't be sure he doesn't have a reason from before he came here." She smiled. "But it would be a passing strange reason, I should think. Now, Lady Isobel sat with her in the night. And the servants Maryon and Maudelyn. Sir John came at least once, I think. They all say no one else was there, but Lady Isobel and the two servants slept, and though Thomasine insists she was awake and praying the whole time, she might have dozed unknowingly."

"Or been so far into her prayers she was unaware of anything else."

Frevisse nodded agreement. "So there might have been others in and out and no way for us to learn of them except to go on asking. Will you come with me? Something that's said may mean more to you than it does to me, or more to both of us if we're both there to hear it."

"Assuredly. Where first?"

Frevisse smiled wryly. "To Dame Alys, since we're so near the kitchen."

The kitchen still seethed with purposeful movement. The ox was browning on its spit, and the baked cakes were cooling on a side table; the smell of baking bread was rich in the air. Dame Alys was in heavy talk with one of Lady Ermentrude's servants near the door. Frevisse, pausing to draw her attention, was aware that the low-voiced running talk all through the kitchen had stopped on their entry, and that faces turning toward them were bright with nervous excitement. Somehow word must have come to them that Dame Frevisse and Dame Claire were looking into this matter on orders from the prioress. Frevisse said nothing, but simply gestured a summons at Dame Alys, who for a change came without complaint or her spoon.

They returned to the slipe, and before Frevisse could say anything, Dame Alys burst out, "So is it true? Someone finally did what the old . . . ," she reconsidered her word and said, ". . . lady has been begging to have done these fifty years or more?"

With a quelling lack of excitement, Frevisse said, "She was assuredly poisoned. Someone has killed her and Domina Edith has set Dame Claire and me to asking questions."

"And there were truly demons come to grab her Hell-bound soul? You saw them?"

"No one saw them," Dame Claire said wearily. "Lady Ermentrude was jibbering in some sort of brain fever and Thomasine said she must be seeing demons. That was all it was, just her brain fever and too much wine. It was before she was poisoned anyway."

"Oh. Thomasine." Dame Alys dismissed the matter with regret but firmly. "As holy a child as I ever hope to meet, but she's not got the sense God gives a Michaelmas goose. So what about Martha then? She was poisoned, too, they're saying."

Frevisse said, "It appears she took what was meant for Lady Ermentrude."

Dame Alys crossed herself, shaking her head. "Greed and temper were always her failings. God's will be done," she added piously.

"But," Frevisse asked, "who made the first milksop for Lady Ermentrude?"

"First one? She had more? The greedy—" Dame Alys stopped herself and said, "I did. Bad enough I had to take the time, and for such as she, but Thomasine is a perfect simpleton at any task not based on prayer."

"What bread did you use?"

"None of my fine new loaves, I assure you! No, since it was to be soaked in milk anyway, I gave her an old loaf I'd meant to use as crumbs for thickening."

"And what milk and honey?"

Dame Alys's thin eyebrows climbed up her broad forehead. "Whatever was sitting on the hob and in the cupboard. It's good enough for us, it's good enough for the likes of Lady Ermentrude."

"And did Thomasine go straight back to the guest house?"

"Now, did I go along and show her the way? I've better things . . ." Dame Alys's expression changed. "Ah, no, that's when the shrieking started and Martha took off to see how close she could get to it, and I sent Thomasine packing after her."

And Thomasine had arrived at Lady Ermentrude's room in Martha's wake; she had not had time to go anywhere else. Unless she had gone to the infirmary on her way to the kitchen. But Frevisse thought she had not had much time for that, not if the milksop was all made in the little while before Lady Ermentrude began to scream.

Dame Alys, unhobbled by doubts, thrust onward. "That old harridan, thinking Thomasine belonged anywhere but in St. Frideswide's! It's God's blessing I don't have to cook another meal for her, but how long is it until that son of hers takes himself off?"

"Tomorrow or the next day, we hope," Frevisse said. "But meanwhile he's set men to mend the chimney and once they do, you won't be bothered anymore."

"It can't happen soon enough. There, I've told you all I know. Can I go back to making sure those numb-wits don't decide to use the rice for flour or some other foolishness?"

Frevisse excused her and drew a deep, steadying breath when she was gone. Dame Claire, with her blessed ability to keep silent, waited while she thought, until finally Frevisse said, "What I'm beginning to want more than anything else is the reason why someone wanted Lady Ermentrude dead right at this moment. Sir Walter is right, this was an awkward time and place to do a murder, and on holy ground beside."

"Is there anything we can do besides asking questions?" Dame Claire asked.

"Not that I know of. And I can't even be sure they're the right ones."

"You can only ask the questions you have. After all, they may lead on to others."

Frevisse half-smiled. "True enough. Let's see what more we can be learning."

Not very much, it transpired.

"I haven't noticed anyone much moved to grief for the lady," Frevisse said, an hour later. "Not even her own son. He seems much hotter for revenge than burdened with grief."

They had managed not to meet Sir Walter face-to-face, but Frevisse noticed, as they crossed the hall again in search of the servant Maudelyn, that more than a few people pointedly shifted out of their way and no one seemed inclined to meet their eyes.

"I think," she said quietly, "that Sir Walter has made his displeasure with us known."

"How long before he demands again we give him Thomasine?"

"He'll want Master Montfort to back his demand this time, so it depends on how long it takes for him to terrify our crowner into it. Not very long, I'm afraid."

Maudelyn proved almost as difficult to run to ground as Maryon, but once cornered, she seemed prepared to talk with them. She was a homely woman, the sort who would be normally cheerful and glad of a gossip, even with her betters. But now her hands twisted in her skirt and she kept her eyes averted. "Yes, I remember what happened as clearly as can be. It was just as I've already told you, and Sir Walter. There's nothing more to be said, I promise you."

"Is there anyone you can think of who would be wanting your mistress dead?"

Maudelyn shrugged. "None."

"She was a kind mistress?"

Maudelyn hesitated, then shrugged again. "She could be right cruel, to me and to everyone around her, when she chose. And she mostly did. It's no wonder—'' She stopped short.

''What? That someone murdered her?'' asked Dame Claire.

A hand over her mouth, Maudelyn nodded.

''Come now,'' said Frevisse in her strictest voice, ''tell us the truth. It may be that we already know what it is you're trying to hide.''

Maudelyn's eyes widened. Her hand slowly came down. ''It doesn't matter, I guess,'' she muttered. ''With my lady dead, I've lost my place anyhow.'' She took a breath and straightened her back. '''Twas me that drank the wine.''

''What wine?''

''In the bottle. I saw it and nobody was paying much attention, so I took it and hid it under my skirt and said I needed to visit the garderobe, and I drank it there and dropped the bottle down the hole. There! I've told you!'' She broke into tears.

Frevisse absently patted Maudelyn's plump shoulder and looked at Dame Claire, who was looking back, both of them dismayed at this destruction of the most solid part of their theory.

''Have you been ill since you drank the wine?'' Dame Claire asked.

''N-no,'' Maudelyn blubbered. Her tears stopped as if her eyes had been plugged with a cork. ''Is it true, then? That it was poison killed her? And it was in the wine? By Our Lady's veil, I drank from the very bottle!''

They assured her that could not be the case, as she was herself still alive, and left her still amazed. When they were out of earshot, Dame Claire asked, ''Now what?''

''I don't know. It seemed so clear the poison must be in the bottle. I should have guessed otherwise when Lady Isobel told me she opened the twin of it for Sir John. Because unless she marked it somehow, how could she tell which was the deadly bottle after they rubbed around one another on that hard ride? It should have been plain to me then that the poison could not have been in the wine.''

The cloister bell began to chime, startling them both.

''Vespers,'' Dame Claire said, relieved. ''We can't do anything more today.''

''Except ask Thomasine if she's remembered seeing anything more,'' Frevisse said as they left the guest house and descended the stairs to the yard, hurrying a little through the soft fall of rain. ''But she won't. She'll repeat she prayed all night and saw or heard no one and there's the end of it. Why does the child bother me so much?''

''Because she's the child you very nearly might have been, if you'd had her childhood leisure to indulge in piety,'' Dame Claire said.

Frevisse looked sideways at her, and found her own first amusement at such an idea sliding into dismay with the discomforting thought that it might be true. Except for Domina Edith, Dame Claire knew more about Frevisse's deep piety than anyone else at St. Frideswide's; and knew better than anyone that it was only her early childhood that nourished a need to be as pragmatic as devout. It was a welcome diversion from such thoughts to see Robert Fenner coming purposefully toward them, reaching them as they reached the cloister gate.

As they crowded under the eaves, out of the rain, Frevisse saw again the large bruise that was discoloring Robert's left cheek and jaw. As Dame Claire reached to touch it, he flinched back from her.

Frevisse asked quickly, ''Was it Sir Walter gave you the bruise? How did you anger him that badly?''

Robert jerked his hand in quick dismissal. ''I was too slow picking up a boot he'd dropped, that's all. His mother was quick with her hands, too, but not as strong.''

''So he's taken you back into his household.''

''Yes. I'm a Fenner after all, and we take care of our own. If roughly, sometimes.''

"Then perhaps you can be of service to us—and Thomasine, if you will."

His grin was as charming as an angel's. And his mind as quick to understand. "You want me to listen to anything I can, and see you hear of it afterwards."

"Yes."

"Gladly. Anything to serve the Lady Thomasine. You're worried for her, aren't you?"

"And so are you, I think."

"I think her very fair and very sweet." A faint blush over his cheeks made him suddenly look even younger than he was. "But I'm also without inheritance and have few hopes and know that even if she willed it, she could not be for me. So all I can be is worried for her. So far it's all Sir Walter's idea to have her out of here, but with a little more pushing, Master Montfort of the little wits and great ambition is going to agree with him. The easiest choice will be the best choice for him, he thinks."

"And that's where Thomasine's peril lies," Frevisse said bluntly. "So if you hear anything you think I ought to know, any of the priory's lay servants will know how to take word to me about it. Will you be able to do that?"

"Yours at your need, my lady," Robert said as if she were a queen. "Will you take Lady Thomasine a letter from me?"

"Never," she said promptly.

He grinned around the worry in his eyes, and said, "Well, there's something else, too." He bowed. "You've been asking questions about who was in Lady Ermentrude's chamber last night. You'd best ask me, too."

Frevisse and Dame Claire exchanged looks. The bell was still calling to Vespers, but there was this task to be done as well. Best talk to him now while he came willing to speak; Domina Edith would almost surely pardon their being late.

"You were in Lady Ermentrude's chamber that night?" Frevisse asked.

"Once. I awoke sometime and went to see if anything

was needed. Lady Ermentrude and the woman Maryon were both sleeping. Lady Isobel was not there, or the maidservant, Maudelyn. The lady Thomasine was praying. I don't think she knew I'd come."

"You did not speak to her?"

"No." But his color deepened, and it was obvious he had stood there awhile, looking. If his look was anything like the way he said her name, it had been a very warm and lingering stare, Frevisse thought, and Thomasine deep indeed in prayers not to have felt it. She asked, "Except for then, and later when Lady Ermentrude died, were you ever in her chamber that day or before?"

A shrewdness in his face told Frevisse he was following very well what her questions meant, but he answered simply enough, "I helped bring her into the hall when she first came. That was all."

"So you saw her very well then," Dame Claire said. "I only came to her after she had begun to quiet. Was she very drunk?"

"Like I'd never seen her," Robert said. "It seemed more than drunkenness, like she was gone mad."

"Brain-fevered maybe," Frevisse suggested. "From the day's heat and her drinking and her anger."

Robert frowned, not anxious to disagree. "She was giddy on her feet and saying her eyes hurt. The sun wasn't particularly bright that I noticed but she said it was hurting her and covered them. Her eyes were all black and swollen, I know that. The blue of them was a thin rim about the black. And she kept hold on one thought all the while as if she were afraid of losing it: she would have Thomasine away from here at once. But she seemed so wild I doubt she really knew what she was saying, just kept saying it, with her eyes all staring, so she looked mad even if she wasn't." His look sharpened on Dame Claire. "I've said something."

Frevisse looked at the infirmarian beside her. Dame Claire's expression was somewhere between excitement and distress, and her voice uneven as she said, "Yes, you've said something." She pulled at Frevisse's arm. "We have to go or we'll be too late even for Domina Edith. Thank you for telling us."

The bell for Vespers had stopped. Frevisse and Dame Claire hurried along the cloister walk. So urgent was her need for information that Frevisse ignored the rule of silence to ask, "What did he say that mattered so much to you?"

Dame Claire pressed her fingers into Frevisse's flesh through the heavy cloth of her habit. "I never heard her symptoms before. I never asked how she was when she first came back here from the Wykehams. Everyone kept saying she was drunk and I never asked."

"It didn't seem to matter. Drunkenness or brain fever. Does it make a difference?"

"I don't think that it was either one. What that boy said about Lady Ermentrude's giddiness, her wildness almost without sense and her bulging eyes all black and hurting her in the sun; Frevisse, if we join that with her screaming afterwards and her seeming to see awful things, then she was already poisoned when she arrived back at St. Frideswide's. I'd swear to it."

Chapter 11

THEY WERE AT the door to the church, already remiss in talking in the cloister and unwilling to be any later for Vespers. They slipped into the church, made apologizing curtseys to Domina Edith, and took their places in the choir.

But once in her place, chanting the verses so familiar they did not need her thoughts, Frevisse felt the creeping impact of Dame Claire's assertion. If she were right, someone had tried to kill Lady Ermentrude not two times but three. And it had to have been someone not of the priory, for none of the priory people went with her to the Wykehams or met her on the way back. So who, then? Someone who went to Sir John's and Lady Isobel's with her—or met her there or on the road on the way back to St. Frideswide's. Whoever it was, came with her into the priory and stayed, to try again—and again.

So some of the questions Frevisse had been asking were no longer ones that needed answering. But at the very least Thomasine could no longer be considered guilty. If Dame Claire were right, even Sir Walter and Master Montfort would have to accept that.

Except this was somewhat subtle reasoning, at least by Master Montfort's standards. He would not take Dame Claire's word for it. He would say she was lying to protect the nunnery and refuse to hear her. Or, being male, he would say a mere woman should not dare to offer some female notion as fact. Montfort, the fool, and Sir Walter, the arrogant fool, would never waste their valuable masculine time seeking the truth when they thought they already had it.

Suddenly Frevisse found the curses in today's chanting of Psalm 109 very applicable. "Let his days be few; and let another take his office. . . . Let his children be vagabonds. . . . Let the extortioner consume all that he has; and let the stranger spoil his labor." And she did not care if that curse fell on Master Montfort or on Sir Walter or on both of them, so well they both deserved it.

But even as she knew the translation of this verse, she knew the later verse, and her perverse mind recited it to her before she could stop it: "His delight was in cursing, and it shall happen to him; he loved not blessing, therefore it shall be far from him." With an inward bow, she begged pardon for her soul's sake, and turned her mind back to Vespers' true purpose, to bring the day toward its close in peace and harmony.

Supper was bread and cheese and hot apple cider against the evening's drizzling chill. Recreation was brief; no one was inclined to walk for long even in the damp shelter of the cloister. They all gathered in the warming room, waiting for Compline, and wishing the rule permitted a fire before October's end. After awhile, Frevisse became aware that Dame Claire had gone out.

When she returned, Frevisse was waiting for her in the cloister. They hurried into the slipe, where Dame Claire said with mixed eagerness and anger, "It was henbane. It's useful for some things if carefully handled and poison if it's not, and it's easily come by. Red face, cold limbs, thirst, incoherence and inability to speak at all, delirium, the apple of the eyes so huge any light hurts them, everything seeming to be colored red. All of those are symptoms of it, laid out clear and plain in my book."

"And every one of them Lady Ermentrude had—"

"Before she ate or drank a single thing here."

"We must tell Domina Edith right away," said Dame Claire, but the bell began its summons for Compline.

Frevisse shook her head and said quickly because all talking should stop with the first ring, "Tomorrow. There's nothing to be done tonight and I'll have time to think on it by then."

Dame Claire nodded agreement; nothing could be done tonight, no matter what was said.

Frevisse tried to lose herself in the brief, familiar service and its quiet, closing prayer, *Nunc dimittis*: "Now, Lord, send your servant away in peace. . . ." They sang it in low voices, a plaintive plainsong softened to silence at the end, bringing with it a sense of rest. Not until they had all made silent procession back to the dormitory and she had stripped off her outer gown and slipped into bed did her mind begin again the relentless search for a question, or questions, that would show her the road to the truth.

But she fell asleep in the middle of her mulling, and did not wake until the cluster of small bells by the dorter door jangled her awake for Matins and Lauds in the dark middle of the night.

When the long service was done and she was back in bed, listening to sleep come back to everyone else, she found she was utterly awake. Thoughts ran at random, taking her nowhere, refusing to be disciplined.

So she heard the clumsy, cautious steps on the stairs from the cloister before they reached the dorter, and catching up a shawl kept for such night-rising, went quickly from her cell toward the small light at the head of the stairs. Old Ela, a servant from the guest hall who rarely ventured so far into the cloister, looked up as if grateful to see her and, unwilling to wake the other sleepers with her message, beckoned at Frevisse, turned, and dragged her lame foot down the stairs again and out into the cloister walk. Frevisse followed her.

"It was you I was coming for, my lady," Ela declared in a whisper. "Only I didn't know how I'd find you in the dark. But the boy said I must try, that I had to come since he could not and it's a desperate matter. Robert, he said to tell you he was, and said I had to come straight away, though he never gave me even a ha'pence for doing it. Is it all right?"

"Very all right," Frevisse assured her. "I doubt he has a ha'penny to his name to spare. What's the desperate matter?"

"He says to tell you that they were talking late over there. But I could have told you that without his word on it; we all could hear that much of it, right enough. Loud, they were, then yelling at each other and then sinking down to soft again."

"Who?"

"Sir Walter mostly. At the crowner hammer and tongs, and him not yelling back much, seems. He was objecting some, I guess, but feeble. Then everything settled and they went to their beds, except that boy Robert, who comes and tells me I have to tell you that they're meaning to take Thomasine in the morning."

Frevisse drew a sharp breath, then steadied herself and said firmly, "That they won't be able to do. We're keeping her close in the cloister."

"That's where they're meaning to do it, Robert said!" Ela relished the shocks her tale was dealing. "When you've all gone in to breakfast and they can be certain where she is, they mean to come in from the orchard, through the infirmary door, and to the refectory and have her and be out with her before anything can be done. Now there's wickedness for you, and against God's own lamb, too, for that's what the child is. Who else shall I be telling? There can be a goodly few of us between them and her when they come, and we won't be bare-handed either."

"Don't tell anyone!" Frevisse said quickly. The last thing they needed was a confrontation between angry, armed priory servants and Sir Walter's men. "Keep this all to yourself."

"But if they think to take Lady Thomasine—"

"They won't take her. Not now that we know their plans. But don't tell anyone else about it or we might start a fight that'll have people hurt who need not be. And don't let anyone know you've come to me, or that Robert ever spoke to you. Sir Walter will surely kill him if he knows it."

Old Ela's eyes opened very wide. "So that's the sort of man he is! A Fenner that would kill a Fenner." She made a sound of disgust.

"And maybe worse than that to you if you're found out. So keep you quiet about this." Frevisse was not above unveiled threats; the fewer people who knew trouble was coming, the fewer there would be to make it worse.

Ela nodded her understanding. "No one will hear of it from me, I promise you. I'm back to my blankets and there I'll stay till I'm dragged out at dawn. God's blessing on you."

"And on you," Frevisse said to her back as the old woman scuttled away along the shadowed walk.

The rain had long since ended, but its chill and damp were still in the air. Frevisse shivered with more than the night chill and turned toward Domina Edith's chamber.

The prioress slept in her own room off her parlor, above the hall kept for her own use. It was not difficult to rouse her lay servant sleeping just inside her doorway, and easier still to persuade the woman that Frevisse must talk to her mistress. The mere fact of Frevisse daring to be there at that hour was almost argument enough. Yet before she went to summon the prioress, Domina Edith called from her bed, "Who is it? What's the matter? Is it Dame Frevisse? Let her in." The servant went quickly to open the door, and Domina Edith continued, "You can go. Take your pallet into the parlor and finish your sleep there. Go, go. Come here, Dame."

Domina Edith had been sleeping propped nearly upright on her pillows. As with so many of the elderly, she slept lightly and awakened easily, and in the small glow from the banked fire, her eyes were fully aware as Frevisse went quickly to kneel beside her bed.

"I pray you pardon me, my lady," Frevisse said.

"Most likely I will. Tell me what brings you so urgently."

"Old Ela from the guest hall just brought me word that Sir Walter means to seize Thomasine in the refectory at breakfast and have her out of the nunnery by force."

Domina Edith's face tightened with mixed anger and grief. "And Montfort supports him in this deed?"

"I gather so. Forced to it, I think. Sir Walter is wanting to have the matter settled so he can be back to Lord Fenner's bedside as soon as may be."

Domina Edith nodded slowly, her eyes contemplative and sad. "Not grief or justice, but only greed and a prideful need that someone must suffer if a Fenner does. Poor man."

"Poor Sir Walter" was not something Frevisse was inclined to consider. She said quickly, "I need your permission to take Thomasine into sanctuary. Church walls should be enough to keep her safe until we can gather what we need to prove her innocent."

"I think the only way you may do that is to find the guilty one."

Frevisse hesitated, then said, "I think we can do that."

"You've learned something that makes it possible?"

"Just before Vespers. I've been thinking on it since and would have told you in the morning."

"It must be drawing on to Prime now."

"But Thomasine—"

"Is a long way from breakfast yet. Tell me."

"Dame Claire thinks Lady Ermentrude was neither drunk nor brain fevered when she rode in here from Sir John and Lady Isobel's. She thinks she was poisoned with henbane before she ever reached St. Frideswide's."

Domina Edith's eyelids sank, hooding her eyes. But very clearly she said, "Another poison altogether, is that the way of it? And given to her before she returned here. A poison that made her seem drunk."

"Dame Claire recited the symptoms of henbane, and they described Lady Ermentrude's behavior exactly."

"So it had to have been done at Sir John's or on her way back to us."

"Yes."

"But there's still no reason we know of for anyone to do it."

"No."

Domina Edith nodded. The hooded eyes closed, and she might have been drifting off to sleep, but Frevisse doubted it and waited, until the prioress raised her head and said, "Three times someone tried to kill her then, and did not care another died by the way. That's wickedness indeed. So you must go on asking questions. Find out who among her people did it."

"Or among Sir John's."

"Or Sir John and Lady Isobel themselves."

Domina Edith said it in the same simple tone she had said all the rest, taking Frevisse unprepared. But she had voiced the same idea herself to Dame Claire, so, "Yes," she agreed after a moment.

Domina Edith nodded. "They quarreled with Lady Ermentrude, and there must have been a reason for it. The pity of it is that we'll never convince our crowner nor Sir Walter until we find the store of henbane and stains of it on the hand that mixed the potion, which we cannot do. So go see Thomasine into sanctuary with my blessing, and I'll see to Sir Walter not disturbing our peace come morning."

"If you send him word he's been forestalled, he'll know someone betrayed him."

"But if I tell my gossiping servant that you've been frightened into convincing me Thomasine should be in sanctuary, then my gossiping servant will surely have word of it all through the nunnery and to the guest halls before we're half through Prime and long before we're in the refectory for breakfast."

That was true enough, and Frevisse nodded acceptance, then curtseyed and left, but did not return to the dorter for Thomasine immediately. Instead she went to the kitchen. The corridor outside it was pitchy black and she groped her way until she reached its door. Inside, the banked hearth fire gave a ruddy glow to the ceiling beams and across the scrubbed-to-polish tables, showing the long lumps on the floor that were the sleeping kitchen help. Frevisse knew where the things were that she wanted, and no one so much as stirred while she gathered them quickly, nearly soundlessly. A jug of water, a loaf of bread, a cracked bowl for a chamber pot, an apple. The last was an afterthought, because it might comfort a frightened child in the cold last watch of the night.

She left as unnoticed as she had come, back through the black corridor to the cloister again and around it to the church. There, as always, a lamp burned beside the altar, and now two candles glowed at the biers, outlining the heads of the two nuns praying there. Frevisse saw one head lift to look toward her, and then bow to praying again.

Frevisse placed the food and drink and bowl behind the altar, then knelt on the step in front of it to ask for help and anything like wisdom that God or St. Frideswide might choose to give her for what she was going to do and what was going to come of it.

Returning to the dorter, she passed silently between the varied soft—and not so soft—snorings and breathings and someone shifting in her sleep, to the farther end and Thomasine's cell. Her eyes were used to the darkness by now; she could see Thomasine curled on her side beneath her blankets, hand under her pillow to cuddle it closer to her cheek, her breathing as tiny as a sleeping kitten's. Frevisse paused a moment, then regretfully touched the girl's shoulder, waited for a response, then shook her slightly. She felt Thomasine awaken under her hand and said very softly,

"Hush, Thomasine. You have to come with me. Dress now and come."

Thomasine struggled upward, fumbling at her covers. Confused, she murmured, "I haven't slept past my time, have I? I didn't mean to sleep so—"

"Hush. No. Just come. You're fine."

She felt Thomasine still hesitating and said more urgently, "I'm taking you to the church. Come quickly."

That reached past the edges of Thomasine's sleep; Frevisse felt her come fully awake. With no word and hardly a sound, Thomasine arose and began to dress while Frevisse gathered up her bedding and the rustling mattress. They finished together, and Frevisse led the way out of the cell. Silently they passed the dorter's length, down the stairs, and along the cloister to the church. This time both nuns stared, but Frevisse signed them back to their devotions.

As Frevisse laid her mattress and bedding down behind the altar, Thomasine asked, in a trembling murmur, "What's wrong?"

"Sir Walter means to break in tomorrow morning and seize you in the refectory. Domina Edith has agreed you should be in sanctuary where he'll not dare touch you."

Thomasine's eyes grew huge, but she made no outcry; after a minute she said softly, "Will I have to leave England? Isn't that what you have to do if you claim sanctuary?"

"That's for confessed felons. If you are proven innocent, you will stay right here."

Thomasine shivered and wrapped her arms around herself against the church's cold. Or against the fear shining in her eyes. "Can you prove me innocent?" she whispered.

"Dame Claire claims your aunt was poisoned before ever she came here the second time. It was poison making her act so wild when she rode in here that day, not her drinking or a brain fever. Someone was trying to kill her before she was anywhere near to you."

Thomasine drew in a startled breath. "Then it wasn't in her wine, with the medicine?"

"The second poison was, and the third, because the first poison wasn't strong enough. Your aunt looked like she was recovering from it and so someone tried again, but Martha died. It was the third attempt that succeeded."

With visible effort Thomasine absorbed the meaning of all that. Around them the church waited, layers deep in silence: silence that was part of the night, silence that was left from years of praying, silence until Thomasine asked, "You know who did it?"

"No. Not yet. But now there's a better chance I can find out."

"And I have to stay here until you're sure?"

"Until I'm sure and we've proven it to Sir Walter and Master Montfort."

"I may stay here in the church? All of the time?"

Frevisse realized that the tension in Thomasine's body was no longer fear, that she was standing eagerly, her face bright with more than just the lamplight. Being confined to the church was going to be no ordeal for her. Frevisse sighed and said, "Yes. Here in the church all the time." The girl's face bloomed with happiness. "Now let's make your bed so you can rest at least."

Together they laid out the mattress and spread the bedding over it.

"I'll leave you now," Frevisse said. "Domina Edith will speak to you in the morning. Until then, rest if you can."

Thomasine nodded, her face still warm with delight. And Frevisse, looking back from the doorway before going out, saw her on her knees before the altar, hands clasped and face raised fervently toward heaven. Better one of us taking pleasure in this than that we all should be frightened, Frevisse thought wearily, and left.

From weariness more than intention, Frevisse fell to sleep as soon as she lay down on her bed. The bell for Prime woke her with the others, and quietly she made herself ready and took her place in the procession to the church. Thomasine's absence was noticed, but she was so often in the church before morning prayers that there was hardly any twitch of curiosity at finding her there when they came in. She had hidden her bed and other things somewhere and was seated quietly in her place, and Frevisse guessed that if the other nuns had heard the rumors of murder and suspicion, her being there in prayer before them was amply justified to all their minds.

The morning hymn began. "Now daybreak fills the earth with light; we lift our hearts to God . . . ," which hardly fitted with either the day or Frevisse's heart. The September dawn was obscured by clouds that threatened rain again before the day was done, and her heart was clouded, too, with the many things she had to do and learn today.

The prayers ended at last. Two nuns stepped to their places to resume prayers for the dead. Thomasine stayed where she was, head bowed. Domina Edith gave her neither word nor look, but began to leave the church, leaving no one any choice to do more than wonder and leave Thomasine behind.

Breakfast was uneasy. Silence was still kept, but clearly Domina Edith's woman had done her work; every kitchen servant came and went from the refectory with half an eye to the outer door and a twitch at sounds that were not there, until everyone had no doubt there was something very wrong and Frevisse would nearly have welcomed a burst of rough voices in the outer hall to break her own tightening tension.

But it never came. Breakfast ended in its wonted way. Domina Edith gave the grace and benediction, and they returned to the church for Mass. Now heads turned openly toward Thomasine where she waited in her place, and Father Henry pattered briskly through his Latin, making clear he was as eager as they to be done with the Mass so they could go to Chapter and find out what was happening.

They proceeded directly from the church to the little

room they called the chapter house, where on a normal day they would meet to deal together on daily nunnery business. Domina Edith kindly waited until Father Henry had taken off his vestments and joined them. Then she told them what was to hand, ending with, "So we forestalled them in the refectory, but Thomasine will remain in sanctuary until all this is ended and she's safe from wrong."

With a sure knowledge of her nuns, she waited while, bright with indignation and outrage, each raised her hand to go on record that she was angry at Sir Walter's unholy boldness and mad injustice, with Dame Alys loudest of them all, swelling with pleasure at having another Fenner to castigate.

Domina Edith had been prioress long enough to judge how long to indulge a thing and when to stop it. The crest of their exclaims was past and they had begun to repeat themselves when she said in her old voice, not seeming to raise it but carrying easily over all of theirs, "Because of this, none of us are to go outside of cloister today except Dame Frevisse, whose duties take her there. For the rest of us, we still have our duties and our prayers to follow and we will do so. Is there any business of the day we need to deal with?"

If there had been, it was forgotten in the present excitement. No one said anything, and firmly Domina Edith ended Chapter, setting them all back to holy silence.

As they filed out, Dame Claire gestured questioningly from Frevisse to Domina Edith. Frevisse gestured back that she had indeed told Domina Edith what they had learned. Dame Claire offered to accompany her again today. Frevisse found she wanted it very much, but less from need than because she was afraid of what she was going to face outside the cloister; so she smiled and shook her head, refusing. The questions she meant to ask today would not need Dame Claire going into trouble with her.

The trouble came as soon as she crossed the yard toward the guest house. She had been watched for, she guessed, because as she reached the top of the stairs, Master Montfort stepped out of the door to block her way. He was swelled with importance and stood there, hands on hips, waiting for her to speak and show she was impressed.

Frevisse gave him a curtsey and stood, eyes down, waiting for him to get on with whatever his business was.

Montfort gave up first and said with blustered authority, "The word is that the novice Thomasine has taken sanctuary by your doing. Is that true?"

"It is by God's doing and with my prioress's permission," Frevisse said meekly. But she did not resist the urge to look up and be gratified by the angry red that welled up in his face.

"So she is in sanctuary and admitting her guilt?" he demanded loudly.

"She is in sanctuary and admitting nothing but her innocence," Frevisse returned, pitching her voice to match his so that it carried across the yard to all the listening ears.

Sir Walter pushed past Montfort. "And you're the one who put her there? Who warned you?"

"Warned me of what?" asked Frevisse innocently. She was aware of Robert among the men crowded into the doorway behind him.

"That . . . that . . . ," began Montfort.

"That we meant to arrest the woman for murder, that's what!" shouted Sir Walter.

Frevisse said in a clear, carrying voice, "Yes, we were told by a voice in the night that you purposed to break into our cloister, where no man should ever step even in humility, much less in violence. It was God's will that we learned it, so Thomasine could be put in safety against your coming."

A disconcerted murmuring swept through everyone listening, and Montfort crossed himself. Even Sir Walter was taken briefly aback, but then he snarled, "Which dreamer among you repeated such foolishness?"

"It was not a dream. And now you have told me with your own words that our message was a true one."

That did not please Sir Walter either. The color of his face began to match Master Montfort's. "I want to see that she's truly claimed sanctuary, and is in it now," he snarled.

"God's church is open to all," Frevisse said graciously and, bowing her head, moved aside to let him pass, but she could not resist murmuring softly, "Only, I pray you, go in by the west door, *not* the cloister."

Sir Walter's breath hissed in sharply, but he bit back his retort and stalked down the steps, some of his men and Robert following him. Master Montfort, trying to regain lost authority, stayed where he was and warned, "You have her tucked away for now, Dame, but remember there's a limit to how long she can cling to sanctuary. You and your prioress are doing yourselves no good this way. Why not make it simpler for all of us and have her out of there now?"

"Because she's not guilty," Frevisse replied.

"Ha!" Montfort exclaimed, and stalked away after Sir Walter.

Frevisse thought of the things her Uncle Chaucer might say when baffled, and they were far more expressive than that. But facing Montfort and Sir Walter had been the most unpleasant thing she anticipated, and now it was done. With relief, she turned to what came next.

The answers came slowly but steadily. By early afternoon she had talked to everyone who had gone with Lady Ermentrude to Sir John's, and learned that the men had had nothing to do with their lady once she arrived there nor been close to her on the ride back or at St. Frideswide's. Maryon and the other lady-in-waiting had been close to her now and again all of those times, and Lady Isobel and her servants had come and gone from her chamber at the manor. All of that Frevisse learned partly from the men, mostly from the other lady-in-waiting, Anne, who was more than ready to leave off her inventorying of Lady Ermentrude's belongings for Sir Walter and gossip with a friendly nun.

"Oh yes," she assured Frevisse gladly. "I remember all of those dreadful two days. No, she didn't stop to drink anywhere at all along the way from here to Sir John's. She rode fast, and my small mare was hard put to hold the pace. And then we had to turn around and ride back the next day. It's a wonder she isn't broken in the wind, poor thing."

"What happened after she arrived at the manor house?"

"Oh, shouting. Not right when she rode in, mind you. They were surprised but they greeted her well. Only she was having none of it, just swept them into the solar and slammed the door to and then started. The shouting, I mean."

"So it was a quarrel? Between Lady Ermentrude and Sir John?"

"Yes, but mostly between her and Lady Isobel. Sir John said little and that almost too quiet to be heard, except once in a while he'd raise his voice to warn theirs down. All that we could hear through the door but not much else." Anne smirked knowingly and leaned closer to Frevisse. "Though Maryon, mind you, could say more. She was that determined to know she slipped right up to the door and put her ear to its crack."

Frevisse nodded. Cat-sly Maryon would be just the sort to do that, she thought. But she kept her face merely gossiping-interested and asked, "What did she hear?"

"A great deal, may be, but she wouldn't say, though I did ask her. But whatever it was, it wasn't what she was thinking to hear. I could tell that by her face at the time."

Puzzled, Frevisse asked, "What was she thinking it would be?"

The woman shrugged carelessly. "Well, I don't know. I was sort of behind her shoulder there at the door—" She caught herself and looked carefully at Frevisse to be sure she was not taking it wrong.

Frevisse smiled and said, "Oh, I know how it must be with you. You had to take an interest in the doings of your mistress. With her uncertain temper, you had to be forewarned, on chance it was something you could help, or at least not make your lady angrier about."

Anne nodded in complete agreement. "You understand it right enough! I thought Maryon was going to grow donkey's ears, she was listening so hard. But all I could hear was 'marriage,' and then she gave me an elbow in the brisket and backed me off. Then in a little while—just a word or two longer, no more—she eased away and said it was no concern of ours, we'd best let them be and that's all I know of it."

"And in the morning? Did they fight again?"

"Oh, they fought nearly until morning, I promise you! And we thought there'd be more of it when they were rested, but Lady Ermentrude had us all up with daybreak and ready to ride. Not a word of thanks or farewell to our hosts, and only time for me to grab a cup of flat ale and a knob of bread before I had to climb into the saddle and be off. It's good luck my mare stood it as well as she did."

"Did Lady Ermentrude drink or eat on her ride back? She came in here rollicking enough."

"She did that." The woman giggled to remember it, then stopped her mouth with her hand as she realized to whom she was speaking. "She had a bottle slung at her saddle bow and she drank now and again, especially toward the end of the journey, and no wonder; she rode like the devil was at her heels in all that heat."

Frevisse nodded knowledgeably, but she felt very far from knowledgeable as she excused herself from the conversation and went in determined search of Maryon.

She found her in the ladies' chamber, sitting on a clothes chest with an embroidery frame on her lap. It held a pretty pattern of flowers and leaves, but Maryon's hands and needle were idle. She looked up as Frevisse approached and laid her work aside. "I heard you were still questioning," she said. "Is Master Montfort going to be pleased with you?"

"As much as he is already." Frevisse did not sit; nor did

Maryon rise. They looked at each other with mutual assessment before Frevisse said, "You've been in Lady Ermentrude's service only a little while?"

For so young and seemingly open a face, Maryon's showed surprisingly little of any thoughts behind it. She said, "This week and a little more is all. Ever since she left Queen Catherine."

"You were in the Queen's service before that?"

"And lucky to be so, surely," Maryon said readily. "As sweet a lady as ever tread earth. But she's not much given to leaving Hertford and I'd a mind to see something of the world so I took service with Lady Ermentrude. Only that's not come out so well, but I'm thinking her grace will have me back if I ask."

"How did you come to be in her service at all? Wales is a ways and a ways from here."

Maryon's slender, dark eyebrows lifted in what was surely a deliberate show of surprise. Then she smiled appreciatively, and dimples showed in her round cheeks. "Now that's clever of you, to know that's where I'm from. Yes, I'm Welsh. My brother's wife is cousin to one of Her Grace's household officers and that's how I came by my place."

"And you left it to see the world."

Maryon nodded but turned her head away so that she was looking slantwise at Frevisse, like a cat. There was too much satisfied knowing in that look and Frevisse asked quickly, wanting to encourage the woman's cleverness while she was so proud of it, "So what did you hear at the solar door when Lady Ermentrude was quarreling with her niece?"

Maryon smiled archly. "You *are* a knowing one! I listened, indeed, but there wasn't much I heard. Something about a marriage in France, or France and a marriage, or something like that. It was a very stout door and Sir John kept quieting them down to where I couldn't hear what was being said."

"They didn't quarrel outside the solar?"

"No, indeed they seemed very careful about that, even Lady Ermentrude, who was never so very careful about most things. Why are you suddenly wanting to know about what happened before she came back here?"

"Oh, for the sake of a riddle," said Frevisse, to show she could be clever, too, and left her.

Chapter 12

THE WOMAN SERVANT who had come with Lady Isobel was seated on the bench outside their chamber. She made no move to stop Frevisse, but Frevisse paused, turned from her intent to talk with Sir John and Lady Isobel because so casual a chance to talk to the woman might not come again.

"God's greeting to you," she said lightly, and nodded her head toward the door. "Your lord is still hurting?"

The woman, obviously bored at sitting attendance here, brightened, glad to talk about troubles. "Indeed he is. Wearying my poor lady with his needs and her so good to him she'll not deny him anything." She lowered her voice and said, leaning forward as if to give a great confidence, "Fancy, a big, strong man like him letting some passing peddler muck with his tooth because he's afraid to have it drawn!"

Frevisse was not interested in Sir John's toothache, but asked without a qualm at her own duplicity, "Do you suppose it was all the quarreling brought it on this time?"

The woman shrugged. "It comes on anytime it feels like, but I'd not be surprised. All that shouting would make anyone's jaw ache."

"They argued all the night, I've heard. And Sir John told Lady Ermentrude to leave."

"Now that's not quite right but close enough. Sir John was the one who tried to quiet it between them, but hardly a word in edgewise they let him have. We could hear them right through the door of the solar most of that evening. But the next morning when Lady Ermentrude came to leave, hardly a word was passed among them, except Lady Isobel sent my lord out to say, nice as you please, that he hoped it would all come right after she'd thought on it and wouldn't she break her fast before she left."

"And did she?"

"Not her! She'd hardly open her mouth to him, and rude when she did, she was still that angry. Said she had wine to steady her after so harsh a welcome and that would suit her till she chose to dine, thank you. Then off she rode, and Lady Isobel was all white and near to tears and decided she and Sir John had best go after her."

"So she accepted a gift of wine from them? Or had she brought it with her?"

The woman shrugged. "Not her! No, she sent for wine, she knew they kept malmsey particular for her. Sent that mincing dark-haired cat to fetch it. But that was Lady Ermentrude for you. Bring the house down with her temper and then demand the best it has to give. I don't hesitate to say it, though she's dead and coffined."

"It sounds as if it was a huge quarrel, and no forgiveness anywhere," Frevisse said.

"No, not like that at all. A huge quarrel, right enough, but it was Lady Ermentrude would have none of making peace. And they came riding after her, didn't they, with more of her favorite wine for a gift. And Lady Isobel sitting up with her that last night. No, it wasn't my lord and lady who didn't want peace."

"But what was it all for? No one has ever said."

Disappointment shaded the woman's face. "Now there's the pity. All that shouting and none of us could make out the sense of it. The solar door's that thick, it muffled all but the noise."

"And no one happened to walk outside the window?" Frevisse smiled to make a conspiratorial joke of it, as if it were the thing she would have thought to do.

The woman smothered appreciative laughter, but her eyes gleamed, showing she was glad to find a nun so ready to forget her dignity and have a friendly gossip. "Well, I won't say it might not have crossed someone's mind mayhap, but outside the solar is Lady Isobel's own private walled garden, and no one quite dared to be going in there like that, over the wall. It would be worth your life to cross her like that. She's a fine lady but she can be sharp when she's been crossed, you know."

Frevisse said with real regret, "And so all that disturbance keeping everyone awake, and no idea at all what they were on about?"

The woman shrugged. "Something about a marriage. That word was said loud enough a few times. And something about it being none of Lady Ermentrude's business. But nothing else clear enough to make any sense. It made all of us in the household nervous, I promise you."

And moreover what a waste, her expression said: a splendid subject for gossip spoiled by an honest carpenter's thick doors.

Frevisse shared her disappointment, for other reasons, and went to knock on Sir John and Lady Isobel's door.

Lady Isobel's voice bade her enter. Except for the very best one, which Sir Walter had now, the guest-hall bedchambers were small and sparely furnished, but Lady Isobel had made this one into her own. A dress lay in careful folds over a stool; a small prayer book was open on the plain table; Sir John's cloak hung evenly from a wall hook, its folds arranged by a loving female hand. Even the air was faintly scented with her perfume.

Sir John lay dozing on the bed, propped up on pillows, one hand still cupped to his swollen jaw, his face pale with pain. Lady Isobel rose with a quick and graceful movement to come between him and Frevisse, saying in her light voice,

"Forgive me. I thought you were the girl come back with the medicine I've begged of your infirmarian."

Frevisse, remaining by the door, said, "I won't stay long. I have only a question or two I need to ask."

"Questions?" Lady Isobel's slight frown hardly marred her smooth loveliness. Frevisse had the sudden—and ungracious—thought that Lady Isobel probably went to a great deal of trouble to keep from marring her loveliness.

"About the quarrel Lady Ermentrude had with you before she returned here."

Sir John stirred and groaned. Lady Isobel looked around at him with concern and a quieting lift of her hand. "It's not the servant with the medicine yet, my heart. It's Dame Frevisse. Just a little longer." Then to Frevisse, with a tiny show of exasperation, "We've told you of that already. We've told everyone. She came on us unwarned and ranting. Her wits were unhinged, by drink or a brain fever maybe, I don't know."

"But what was she ranting about?"

Lady Isobel drew a deep sigh. "She was demanding that our marriage be ended. She kept demanding it over and over and never listened to anything we tried to say. She frightened me and made no sense at all."

"What was her thought behind the demand? Did she ever say?"

Lady Isobel firmly shook her head. "No more than her mad thought that Thomasine was brought here by coercion. If there was more to it, she was so incoherent I never discerned it."

"You know that Master Montfort wants to arrest Thomasine for Lady Ermentrude's death?"

Lady Isobel put her fingers to her lips. Her face was grieved. "I can't believe she would do something like that. How could she have been so desperate? She's meant to enter St. Frideswide's since she was old enough to say so. I suppose Montfort thinks it was our lady aunt insisting she should not that frightened her more than she could bear. But how someone set on being a holy nun could bring herself to do it—it passes thought.''

''You think she might have done it?''

Lady Isobel looked at her with wide and bewildered eyes. ''You think perhaps she didn't? Sir Walter and Master Montfort seem so sure. And Master Montfort is a very knowing man in matters such as this.''

Frevisse managed to keep her voice untouched by her incredulity. ''Master Montfort—''

Sir John moved on the bed, making a small, painful sound, then mumbling, ''Who . . .''

Lady Isobel went to him quickly. ''Hush now, my dear, hush. I know it hurts but more medicine will be here soon. Dame Claire promised. Then you'll have ease and can truly sleep. I know you need your silence. The lady is going now.''

That was more than a mere hint, but Frevisse asked, ''Have you ever been to France, you or your husband?''

Lady Isobel, still bent over Sir John, her hand on his forehead, did not even look around. ''France?'' she said distractedly. ''No. Why should we ever want to go to France? Lie easy, my love. She's going now so you can rest.''

Frevisse went with outward grace, a brief farewell, and the unsettling realization that Lady Isobel was willing to believe that Thomasine had killed their aunt.

She was at the guest hall's outer door, at the head of the steps to the yard and intent on taking what she had so far learned to Domina Edith, when Master Montfort said officiously from behind her, ''Dame, we wish to speak to you.''

She stopped and turned. Her single long look at his nervous, determined face and Sir Walter's angry one behind him told her enough, but very politely, controlling her own voice and face, she said, ''Yes, my lord?''

''We must needs talk with you, Dame,'' Master Montfort said.

"At your service, my lord." Deliberately, calmly, she met his eyes, looked past him to Sir Walter and added, "But in God's first. It is coming on the hour of Sext and I must go to the church."

Sir Walter's lips clamped angrily tight. "To give comfort to your little sanctuary nun? I've posted my guards. There'll be no stealing her away from the nunnery without I know about it. And word has gone to the sheriff, so when her sanctuary time is up, he'll have the girl anyway. Why draw this out for everyone? It's your doing that put her there—"

Lifting her voice to be heard across the yard and into the hall, Frevisse said, "And let you be grateful for it since it kept you from breaking both England's law and the law of God's Holy Church."

Sir Walter began to color again. Frevisse reflected that a man so easily angered to red would never make old age. She knew that nothing would satisfy him except having his own way, so that she might as well not even waste more time quarreling with him. Making sure her voice still carried to everyone, she said, "I have duties now. I pray you excuse me to them."

She made to turn away from both of them. "God's teeth!" Sir Walter swore. "Take her, Montfort, you fool!"

Frevisse grabbed up her skirts and bolted down the stairs toward the cloister door.

Behind her Sir Walter bellowed, "Hold her! One of you down there! Stop her!"

There were men scattered across the yard. A few began to move, but uncertainly, not clear on whether he meant her, and how they were supposed to lay hands on a nun. Only two were quick enough to intercept her. One was a large man who only needed to move a few yards sideways to block the cloister door. As he moved to do so, Robert came suddenly at her from the side. He grabbed her by the upper arms and said fiercely under his breath, "Fight me," as he swung her around and staggered toward the cloister door as if carried by the force of her running.

Frevisse jerked an arm free and clouted him over his ear. He staggered and ducked, and they lurched forward, almost into the large man in their way. He shifted sideways, circling to try and catch hold of her, too. Robert yelled, pushed her away, and grabbed for his ankle as if he had been kicked. Hopping and yelping, he managed to lurch into the other man, staggering him off balance and bringing him down in a heap with Robert on top.

Frevisse flung herself at the door, but even as the latch gave under her hand, hands grabbed at her from behind, dragging her back and spinning her around. The other man and Robert still lay on the cobbles. It was Sir Walter, quicker than all the others. He hauled her away from the door, out into the center of the yard.

"Boldly done, Dame. But I have you now and here you'll stay. If we can't have the novice, then the nunnery can't have you, unless your prioress thinks again and offers a fair exchange."

"A fool's exchange," Frevisse retorted breathlessly. "And you little know our prioress if you think she'll make it. Nor the bishop either. You'll find yourselves excommunicate if you go on this way."

"Damn the bishop, and that silly old woman your prioress! My mother's murderer does not go free!"

"I beg your pardon for intruding," a familiar voice said quietly at Sir Walter's back. "I don't think you heard me come."

Sir Walter spun around. Thomas Chaucer was standing dismounted beside his horse under the gateway from the outer yard, his mounted men behind him. He was regarding Sir Walter coolly, not seeming to see Frevisse at all. His gaze traveled around the yard and up to Montfort, still gaping at the head of the steps. Chaucer nodded to him in polite greeting and then strolled forward to Sir Walter. At his moving, Montfort hasted down the steps, reaching Sir Walter just as Chaucer was saying, with mild interest, "Is there some sort of trouble here, my dear?"

Frevisse, in her great relief, had to hold an urge to laugh at Sir Walter's face as, confronted with so important a man as Chaucer, he struggled to curb his anger. Very evenly she said, "A little trouble, Uncle, but it's being sorted out, I think."

Sir Walter jerked away from Montfort's, plucking at his sleeve and demanded, "What are you doing here, Chaucer?"

The question was more peremptory than polite. Montfort made a choking noise of protest. Sir Walter far outranked Chaucer in title and birth, but Chaucer's power and connections went far beyond any Sir Walter could claim. The part of Sir Walter's mind not taken up with his anger knew it, but for just now he plainly did not care. "What brings you here?" he repeated.

"Your mother's death, surely," Chaucer said, unoffended. He looked casually around the yard again. "I heard she'd suddenly died and I came this way in hopes of offering condolences to you before you took her body home to burial. Is there a problem?"

"There's murder. My mother was murdered and this woman is keeping the murderer from us."

Chaucer looked at Frevisse in surprise. "Are you, my dear? I raised a niece in my own house who would behave like that?" Without waiting for her answer, he turned to Sir Walter. "Your mother was murdered?"

Sir Walter's face was shifting expressions rapidly. But he answered belligerently enough, "Poisoned. By their novice. And now she's taken sanctuary to keep from justice."

"Poisoned," Frevisse agreed quickly, "but not by Thomasine."

"Then who else?" Sir Walter snarled. "Who else had chance and reason both for doing it?"

"That little mouse of a child I saw last time I was here?" Chaucer's tone was still mild, as if no one's voice had been raised. He glanced at Montfort, who nodded to show he agreed with Sir Walter then bowed to Chaucer. "Really, my dear Frevisse, if she's taken to poisoning, I wouldn't think you'd want her anywhere about.''

Frevisse bit the inside of her lip. Chaucer's light response made anger and confusion mix across Sir Walter's face. Chaucer held out his hand to Frevisse and said, ''But I've come a weary way this morning, and missed my dinner in the bargain, and would pay my respects to your lady prioress, my dear. Is there possibly more of that wine I had last time I was here? It was particularly good, I thought.''

It was a prompt Frevisse was ready enough to follow. As smoothly as he, she said, ''Of course, Uncle,'' and took the one step that put her beside him.

''You'll pardon us, my lords?'' Chaucer asked.

Whatever they were thinking—and judging by Sir Walter's face it was nothing pleasant—there was no reasonable way of stopping him. They made small bows, their men did likewise, and then Chaucer had her to the doorway and through it.

With a gasping laugh, Frevisse shot home the bolt, locking the door with herself and Chaucer safe inside.

''I suppose this can all be explained?'' Chaucer asked as she turned back to him. ''Wrestling in the yard with young men, quarreling with nobility, sheltering murderers. This is the way you spend your holy days, Frevisse?''

''When needs be,'' Frevisse said. ''But I'm hoping to change my ways. Weren't you a little obvious in 'my dearing' me just now?''

''I was afraid anything more subtle would be lost in the thickets of Sir Walter's brain. I notice you 'uncled' me readily enough. What's all this about?''

Frevisse said, ''Come with me to Domina Edith. I have to tell her what I've learned today. So doing, we'll both tell you what's been happening.''

The parlor was drowsing in its comfortable sameness as they entered, except that Domina Edith, leaning heavily on the arm of young Sister Lucy, was turning from the window.

''I saw only the last of it,'' she said. ''You were well

come, Master Chaucer, and have mightily displeased them. You see something of the trouble we're in of a sudden."

"The sight of Dame Frevisse beset with a Fenner and Master Montfort tells me enough to make me want to hear the rest, I promise you."

With Frevisse's and Sister Lucy's help, Domina Edith sank carefully into her chair. When she was settled, she bid Sister Lucy go, saying Dame Frevisse would see to her until Sext. When she was safely home, Domina Edith fixed Chaucer with a firm look.

"There have been two murders done here, Master Chaucer." She then explained, concluding, "Sir Walter has decided our novice Thomasine is the guilty one and is determined to see she suffers for it."

"And you're sure she is not?"

Domina Edith cocked her head toward Frevisse. "You and Dame Claire know that part best. Tell him."

It was a relief to lay everything out in simple steps to someone not entangled in the mess. Frevisse said readily, "From all the symptoms on Lady Ermentrude when she rode in here that second day, she was poisoned before she ever reached St. Frideswide's. Dame Claire swears it is true, and believes the poison was henbane. It was when that failed that the killer went to nightshade, and killed first Martha Hayward and then Lady Ermentrude. So certainly Lady Ermentrude died of poison given her here in St. Frideswide's, but assuredly she arrived already poisoned. I'd been trying to learn who could have poisoned her wine the night before she died since only a few people were near her. When we learned of the henbane, I had to learn who was with her both at her niece's and here."

"And you've done so?"

"As nearly as possible, I think."

The cloister bell began to chime for Sext. Domina Edith sighed. "I confess myself strongly tempted to miss my prayers this time to hear more of this. But Heaven takes precedence, and I've learned too many times that prayers both aid and comfort me in worldly matters. Do you stay and talk, Dame Frevisse, about this with Master Chaucer. His greater knowledge of the world may be the boon we've needed. I give you leave to stay here with Master Chaucer and miss Sext because matters are becoming worse and the sooner there is answer to this matter, the better. Only call for Sister Lucy to come for me, if it please you."

Chaucer withdrew to the window to wait while Domina Edith was helped from her chair and out of the room. Her shuffle of footsteps faded down the stairs, and Frevisse found she was thinking the brief verse that belonged to Sext's prayers day in and out: "Incline to my aid, O God: O Lord, make haste to help me." With an inward, unhappy smile at how apt that was, she turned to Chaucer.

"It's all in bits and pieces, Uncle, with none of it giving an answer I can hold to. Some several people could have killed her but what I need to know now is the reason for her dying. It must have been a sudden one, something beyond the ordinary, because Lady Ermentrude had been like this for years."

"You mean dead?"

Despite herself, humor twitched at Frevisse's mouth. "Be respectful. I meant offensive."

"That's much more respectful, yes."

A moment of laughter warmed between them, then faded. Quietly Frevisse said, "The question I can't let go of is, what changed? Why suddenly now did someone decide Lady Ermentrude was no longer bearable? Why suddenly now did she need to be dead? We have to find it out, and who did it, before it tears any further at St. Frideswide's peace."

"Perhaps it wasn't Lady Ermentrude they were after. Perhaps Martha was the intended victim. Tell me about her. Was she anyone in particular, this Martha Hayward? Anyone Lady Ermentrude knew?"

"Before she came here, she was in Lady Ermentrude's kitchen, a position of no great importance, but she would talk of her mistress as if she were her chambermaid. Lady Ermentrude found her a place here when she was reducing her servants after her husband's death."

"Has she been much in contact with Lady Ermentrude of late?"

"Not at all, that I know of. It seems only chance brought her instead of someone else to watch at Lady Ermentrude's bedside then."

"How did she die? Where?"

"There in the room. Of poison. She had a tendency to greed and it seems she drank some of the drugged wine and gobbled the milksop meant for Lady Ermentrude. The poison was in one or the other."

"Hmmm," said Chaucer. "So Lady Ermentrude was given the rest of the goblet's contents later?"

"No, a fresh mixture was prepared for her, and after she drank it, she died. And so, it seems, did her monkey."

"Ah. Then it was indeed Lady Ermentrude they were after. Tell me what you've learned, and what you suspect." He sat down, to show he was willing both to wait and listen. "Lady Ermentrude left almost as soon as I did?"

"I saw you out the gate and as I turned away, Lady Ermentrude was coming, intent on leaving."

"You don't know why?"

"She never said, simply rode off with a few men-at-arms and two of her ladies because she was in haste, she said."

"And she went direct to—"

"To Thomasine's sister and her husband. Sir John Wykeham and Lady Isobel. I believe you know them?"

"He was in my ward. I helped to arrange their marriage."

"Lady Isobel says that Lady Ermentrude arrived all in a taking and told them their marriage had to be undone. When she and Sir John tried to reason with her, Lady Ermentrude flew into a mindless rage and fought with them far into the night, then in the morning stormed away, intent on returning here. She was still in such a temper she refused to eat, only drank some wine brought from Sir John's stores. Sir John and his lady followed after her, in fear she would do damage to herself or make herself ill, she was so angry.''

''Does Sir John tell the same story?''

''Sir John is telling nothing at all. His tooth is paining him and his jaw is swollen, but he heard what his wife said to me and made no denying gesture to anything.''

''What do you think of them?''

Frevisse said cautiously, ''He seems an easy man, and kind. He and his lady are most fond of one another, but . . . Lady Isobel seems utterly willing to accept that her sister killed Lady Ermentrude, though it pains her to think it.''

''Have you pointed out that Thomasine couldn't have done it?''

''No one knows about the henbane except Dame Claire, Domina Edith, me, and now you.''

''A quarrel lasting well into the night and yet so little to be said of its details seems unlikely,'' mused Chaucer. ''Have you asked anyone else what they might have heard?''

''I've questioned two servants who were there, but the door to the solar where they argued is regrettably thick and the window protected by a walled garden. All that was heard besides Sir John trying to quiet them was something about a marriage and France and the need to undo it.'' Chaucer's expression changed. ''What are you thinking?''

He did not reply directly, but asked, ''Lady Ermentrude said nothing about marriage when she returned here? Nothing at all?''

''No, what she wanted was to take Thomasine away. That's all she said before she went into a sort of screaming, gibbering fit, and then collapsed into exhausted sleep or unconsciousness.''

''But you're sure Lady Ermentrude was already poisoned before then.''

''Very sure. What we thought was drunkenness when she arrived was the effect of henbane.'' Something shifted and slipped into place in Frevisse's mind. "Henbane," she said.

But Chaucer was not listening; he rose to his feet and went to the window to stare out at the sky. "I thought there would be more rain but it's looking to break to sunshine soon. That will be good for the harvest, I'm thinking."

"You're thinking something else as well," Frevisse said.

Chaucer turned back to her, his face grim, untouched by any of his wonted humor. "What I'm to tell you goes no farther than yourself." She nodded and he continued, "When I went from here the other day, it was to Hertford and the Queen I went, not my own business. And I went because of what Lady Ermentrude was stupidly hinting at that afternoon. About secrets and trouble in the Queen's household."

Frevisse cast back to what they had talked of that afternoon when Lady Ermentrude had come. There had been no seeming importance to any of it at the time, and she had not thought on it since, but, "Yes, I remember. You knew what she meant?"

"I didn't know then. I know now. Her Grace the Dowager Queen, daughter of King Charles VI of France, widow of King Henry V of famous memory and mother of our present King Henry VI of England, has been married this half year past to a Welsh esquire of no family worth mentioning, an officer in her household. Before spring comes, she'll bear his child."

Frevisse felt her mouth open, then drew it sharply closed on every question or comment that came into her mind. A queen's marriage—a widowed queen's as well as any other's—was a matter of state, to be talked over in councils, debated and decided on by the lords of the government for the best ends of the realm. It was not a thing done in secrecy, as this one must have been, and never with a nobody of both foreign and ordinary birth. And if there was going to be a child, it was a secret that had to come out, and when it did there would be a scandal that would taint anyone connected to it.

"So it's no wonder Lady Ermentrude was leaving her service," Frevisse said. "To escape what will come when the marriage is disclosed."

"Exactly. Loyal to her own well-being to the end. Though she wasn't the first or last to find an excuse to leave."

"But how did you find it all out?"

Humor glinted again in Chaucer's eyes. "I went and asked Queen Catherine, of course."

"Just . . . walked in and asked her?"

"It seemed the straightest way," Chaucer said. "I told her of meeting Lady Ermentrude and that if there was indeed something afoot, she might be well advised to let me know of it because I don't want more upsets in the government than are already there, and if this were a secret I could help her keep, I would, if I knew it."

"And she told you."

"She knows me. And I met this Owen Tudor of hers for good measure. He may not have any birth to speak of but Her Grace has a fine eye for a well-made man. Small wonder our King will have a half brother by spring. Or a half sister. But none of this is talk for your ears. And it had certainly best never come out of your mouth."

"No fear of that," she said fervently. "And this somehow concerns Lady Ermentrude?"

"I warned Her Grace what Lady Ermentrude had said and nearly said, but Queen Catherine knew her well enough and had made sure before she left that there was someone paid among her women to keep eye and ear on what she did. If she looked like becoming too free of tongue, she was to be reminded there were ways she would suffer, too, if the Queen did."

"Or be silenced," Frevisse said. Thomas did not even nod; he would not admit a queen might even think of giving order for a murder. "Maryon," she said.

"That's the name Queen Catherine gave me, yes."

Frevisse felt a momentary, airy relief that it could all be so simple. Then she lost the feeling. "Maryon wasn't here in the parlor to hear Lady Ermentrude be nearly indiscreet."

Chaucer asked, "Was she with her to the Wykehams'?" At Frevisse's nod he looked grimly satisfied. "Then Lady Ermentrude said something on the ride. Or for all we are knowing, her almost indiscretion here wasn't her first. She may have been doing it ever since she left the Queen, and with one thing and another, Maryon may have decided the risk was great enough to warrant her death, and at the Wykehams' was her first chance."

"The marriage that Lady Ermentrude wanted undone!" Frevisse said excitedly. "It wasn't Lady Isobel and Sir John's, it was the Queen's! But why would she have told them about it?"

"I've no idea on that, but I mean to ask them very soon," Chaucer said grimly. "At any rate, Maryon must have heard enough to think it best to end her then."

"There's no question of the Wykehams' marriage being doubtful?"

Chaucer made a dismissive gesture. "We managed it between us, Lady Ermentrude and I, since Lady Isobel's father was already ill then. All things were rightly done and they're firmly married. That at least is certain."

"So if now Sir John and Lady Isobel are insisting it was their own marriage they were quarreling over, it would be because they're frightened and trying to cover the real cause of it. But then why . . ." Frevisse fell silent a moment. Chaucer waited until she firmly said, "But then why did Lady Ermentrude come back here insisting Thomasine had to be taken from the nunnery? That's not of a piece with the rest. It doesn't make full sense."

"We don't have to make full sense of it," Chaucer said. "It may have been the henbane working in her, so there'd be no sense to anything she did. For our purposes, we only have to be sure of who did the poisoning. And that brings us to the little problem of how I am to take the woman Maryon from here without Sir Walter knowing it."

"Without him knowing it?" Even as she echoed him, Frevisse caught at his unsaid thought and felt her face, like his own, go very still and unrevealing. Carefully she said, "He has to know it. How else do we call him off Thomasine?"

"The matter of Thomasine will have to wait. The matter of the Queen's secret is more important. If we accuse this woman Maryon, our reason for it has to come out and that is not possible."

Frevisse's chin came up. "Then Thomasine remains in danger of her life?"

Chaucer held out his hand and said quickly, "No, assuredly not. All I need do is have the woman away from here without Sir Walter or Montfort having their hands on her first. Word can be sent back what I've done and then the priory and Thomasine will both be clear. It's Montfort's questioning her we can't have. Once away, she's the Queen's concern, and the Queen can deal with both Montfort and Sir Walter. But I have to have the woman out of their reach."

There was sense enough in that, and ways out for the priory and Thomasine and Chaucer and the Queen all at once. Frevisse sighed and asked, "How?"

He had already thought that far. "At my asking, Sir John will surely be willing to help. There's no reason for him to stay longer. He can claim his own pain, or his wife's concern for their children, and make his departure in the morning. The woman Maryon can go with them, as if Lady Isobel had taken her into their household. But she'll be under Sir John's arrest, and he'll keep her for me until I can come, no more than an hour later. I think Sir Walter and good Master Montfort—"

Footsteps heavy with hurry and clumsiness beat suddenly on the steps outside the open door.

"*Benedic—*" Frevisse began, but the servant Ela flung

into the room without waiting. All panting and red-faced, disheveled from her limping haste, she gasped out, "They're going to take her! Sir Walter's men, they're all outside the church and they're going to break in and take her!"

Chapter 13

Ela clutched at Frevisse's sleeve. ''When I saw what they were doing, I went the back way round, into the church! To Domina Edith. She said I was to come get you! And him!'' She gestured wildly at Chaucer. ''She said to hurry!''

''Damn him,'' Chaucer said without passion, and went for the door.

Jerking her sleeve free from Ela's fingers, Frevisse followed him, overtaking him at the foot of the stairs as he hesitated, unsure of the way.

''Here!'' Frevisse said sharply, shoving open the door into the open cloister walk. No men were supposed to come so far into the nunnery, but it was the shortest way to the church from here. ''Your men?'' she asked. ''Can they be of use?''

Chaucer shook his head. ''There'd only be blood shed to no purpose. I'll have to stop him with words or nothing.''

Breathless with fear as much as haste, Frevisse nodded, gathered up her skirts and ran. Chaucer followed her.

The cloister door to the church had been left wide in Ela's haste. Only the sudden shadows of the church after the gray daylight of the cloister slowed them as they entered. And then, together, they completely stopped, held by the same shock that already held Sir Walter and his men in crowded disarray in the church's short nave.

It was easy to forget among the quiet patterns of St. Frideswide's that its nuns were the daughters, granddaughters, sisters of men who held their inheritance by right of arms and battle skills. As nuns and women their daily life held little need for their inheritance of courage, but their blood remembered. With no weapons but their own anger and courage, they were standing in a closed rank of black and veiled white across the center of the choir, between Sir Walter's men and Thomasine. She stood alone at the top of the altar steps, beside St. Frideswide's altar, her right hand stretched out to touch it. Head raised, she was staring out at the men come to take her, and there was no show of fear in her at all.

In front of them all stood Domina Edith. She should have seemed small there, between Sir Walter's men and her grouped nuns. But her age was like a mantle of authority, and she was not frail but fierce, her hand raised defiantly against the men, forbidding any of them to come so much as one step closer.

And behind her the nuns chanted in powerful unity the *Dies Irae*, the promise of God's wrath, judgment, and doom on all men who crossed His will. Their voices rose together, flinging the words at Sir Walter and his men, making God's wrath their own terrible weapon. "*Dies irae, dies illa. Solvet saeculm in favilla. Quantus tremor est tuturus, Quando judex es venturus. Cuncta stricte discussurus!*" A day of wrath that day will be, the world dissolved in glowing ashes. Trembling before the Judge's throne, no sin going undiscovered, all sinners brought to their deserved fate.

As they chanted their defiance and a warning of God's wrath, somewhere outside the day's clouds shifted, letting a long and single golden shaft of brightness sweep the length of the church's darkness, from the western window to Thomasine, where she stood above them all. She shone in its sudden brightness and, as if to answer it, raised her face, shining, into it. With pure and simple loveliness, as if she were seeing something more wondrous than any fearful thing before her, she smiled, and reached out into the light and emptiness in front of her, toward something there that no one else could see.

Beside her, Frevisse heard Chaucer draw in his breath through shut teeth. She could not have taken her own eyes from Thomasine to save herself.

But his startlement and her wonder were nothing to the effect on Sir Walter's men. They had been ready for scurrying, frightened women and the huddling, unnerved novice some of them had glimpsed in the courtyard. Not for this. The rearmost of them began a furtive slipping backward out of the great door behind them. Others started to draw back after them, their fear of staying there stronger than their obedience to Sir Walter.

He was still at their head, already stirring out of his own frozen pause. He had his anger to protect him a little, but he must have felt their going and swung around on them. "This way, you fools!" he ordered and started for the altar again. Only the men nearest to him followed, and among them only Robert Fenner kept close at his back. The others let distance spread between them and Sir Walter and somehow after a few steps were not following him at all but staying where they were, uneasy on their feet, the farthest ones joining the drift toward the door.

Sir Walter was almost to the choir before he realized how alone he was. With an oath he swung around. "Buzzard-hearts! You're going to let a pack of howling women stop you?"

Domina Edith moved her hand. The singing fell away to silence behind her, letting Sir Walter's voice grate into the charged stillness.

"Come back, you bench-bred bastards! You're supposed to be men!"

"And we want to stay that way," an anonymous voice said out of the clot of men around the doorway.

"Step out and say that to my face!" Sir Walter roared, but there was only an uneasy shifting of the men nearest him and no obeying. "The boy here is the only man among you and I'll remember it!"

He clapped Robert on the shoulder and swung around to face the nuns and Thomasine again. But Chaucer moved forward now, not directly into his way but near, saying quietly, "My lord, think well what you are doing."

Sir Walter snarled, "My mother's murderer stands up there and I'll have her to justice!"

But he did not move forward, and Chaucer said, "You blur the wrong done to your mother by making another injustice."

"I'll risk that to gain her murderer there!" Sir Walter pointed violently at Thomasine. The sunlight had diffused by now into simple afternoon light, but she still stood motionless beside the altar, enraptured and unaware of him. Sir Walter's gesture lacked some of his former force, Frevisse thought. The crest of his anger was breaking on the nuns' defiance, his men's unwillingness, the sight of Thomasine, and the risk of the Church's anger. It was one thing to override Montfort, another to cross wills with Chaucer, who had the weight of law at his back, the royal council's good will, and nothing to lose by defying him.

He hesitated, looking from Chaucer to the nuns and back again, as if unsure where the greater threat now lay. Behind him more of his men disappeared through the doorway, leaving only Robert and three others. Frevisse for the first time looked fully at Robert.

He must have come intending to protect Thomasine if he could. Now he stood, unmoving, lost to all the sound and movement around him, looking at her. But while Thomasine was beholding something only she could see, Robert was looking at her with all his heart, knowing that he had lost her. All hope of having her died in his eyes as Frevisse watched, and he was no more ready than the rest of them when Sir Walter suddenly, savagely, slapped him on the shoulder and said, "So keep her for now! But don't think you'll be having her out of here and clear away. My men are still here. I'll close this place so tight no one can go without my knowledge until I have the bishop's writ for her!"

Stiff with rage and defeat, he spun away. Numbly Robert followed him, not looking back.

Outside the door, Sir Walter's voice rose, roaring at his men, but this faded and was soon too remote to matter. In the stillness the nuns began to feel their victory, and a little spate of excited talking started. Domina Edith silenced it with a sharp gesture. "Not yet," she said. "Thomasine . . ."

She turned as she spoke, and the others with her. Thomasine, come back to herself from wherever she had been, was shivering. Her eyes had lost their focus, and she stared blindly back at the nuns as if unable to see them, then abruptly sat down on the top step.

The women began to surge toward her, but Domina Edith said, "Let her be. Dame Claire only is to touch her. The rest of you go to the common room. We're not done yet with Sir Walter and praying will do Thomasine more good than your smothering her. Go and pray."

They went reluctantly, forming their familiar double procession line to leave the church.

Dame Claire knelt beside Thomasine, patting the girl's cheek and speaking softly to her. Thomasine, dazed, did not resist or particularly respond.

Frevisse, with a glance at Chaucer, went over to Domina Edith. Chaucer followed. Domina Edith looked around and said with her familiar mildness, "My thanks, Master Chaucer, for your timely help."

"It was more your doing than mine, Domina. And the child's." He nodded toward Thomasine. "She spoke bravely for herself without saying a word."

Domina Edith nodded. She had seen Thomasine when

she turned to signal her nuns to silence. She sighed. "Yes. And every one of those men saw it. Now she, and we, must needs live with it. As well as with Sir Walter."

"Sir Walter at least is a matter I can help," Chaucer said. "We talked, Dame Frevisse and I, and have the answer that will rid you of him. We know the murderer."

Domina Edith and Dame Claire lifted eager faces to him. Only Frevisse, kneeling now on Thomasine's other side and holding her hand, continued to watch the girl's face. Her eyes were still closed, but she was more conscious than she was showing; her fingers had tightened around Frevisse's when Domina Edith spoke of her.

"You know?" Dame Claire exclaimed. "Then why didn't you say so to Sir Walter?"

"Because more than only Lady Ermentrude's death is involved. I must needs have the murderer out of his reach before he knows the truth. He can't be talking to her."

"Her?" Domina Edith and Dame Claire both echoed. Their gazes swung disbelievingly to Thomasine.

"Assuredly not. Someone not part of St. Frideswide's at all. All I need to do is to talk to Sir John and ask his help. With it, I'll have the woman out of here by tomorrow's dawn or a little later. And soon after that, you'll be free of Sir Walter."

Domina Edith considered his words before nodding. "I entrusted the matter to Dame Frevisse and to you. Let my trust see it through to the end."

"Then by your leave," Chaucer said. He turned to Frevisse. "You'll come?"

"I'll stay here a time. No need for both of us to disturb Sir Walter's peace."

"Such as it is," Chaucer said dryly and bowed his leave to Domina Edith. "I'll talk to Sir John and Lady Isobel in their room and, if they agree, see them on their way, then come back and tell you how it goes."

"But not why," Domina Edith said.

Chaucer's grin was appreciative at her sharpness. "But not why," he agreed.

When he was gone, Domina Edith sighed again. The strength of the moment was going out of her and she looked as if she wished for Sister Lucy to lean upon. But she turned her attention to Thomasine and asked, "Is she better?"

Dame Claire nodded, but it was Frevisse who, slipping an arm behind Thomasine's shoulders, sat her firmly upright and said, "We need to talk. Heed me, Thomasine."

Thomasine obeyed. Her gaze was still cloudy with shock and strain but sensible enough as she looked at Frevisse. "I saw . . . something," she whispered. "In the light. I knew I was safe. I wasn't afraid at all."

"I know you weren't," Frevisse said.

"Is she well enough to talk?" Domina Edith asked.

Thomasine turned her pale face toward her reassuringly. "I'm quite all right," she murmured.

"Right enough," Frevisse agreed. "We need to talk, you and Domina Edith and I."

Dame Claire rose and went down the steps. She took Domina Edith by the arm. "You should sit," she said and guided her across the choir to her stall.

Domina Edith sank down gratefully onto its seat, but her attention was on Frevisse now. "You're troubled by something," she said.

"There are still things I don't understand about the murders," Frevisse said. "Among them, why did Lady Ermentrude decide so abruptly to leave St. Frideswide's? Do you remember what we talked of that day Lady Ermentrude came, in the parlor with Master Chaucer?"

Domina Edith pursed her lips and clearly cast back in her mind before she nodded. "I think so. Much of it."

"Then I want to talk it again, with Thomasine to listen and hear if anything sounds wrong, or means something more to her than it does to us. Do you understand me, Thomasine? Can you do that?"

Thomasine's face cleared of all its vagueness. She was

fully back to them, and some of Frevisse's urgency was reaching her. "Yes," she said. "I'll try."

"Then what did we talk of?" Frevisse asked Domina Edith. "Thomasine, I think, after she had left. Briefly. And my being new as hosteler. None of that can signify. It has to have been something outside of St. Frideswide's."

Domina Edith thought. "France?" she said at last. "Master Chaucer was telling us he was bound for France shortly. We gossiped of that. And of the King. And that Lady Ermentrude was angered at being ill-received at Fen Harcourt. I remember that."

"Moleyns," said Frevisse with sudden memory. "Chaucer is going to collect Lord Moleyns's heiress. We talked about her. And someone else." It was names she wanted. Or events. Something to stir Thomasine's memory, unless she was imagining there was anything to be stirred. She had only the henbane to lead her on and maybe it was a false clue.

"William Vaughan," Domina Edith said firmly. "A young man named William Vaughan who made a French marriage and left a child that Lady Moleyns has had the raising of."

Frevisse was aware of Thomasine suddenly tense in the circle of her arms. "That means something to you, Thomasine?"

Thomasine frowned, then shook her head. "It can't have been the William Vaughan I knew. Knew of," she amended. "He died."

"So did this one. At Orléans siege, trying to save Lord Moleyns."

"Then it's someone else. The William Vaughan whom Isobel knew died of sickness two years or more before then."

"Your sister knew him? Not you?"

Willing to be helpful but clearly not understanding what difference it made, Thomasine said, "He was an esquire in Lady Ermentrude's household when Isobel was there."

Frevisse said, "Then he would be the same. Master Chaucer was asking if he had relations yet living and if Lady Ermentrude knew them since he had been in her household."

"Oh, no." Thomasine sounded very certain. "Because he couldn't have married in France, because . . ."

She stopped; against Frevisse's encircling arm she was now utterly rigid. When she said nothing else, Frevisse asked carefully, "He couldn't have married because of what?"

Slowly, drawn by Frevisse's will more than her own, Thomasine's head turned until she was staring wide-eyed directly at her.

"Say it," Frevisse said softly, not daring to startle her but needing to hear it.

Thomasine failed to respond. She was not, Frevisse realized as she watched a motionless struggle take place behind the girl's eyes, a fool; it was simply that all her thinking had always been turned toward the Church and her nunhood. Now her mind was turned toward something else with the same intensity and depth, and what she was thinking was beginning to frighten her.

Frevisse asked again, "Why couldn't William Vaughan have married in France?"

"Because . . . ," Thomasine held back, then dropped her gaze away to the tiled floor and said, ". . . because he was betrothed to Isobel before he went. They did it secretly. He was to make his fortune and come back to her. He couldn't have married anyone else. They were betrothed."

And a betrothal was as binding as the vow of marriage. Once made, however lightly, only death or an act by the Church could free the couple from one another. If Lady Isobel had been betrothed to William Vaughan, and he was still alive when she married Sir John, then her marriage was no marriage and her children were bastards.

Which could be reason enough to kill.

"It was a secret betrothal? No one knew of it except themselves? And you? How did you know of it if you didn't know him?"

"The one time I visited her at Lady Ermentrude's, he had just gone to France. Isobel was all full of thoughts of him and talked to me because there was no one else. So I knew about him and that they were betrothed. But later she heard that he was dead."

Thomasine straightened up earnestly, free of Frevisse's arm. "So it's all right, it must be! Before she married Sir John, she'd heard from William Vaughan that he was ill and dying. That's how she knew she was free to marry Sir John. Lady Ermentrude had arranged for their marrying and Isobel was finding reasons not to, until she heard William Vaughan was dying and then it was all right. I remember how glad she was, because she'd fallen in love with Sir John by then and been so afraid she would lose him. She told me so."

"But no one else knew of the betrothal? Not Lady Ermentrude?"

Thomasine hesitated before saying uncertainly, "I think she might have. Isobel might have had to tell her, because she was running out of reasons for not marrying Sir John. There was a while they fought about it, and," with some wonder that she had never thought about it before, "then she agreed she didn't have to. And then, as if the saying no had never happened, they were married all of a sudden."

Thomasine looked at Frevisse, her eyes sad. "But Isobel never heard that he was dead. All she ever heard was that he was dying. He wrote to her, saying he was. She showed me his letter, and was sad about it for a day, and then her marriage to Sir John went forward. She never truly heard that William Vaughan was dead."

Isobel had simply hoped it were true, Frevisse thought, as usually it was when someone was pronounced dying. Very possibly Lady Ermentrude, not taking her resistance lightly, had pressured her into telling why she was avoiding marriage with Sir John. Which would explain why Lady Ermentrude had been so suddenly set on going to her that afternoon after they had talked of William Vaughan. The marriage she had been raging about to Sir John and Lady Isobel had indeed been theirs, not the Queen's.

Was it in that raging that Sir John learned their marriage was no marriage? Or had he known earlier? Whichever, he wanted it kept a secret as much as Lady Isobel.

And that explained why Lady Isobel was willing to accept Thomasine as the murderer, because Thomasine's death would break the last link between herself and William Vaughan now that Lady Ermentrude was dead.

And Chaucer—the one person who could keep Sir Walter from executing Thomasine—was gone to ask their help in saving her.

The pieces went together in Frevisse's mind with the silver chink of dropping coins. They had not finished falling before she was on her feet and running.

She wasted no time returning through the cloister. The church's west door into the yard was the shortest way, and she took it. There were men in the yard, soldiers and servants both, mostly in sullen little clumps along the walls. No one moved to stop her, and the single man at the top of the guest-house steps gave way before her rush as she thrust past him.

She had one glimpse of Sir Walter in red-faced argument with Montfort as she crossed the hall, but they were nowhere near enough to stop her, and if they shouted an order to any of the scattered servants, she did not hear it. She was in the passageway and at Sir John and Lady Isobel's closed door. She struck it hard, twice, with her fist, even as her other hand found the handle. With fist and hand, she shoved the door wide open, bursting into the room. Her own grip on the door handle stopped her there; for two strong heartbeats she was as motionless as the two men and Lady Isobel standing across the room, Sir John's hand still on the wine bottle he was setting down on the table, Lady Isobel still reaching out to Chaucer, who held, half-raised to his lips, the goblet she had just given him.

All of them were staring at her.

With a deep, unsteady breath, Frevisse drew back into her dignity, straightened, and said, "Thomas, I wouldn't drink that if I were you."

Chapter 14

THOMASINE SAT DOWN in the far corner of the window bench in Domina Edith's parlor, her hands folded in her lap, her gaze on the sunlit, empty yard below. Sir Walter and Master Montfort and all their men were gone. Sir Walter had taken Lady Ermentrude's household with him. There had been a great clatter, with shouting and creaking of wheels and clanking of harness, but now there was only the mid-morning silence, with, distantly, the calling of workers in the fields. Everything in the past few days might not have happened, except for Martha Hayward's coffin waiting in the church for someone to come and take it to her people.

But here, in the first deep quiet since yesterday, Domina Edith had asked Thomasine to come to the parlor, and told her to sit while she and Dame Frevisse and Master Chaucer talked together. Thomasine heard their voices as a wordless mutter, a background to the quiet, glad to have her Benedictine peace wrapped round her again.

Lady Ermentrude's coffin and mortal remains had gone with her son and with her murderers. Sir John, bound to his horse and his hands tied behind him, Lady Isobel at his side and guarded, had ridden out behind the coffin on its cart this morning, with Master Montfort's men on all sides of them, taking them to Oxford and the royal justices.

Thomasine, at her request, had spoken to Isobel before they left. Thomasine had known by then what had happened. The other nuns had been told as much as they needed to know at recreation time before Compline yesterday, but she had been taken to Domina Edith and told all of it. So she had known as she stood there, looking at her sister and Sir John, that Isobel had killed two people, had tried to kill her, and only barely been stopped from killing Master Chaucer; that she had done all that while she fretted over her husband's toothache, and talked of being grieved, and that Sir John, weak and insecure, had helped her.

But the soul-deep quietness and surety that had come with Thomasine out of the golden-hazed, half-remembered wonder in the church had still been in her then. It was in her now, keeping her from horror and even anger. She had felt compassion and sorrow as she stood in Isobel and Sir John's room with the guards at the door and told them she would pray for them, and asked if there was anything else she might do.

Isobel had been dry-eyed then, but the marks of tears were on her, and she had clung to Sir John's hand as tightly as he was holding to hers.

"My children," she had said, her voice uneven with grief. "This was done for them. All of it for them. Tell her, John. Tell her how it was all for the children."

Sir John lifted his head. His gaze wandered, never quite finding Thomasine before he vaguely answered, "Yes," his look turned toward the barred and shuttered window.

Isobel's hand tightened on his, but her gaze held, burning, on Thomasine. "People will try to make them suffer but they're innocent. And their inheritance is in doubt. You're meaning to be a nun. Go on with it, and make no claim on their inheritance. Don't rob them. Promise me that."

"Assuredly."

The promise came easily, sincerely, but Isobel leaned forward, a harshness of anger in her voice, saying, "It's a promise you must keep. We'll have our marriage legalized before this . . . ends. They'll be legitimate then, and nothing, *nothing* will come to you or your clever nuns that brought us to this. John, tell her that."

Her knuckles showed white around his hand, and he looked at her, but then away.

"John," she insisted.

And he said, "Yes," but whether in agreement or only answering her tightened hold on him, Thomasine could not tell.

"And keep away from them. They are not to come to you, or you to them, so you can tell them lies about us. I'll see to that before—" She had held back the words that had to come after that, and turned her face away, with maybe tears in her eyes again, but certainly grief as she said, "Go away." No apology for anything that she had done. No regretting anything but failure.

Thomasine had gone. Except for what his wife had told him to say, Sir John had not spoken at all, and at Thomasine's last sight of him, he had been staring downward, slowly moving his head from side to side as if disbelieving what had happened.

Now, in Domina Edith's parlor, while the prioress spoke in her soothing murmur to Dame Frevisse and Master Chaucer, St. Frideswide's peace seemed a more fragile thing to Thomasine than it had been before, a less sure protection than she had thought it was. But it was real, and so was the golden quiet in herself that she knew Isobel had never known. Nor ever would, too bound as she was to her worldly desires to learn that the only way to securely hold anything was to let go of wanting.

Across the parlor Master Chaucer said, "Most of the lady's anger seems to be at William Vaughan for not having died when he was supposed to. She seems to feel the fault is his. His living after he wrote he was dying forced her to the murders."

Dame Frevisse shook her head, not in denial but in regretful agreement, and said, "She and Vaughan thought they were in love and made promises to one another. But their 'love' failed to last beyond their parting. He hardly wrote to her after he left, she said. The message that he was dying was his last. Knowing men—and I beg your pardon, Uncle—I would guess William Vaughan had been as busy forgetting her as she anxious to forget him, until he was ill and sure he would die. He sent the message because he wanted to let her know, if she hadn't done anything about it in the meantime, that she would shortly be free of her vow to him—and possibly to make her feel at least a little sorry for him, dying of flux in a foreign land. When he recovered he felt too ashamed to write and say he was still alive, still out of love with her, that she was still bound by the hasty words they had spoken to one another so long ago.''

''And then he went on to father a child on another woman,'' Domina Edith murmured. ''As careless in his affections, seemingly, as in his promises.''

''As careless as Lady Isobel,'' Master Chaucer replied. ''She had no right to be making such a betrothal with no one's knowledge. And less right to agree to marrying Sir John without being certain she was free.''

Softly from her corner Thomasine said, ''She was in love with Sir John. She's still in love with him.''

''She's destroyed him,'' Dame Frevisse answered quietly.

Master Chaucer nodded. ''The pity is that if she hadn't told John of her other betrothal before they were married, it would be held he married her in full good faith and that their children were, at least, legitimate. But because she told him and he knew of the other betrothal as well as she did, their marriage was invalid from its start since William Vaughan was alive when it was made. They didn't know that, though, and would never have known it if Lady Ermentrude hadn't taken it upon herself to bludgeon them about it after she heard that Vaughan died three years later than they had thought.''

Thomasine dared to ask, "So it's certain my lady aunt knew about the betrothal?"

Master Chaucer nodded. "She had it out of Isobel, when Isobel's reasons for not marrying Sir John grew ever more feeble. You know at least as well as the rest of us how she would demand an answer to her questions."

Thomasine nodded, and was a little surprised to find no trace of resentment in herself. Poor Lady Ermentrude, was all she thought.

Master Chaucer continued, "All this touched her on her pride. It was she who came to me about the marriage, she who was all puffed up about how smoothly the arranging went, and she who felt most abused by this sudden impediment to her plans—an impediment that came about while Isobel and William were in her care, to her greater discredit. Then, just as she must needs tell me about it, Isobel received the letter from William and shared its contents with her."

"She ought not to have told Sir John what the problem was," remarked Dame Frevisse.

"But Lady Isobel wanted him to know she was not refusing him because she wanted to," said Chaucer. "So she told him her secret, and what they would have made of it, I don't know, but word came of Vaughan's 'dying' and the matter was suddenly all easy for them."

"It was only our chance talking here that afternoon that gave the truth about William Vaughan's dying to Lady Ermentrude," said Dame Frevisse, "and set the matter on its way to her death."

"I only spoke of it to keep her mind from planning to bother you," said Chaucer with real regret. "She was a great meddler and a proud woman. She wasn't thinking of Lady Isobel or Sir John when she rode off to tell them. She was thinking of herself and of what blame might come to her at the undoing of their marriage. She never gave them time to think of a quiet way to fix matters, just let her temper take high hand. And Isobel's came back to answer it."

Domina Edith's tone was regretful but firm. "Sin will out, and its price is terrible."

"But they hadn't knowingly sinned," Thomasine said earnestly. "Even Lady Ermentrude was in the right in going to warn them their souls were in danger."

Domina Edith looked at her, her eyes deep with age and knowing, so that suddenly but very surely Thomasine realized how much of the prioress's quietness came not from the weariness of age but from years of watching other people's lives, and her own as well, and thinking on them while she did.

"They did not knowingly sin in their marrying," Domina Edith agreed quietly. "Nor did Lady Ermentrude in going to tell them of William Vaughan. It was Lady Ermentrude's prideful arrogance toward them and her wrath when they would not bend to her will that were her sins. And they did sin knowingly when they chose to kill her instead of bending to the necessity of facing their wrong." She looked at Thomasine. "That's what all her resolve was to have you out of here. She was in a fury with them and their foolish insistence that they would not undo their marriage. She determined to punish them by taking you out of here and seeing you married, so your legitimate children would inherit the family lands and deny them to John and Isobel's children."

"And since her eyes had been uncovered to their greed and wickedness," added Chaucer, "she decided they must have forced you to come here, and bribed St. Frideswide's to keep you against your will."

"But I told her over and over I wanted to come," protested Thomasine.

"And Isobel told her William Vaughan was dead."

Domina Edith said to Dame Frevisse, "I saw how you came to know that she was poisoned before she left their manor. Master Chaucer was so certain it was Maryon. Why did you keep looking for another answer?"

Dame Frevisse's face was marked by weariness. The

confrontation of first Sir John and Lady Isobel, and then of Sir Walter and Master Montfort, had been mainly hers to bear. What came afterward had gone on well into the night, in a welter of angers and questionings until everything had been understood enough to satisfy both Master Montfort and Sir Walter. Then she had had to spend this early morning seeing to their guests leaving. Small wonder her smile was faint as she answered, ''It was Sir John's toothache. Once Dame Claire was certain Lady Ermentrude's first illness was from henbane, there was the question of why that poison. If Maryon was the poisoner, why had she chosen so uncertain a poison? Surely she would not have dared poison Lady Ermentrude without firm instructions from the Queen. So she would have had a sure poison to hand. Henbane is more likely to derange a person than outright kill them so it's not as useful as some others. But Sir John had talked of his toothache being treated by a passing peddler whose cure was a smoking sham. Henbane is the base for that deception. The peddler would warn them not to attempt to repeat the cure, as henbane is poisonous. That's what put it into Lady Isobel's head. Henbane is a common weed, underfoot in any yard. That was Lady Isobel's problem the morning Lady Ermentrude sent for the wine. No time to brew a deadly simple, or slip away to the woods, where the more deadly nightshade grows; she needed something quickly. So she used the henbane, hoping it would be enough to kill, but followed after, when she had the nightshade, on the chance she would have to try again.''

''But how did you come to think of Isobel in the matter?'' asked Master Chaucer.

''Because so far as we knew there was no reason for Lady Ermentrude suddenly deciding to go on to the Wykehams that afternoon. She simply did, and fell to raging at them as soon as she was there, then rode back here, still furious, for no real reason so far as we could tell from what anyone could tell us. It was easy to accept she was in some sort of brain fever all that while, unreasoned and half-mad. And that someone took advantage of it to kill her after she returned here. But it wasn't until Dame Claire realized Lady Ermentrude returned here already poisoned that it suddenly mattered very much why she had gone to the Wykehams in the first place. I could only guess that something we'd said here that afternoon had set her off. When Thomasine told me her sister's secret, I finally knew what had happened."

"And Sir John knew what his lady was about?" Domina Edith asked.

"Not the first time. But afterwards, with the nightshade, he knew. I think he would have stopped her if he could, but she's the stronger of the two of them."

Domina Edith sadly shook her head. "All to save their children from disgrace."

"No," Master Chaucer said. "It's only a small legal matter for the Church and Crown to make a marriage like theirs lawful and legitimize their children. There would be some bother and maybe laughter but no long-held disgrace and afterwards everything would be righted. It was the price Lady Isobel objected to. Such legalities are expensive."

"But they could have afforded them," objected Thomasine. "There must have been a way they could have managed it no matter how expensive."

"Yes, but Lady Isobel had another purpose for the money. Since your father's title of Lord was entailed through the male line only, it died with him, unable to pass through your sister's blood to her sons."

Thomasine nodded. She knew that. Master Chaucer continued, "Your sister was hoping to buy the title back into the family. For Sir John in her right, or for their eldest son. Titles can be had from the Crown for a price but, like all legalities, they're expensive. She and Sir John could afford either the title or having their marriage made legal, but if they had to pay for one, they'd not have been able to pay for the other, not for a long while yet, perhaps not ever. Your sister is a proud woman, not willing to face even casual slurs on her marriage. But above all, an impatient woman, who wants what she wants *now*, not later."

"The way she wanted William Vaughan," Domina Edith said softly. "And then Sir John. And wanted Lady Ermentrude dead. A very dangerous thing is impatience. Even when it is for something good. Like the taking of one's vows."

Thomasine looked at her, startled. But the familiar fear did not come with it, so that she actually saw the laughter quirking at the corners of the prioress's mouth, and Dame Frevisse's. A little uncertainly, she smiled back, then bowed her head and said, "It's almost too late to be impatient now."

They laughed at her then, but gently with the kindness of understanding, and to her surprise, Thomasine found that the laughter did not hurt.

A while later she stood beside Dame Frevisse in the yard as the last of Master Chaucer's men disappeared beyond the gateway after him. At her back St. Frideswide's silence was waiting for her, a promise of prayers and peace, but for just now she was more aware of the doves coming back to the well on their rustling wings, unafraid of two nuns at the cloister door.

Over the fading sound of the horses' cantering hoofs she could hear the creak of carts on the track from the fields. The rain had been too slight to hurt the harvest and the fields had already dried. Someone beyond the wall called to mind the rut or they'd have the load over, and Dame Frevisse asked mildly, "Did you talk to Robert Fenner before he left with Sir Walter?"

Slightly disconcerted by the unexpected question, Thomasine answered, "Yes. When I came from speaking to Isobel this morning he stopped me and we spoke."

"What did he have to say?"

"That he was sorry about my sister, and that he hoped I would be happy when my vows were taken."

"And anything more?"

Puzzled, aware that Dame Frevisse was watching her face as if in search of something, Thomasine answered simply, "No. Should there have been?"

Dame Frevisse watched her a moment more before looking away. "No," she said. "There should not have been."